Tye smi
back to his c

love you, Maria," he whispered in her ear. "You know, it's time for me to settle down. You don't have to live in a room at the inn or a house with your sister. My ranch house is too large for one man. Let's get married. We could raise some cattle for me and some chickens for you. And a passel of kids for both of us."

"And I'd lose my job. You know the school board is opposed to having a married woman for a teacher." She twisted her head up to look at him.

"Forget the dang school board—"

"Tye—" Maria glanced at the dance floor and spotted Millie moving toward the door on the other side of the barn. She wiggled free from his embrace, turned toward him, and pulled his face down to meet hers, her lips touching his. She kissed him soundly, brazenly. "Hold that thought, Rancher Ashmore. We need to discuss this, but there's something I have to do right now. Right this minute."

"What? Hellfire! Where are you going?"

To catch a murderer. Maria smiled. "I need to talk to Millie Hanson. It's really important."

"For the love of Pete! Why now?" he asked in disbelief. "Maria, I'm trying to propos—"

"Please, Tydall. Not now. I've waited all evening to corral Millie and talk to her alone, away from the clutches of Aunt Emma." Before he could utter another word, she slipped away and disappeared across the barn floor, threading her way among the dancers.

Praise for Judy Ann Davis

"Storyteller Judy Ann Davis weaves her award-winning tales to make her readers laugh, maybe cry, but always able to relate to the unique characters and the dilemmas they encounter."

~Long and Short Reviews

~*~

"With her fast-paced, but easy reading style, Judy Ann Davis, takes you back to the Old West in the Colorado Territory. The novel [*UNDER STARRY SKIES*] has action and adventure—with a generous touch of humor. The author provides enough twists and turns to provide a captivating mystery, western, and romance. And you'll have no trouble finding colorful characters to carry the tale forward, including a wily renegade Indian called Two Bears."

~J.F. Burten, freelance writer & editor

Under Starry Skies

by

Judy Ann Davis

This is a work of fiction. Names, characters, places, and incidents are either the product of the author's imagination or are used fictitiously, and any resemblance to actual persons living or dead, business establishments, events, or locales, is entirely coincidental.

Under Starry Skies

Cover Art by *RJ Morris*

The Wild Rose Press, Inc.
PO Box 708
Adams Basin, NY 14410-0708
Visit us at www.thewildrosepress.com

Publishing History
First Cactus Rose Edition, 2014
Print ISBN 978-1-62830-364-3
Digital ISBN 978-1-62830-365-0

Published in the United States of America

Dedication

In memory of my father, Frank Lashinski,
who was a gentle, peaceful farmer
in love with the land and all its creatures.

Chapter One

Colorado Territory
1875

Abigail O'Donnell stood at the station of Canon City Landing and watched the group of men hoist the two cherry coffins from the freight wagon to a smaller dray. She silently prayed no one would suspect there was anything but bodies inside. Especially now when she was only forty miles away by water from Pueblo and five more days by wagon from Golden, her final destination.

Several feet beyond, Amos, her old traveling companion, glanced nervously at her before singing out some words of caution to the laboring men. The late summer sun reflecting off his ebony face made his skin shine like polished marble. Nearby, the dray stood ready to shuttle the coffins just a short distance down the spongy riverbank to a waiting flatboat rocking gently on the glassy waters of the Arkansas River.

"Easy men, easy. Let's not jolt the souls out of Joshua and Adam before they greet their Almighty Maker," Amos's deep baritone voice rumbled above the passengers milling about the front of the station. "Step aside, folks, step aside. Let's show the dead some respect as they make their journey to their final resting place."

The sea of faces parted as soon as the first coffin was lifted from the wagon bed.

A surly farmer groaned under its weight. "Good thing the Lord takes only their souls. He'd have a tough time getting these two into heaven!" He hoisted the edge of the coffin onto the dray and sucked in a cleansing breath. "Maybe we ought to take them one at a time. We'll bury this rig up to its axles. Why, they must weigh well over two hundred fifty pounds each!"

"Closer to three, I'd say," a second man complained, stopping to wipe the sweat from his brow with the sleeve of his shirt. From the canvas trousers and stout boots he wore, Abigail suspected he was a farmer as well, or maybe a lumberman.

"Sure 'nough, these were big men," Amos agreed. "Big bodies, big hearts, even bigger souls, praise the Lord! And once gallant Union soldiers, too."

Minutes later, when the coffins were safely loaded onto the boat, Abigail breathed a sigh of relief and searched the area for her younger sister. It wasn't difficult to pick out Maria's dark midnight hair from among the ragtag-looking group of people who were there to collect supplies and mail from the freighters arriving from Salt Lake City to the west and from St. Louis to the east.

Even those dressed in Sunday best were a pitiful lot, wearing clothes well-worn and outdated. The War had taken its toll on everyone, both North and South. Although it was over, goods, tools, and supplies were still in short supply in the Colorado Territory with all the miners pouring into the area in search of silver and gold.

Behind her, she heard Amos come lumbering up,

huffing like a steam engine. He stopped beside her and tried to catch his breath.

"Miss Abby," he said, battered hat in his gnarled hand. "I think I'll mosey around a bit, maybe find someone who might help us for a few coins. We can't take those coffins downriver alone."

Abigail nodded, watching Maria as she wandered down the grassy riverbank below the station toward the crude flatboat. They had been lucky to rent it for only three dollars when they arrived at the landing. It belonged to a merchant upstream who had been planning to dismantle it and sell the wood for scrap in Canon City.

Abigail's stomach rumbled in an unladylike fashion. Yesterday morning, they had spent the last of their allotted coins for food—two loaves of stale bread from a German family heading south. They agreed to save the rest of their pittance to try to hire a river man.

For a brief moment, Abigail stared at the rolling river where the flatboat, now loaded with the caskets, bobbed like a square cork on a sea of cobalt blue. Memories of her father's recent burial, just four months ago, came flooding back. His casket had been similar, if not a trifle more ornate. His sudden death from a weak heart had come as a shock to all of them. His list of debtors had been a jarring blow as well. Even though he had once been a prosperous merchant, he had left Maria and her very little, having generously given credit to the poor who couldn't pay and to those who didn't intend to ever pay. Their traveling trunks held more books than clothes or household goods.

When the old black man started to walk away, Abigail called after him, "Amos, wait!"

He turned. "Yes, Miss Abby?"

"Please don't beg," she said in a quiet voice. She hated the thought of being poor, but she dreaded even more the thoughts of having to beseech others for their welfare. She waited until Amos rounded the corner of the station before she climbed the steps to the platform encircling the building like a giant hoop skirt and entered through the front door.

If it hadn't been for Uncle Henry, her late mother's eldest brother who operated an inn with a barroom in Golden, she didn't know what they would have done. As soon as he heard of their father's death, he had urged them to come live with him. Knowing the town needed a school teacher, he had made the proper arrangements to secure a position for her sister.

Uncle Henry had no children. An old bachelor at the age of fifty, he had married Emma Foster, some fifteen years younger, just as the War broke out. Abigail remembered her father saying Uncle Henry had captured the most beautiful widow in the territory. Emma's family had relocated from Georgia to farm the rich, silt-covered lands along the South Platte River running through the Territory like a lazy blue ribbon. Emma's first husband had been a miller who drowned before their second anniversary.

Inside the station, only a few people loitered, and Abigail quickly located the manager sorting the mail. Explaining both her plight and her need for frugality, she inquired about hiring help for their trip downriver.

"Sorry, miss," he said, shaking his head sadly, "the regular operator is off getting his eldest daughter properly married, and I don't know of anyone around here who'd be fool enough to take all that baggage, two coffins, and three people to Pueblo, let alone on to Golden—and on their good word alone with only the promise of payment. Times are tough."

Abigail felt her cheeks burn in embarrassment. "But upon our arrival in Golden, I assure you, my uncle would pay whatever costs we might incur." She turned away to quell her threatening tears while she surveyed the room around her. Crude, but solidly built of logs and mortar, it was weather-tight to protect the crates, boxes, and barrels which lined its perimeter, awaiting destinations further inland. Beside her, an open door led to the rear platform where two lone crates, like sentries, faced the river beyond. Abigail forced herself to take a steadying breath, determined not to betray her anxiety. They had already been traveling over three weeks since they left Utah, and she was not about to cave in to fear or despair. She turned back around, her gaze finding the station manager's face again. "Surely there must be some goods or supplies in need of transportation to Pueblo, too."

He rubbed his chin, lips pursed. "Most of these goods are headed for the settlements in the south, miss. Two freighters are due in the day after tomorrow to clean this place out." He peered at the platform. "Outside, there are some crates, but I don't think you'll want to take them. Oh, and there's a mailbag here waiting to go downriver to Pueblo. But all I'm obligated to pay is two dollars, mind you, for the entire bag. One dollar to be paid now, and one to be collected at the stage office when it's delivered."

"Two dollars?" Abigail's heart leaped wildly. She couldn't believe her good fortune. "You mean, if I can locate someone to navigate our boat to Pueblo, you'll pay *me* a dollar to take the mail with us?"

"Why yes, miss, but only one. And one dollar when it's delivered. No more. You'll need to hire someone handy with river skills."

She nodded and gestured to the side door where the two squat crates sat covered with a thick, oily canvas. "What are those?"

"I've orders to pay ten dollars apiece to anyone willing to take them, but I'm warning you, you don't want them. Over a dozen men have declined the offer so far."

Abigail stepped onto the platform and peeled back a portion of the canvas. Bold letters, painted in red, stared at her: *DANGER! Handle with care. Nitroglycerin.*

Lips pursed, she looked at them for a moment longer, then ducked inside, and spoke with more confidence than she felt. "I'll take them."

The station manager's old eyes flickered in surprise. "That's some pretty dangerous goods to be totin'."

She smiled. "My father once said, '*Those who never dare, never do.*'" After all, what choice did she have? She dismissed the impulsive part of her brain warring with the more rational one. They needed money for food. They had to hire help. And once they arrived in Pueblo, they would need more money to rent a wagon to take them to Golden. There was no turning back now. Her aunt and uncle were waiting for them.

Beside her, a short, thick-waisted man in black trousers with wide suspenders was filling out a weigh slip. "I saw Tye Ashmore yonder, miss." He tilted his head toward the river. "He comes to the landing every so often to deliver horses or gather supplies from the freighters, and he has been known to handle a few boats in his time, if you catch him in the right mood, that is. He has a ranch somewhere north of here with his brothers. Near Golden. Along Cherry Creek."

Abigail quickly gathered the mailbag and the money the station master counted out. "Thank you, sir. How will I recognize Mr. Ashmore?"

"Tall. Dark haired. Ain't much of a talker." He paused. "He's usually dressed in buckskins and walks with a limp while his leg is healing from tangling with a wild bronc. Last time I saw him, he was skipping stones on the river down below the station, just upstream from where your flatboat is tied."

Abigail nodded to the stranger and turned to leave.

"Oh, and miss, I'd watch out for that speckled blue herding dog of his. The dark marking around its one eye makes him look like a pirate with four legs. I heard tell if he gets riled, he can get as cantankerous as his owner."

"I will. Thank you again for the advice." She smiled graciously, then gazed at the station manager. "Would you please secure the canvas on those crates? I'd prefer not to advertise the wares."

"Ah-hh, I see." The station manager nodded knowingly and winked. "Why, yes, of course. I'll tie 'em down so secure even a field mouse won't be able to crawl under."

"I appreciate it." Relieved, Abigail left the station and stopped for a minute to get a feel for the land. Outside, the day was warm and sunny. Not a cloud skidded across the bright blue sky towering over a sea of aspen marching up the river, their coats just beginning to turn a rich gold. In the marshes upstream, a duck complained. Somewhere along the riverbank, someone had started a campfire, and the smell of wood smoke mingled with the breeze. Several yards in front of her, a tall, lean man stood near the water's edge, staring into its shadowy depths. He wore a simple cotton shirt beneath a buckskin jacket, too heavy for the unusually warm weather. A gun was strapped to his hip, and a rifle lay among his belongings on the bank. His hair, dark as fine onyx, sparkled under the sun's rays, framing a pensive lean face. When he turned to walk farther up shore, Abigail noticed his faint limp. She stepped off the platform and hurried after him.

"Tye Ashmore?"

The man turned abruptly.

"I've heard you might be heading downriver."

"Might be." He eyed her warily. His eyes were dark, almost brooding. They were the kind of eyes that would never betray his deepest thoughts. His tall, muscular frame reminded Abigail of a sleek timber wolf, guarded and distant.

"Station manager tells me the regular flatboat operator is off today. We need to get to the dock at Pueblo and then to Golden. Perhaps you'd be willing to lend a hand?"

Abigail watched his gaze drop to the mailbag, and he muttered something indiscernible, maybe undesirable, under his breath. "No, miss, I'm sorry."

"I'm willing to pay."

He shook his head. "Not interested."

Disappointed, she stared at him. This was not what she needed to hear. There was no way they could stay overnight at Canon City. Little more than a crossroads for those headed north or south on the Arkansas River, it had once been a stop for early travelers and Ute Indians who crisscrossed the lands and used the hot springs located nearby for medicinal purposes. The landing contained only a sparse outcropping of buildings. It wouldn't be easy to find a place to stay or eat—with or without money. Wearily, she turned back toward the station.

"Wait!" he called after her. "No offense, but I'm just not fond of dead people. I'd be willing to take the mail off your hands."

She swung around. "Oh, no! I've just agreed to deliver it safely to Pueblo for two dollars. The cash can line my pockets just as easily as yours." She took a breath and paused, searching for the right words to convince him to change his mind. "If it's the coffins you're afraid of, I assure you, my dear cousins are harmless. They did not die from any fever or contagious diseases. Adam and Joshua are as clean as a new bottle of Canadian whiskey. They were killed in an unfortunate wagon mishap, God rest their souls. And to think, after surviving the horrors of the War. The irony of it all!"

Tye walked to where she stood. "It'll cost you some cash," he drawled, a scowl cutting a valley of creases onto his suntanned forehead. "Five dollars for you and your companions, and five for the coffins and baggage. Ten, total."

Abigail hesitated, frowning. It was a considerable amount to part with. Yet, there was no place for them to stay until tomorrow unless she could convince the tender at the stable to allow them to use the hayloft. "You cut a hard bargain, Mr. Ashmore," she finally said. "My name's Abigail O'Donnell."

He ignored her. "Let's see the cash, little lady."

"Oh my, certainly." With reserved anger, Abigail set the mailbag aside, tore open the strings on her reticule, and dropped one of the gold eagles the station manager had just given her into his outstretched, callused palm. She looked him squarely in the eyes as she spoke, "Now a deal is a deal. Please get the boat loaded and be careful with the two crates on the platform. My mother's finest crystal and bone china are packed inside. Even the slightest jolt could shatter them, Mr. Ashmore."

He snickered and removed his hat. A head of unruly dark hair tumbled out. He bowed, and waved his hand like a gentleman of royalty before replying, his voice full of mock sarcasm. "As you wish, my lady, but first, if you don't mind, I'd like to take my own belongings aboard." He limped down the riverbank and gathered his saddlebags, rifle, and ring flask.

Amos came to stand beside her, shoving his hands into the back pockets of his baggy trousers fastened to his tall, stick-like figure with an oversized worn belt. "What's in the crates, child? Tell me you didn't get yourself mixed up in some devilish scheme already?"

"Just some explosives headed for Cripple Creek."

"Nitroglycerin? Oh, heavenly Father. Oh, Mother of mercy!" The old man's gnarled hands flew into the air, the whites of his eyes rounding into two full moons. "Who talked you into that cockeyed idea?"

"Hush, Amos, will you? I haven't told Mr. Ashmore yet." Abigail threw her hands out and caressed the air, palms down. "It's safe. I checked the crates myself. There's enough straw to secure those bottles and feed a plow horse."

"Mercy, mercy, child, I don't care whether it's in straw or ten tons of fresh goose feathers. You got to be plumb crazy to ride a river with cargo like explosives."

"Hush, I said!" She shot him a warning look and whispered, "If Mr. Ashmore hears you, he won't agree to help us. He's not the most friendly or trusting man I've ever met. He thinks the crates are filled with bone china and delicate crystal. And the river will certainly be a lot smoother than some old rutted, backwoods trail, for heaven's sake."

"Nitroglycerin ain't fussy about where or how it blows, Missy. If you think the man isn't friendly now, I don't reckon he'll be any more pleasant when he finds out the truth." He shook his head. "I ain't goin', no sir-reee."

Abigail squinted up at him. "Well, that's your choice, Amos. I suggest you light out this very minute and start walking or hitch yourself a ride. We're going to need help unloading those coffins when we get to Pueblo. We can't allow them to bob around on a clumsy boat all night, and certainly not with explosives as bunk mates."

"If the boat blows to pieces, you won't have to worry about your poor cousins," Amos said sourly.

Abigail grabbed his sleeve and shook it. Her words came out in a soft hiss. "Now listen. We've just been paid ten dollars apiece to get those crates a mere forty miles downstream. I've had to pay Mr. Ashmore half of it for his help. With money from the remaining crate and two dollars for the mail, we can at least face my uncle without feeling like a passel of paupers. In fact, we might be able to get something decent to eat in

Pueblo before we start raiding his pantry like starving crows. Think about it."

"Begging your pardon, Miss Abby, with what you're totin' we have a good chance of never eating again."

Together they watched Tye Ashmore stride up the bank toward the landing's platform and the covered crates. "Hold up, there, mister!" Amos called out, brushing past Abigail. His bowed legs high-stepped across the grassy bank. "Let me lend a hand with that there boney china and crystal. Gotta be gentle with it! Mighty gentle. Takes two people to do it right."

A thin smile played on Abigail's face as she followed the antics of the old man. It was the fastest she had ever seen him move in the last five years. Elbowing Tye Ashmore aside, he delicately lifted one side of a crate, babbling instructions to the younger man in his soft deep voice.

A northern free slave for many years, Amos had been hired by her father to help with the household after her mother died of pneumonia when they lived in New York. He had no family. He had never once mentioned his exact age, but Abigail guessed he was closer to seventy than sixty.

Minutes later, Abigail picked up her skirts and headed down the bank toward the flatboat. Tasks finished, Tye Ashmore had moved aside and was now in deep conversation with her sister. Abigail wondered how they both would react when she told them about the contents of the crates. And she'd have to tell them soon. Just not too soon—once they were well out on the river and the idea of returning was impossible.

"I imagined the new school teacher to be much

older." She heard Tye say as she hurried to where Maria stood. "To be honest, I didn't know the town's selection committee had made a decision."

Maria flushed a deep crimson. "I'm almost twenty-two, and I have the proper credentials, I assure you. I attended the Harris-Stow Normal School in St. Louis, and I've already taught for a year in Utah." She bent down, took her sketchbook from the top of her trunk, and pressed it possessively to her breast. "And just how old are you, Mr.—?"

"—Ashmore. Tydall Ashmore, but I prefer Tye. I'm twenty-eight." He studied her thoughtfully for a moment. "And I'm certain your credentials are the finest. It's the rowdy youngsters of our miners, trappers, and ranchers that you may need some help with. But rest assured, you'll have a dozen men rushing to your aid, no doubt. It's not often Golden gets two attractive women for the price of one." He reached down and lifted the trunk to his shoulder like it was a box of air.

Abigail interrupted with a soft snort. "If you, Mr. Ashmore, keep moving at your present pace, I fear the school year will be half over before we arrive."

He turned and glared at her, then placed the trunk on the boat and spoke to Maria. "Is your sister always so... so..."

"Bossy?" Maria asked.

"I was looking for the word *impertinent*." Tye took Maria gently by the elbow and guided her aboard the boat rocking gently on the water.

"Yes. And maybe just a tad temperamental." They shared a smile. "Abigail was born with a short fuse. She's older than I am by three years, so she erroneously believes she's always in charge."

Once the women were seated, Tye whistled shrilly. From among the reeds along the riverbank, a compact muscular dog with a mottled coat of white and blue black came barreling up the ramp. A dark black patch of fur encircled his left eye. He stopped and sat obediently at Tye's side, tail beating a staccato tune on the weathered boards. He looked up with deep brown, expectant eyes, waiting for the next command. Tye Ashmore bent, rubbed the dog behind his ears, and pointed to a place at the front of the boat. The dog obediently ambled toward his spot but paused as he reached the first tarp-covered crate. He sniffed it and growled low in his throat.

"It's all right, Swamp," Tye said and heaved a weary sigh. "It's only china and fine women's doodads. I guess this trip will be much more than we originally bargained for, huh, partner?" He pointed to the spot again, and the dog looked suspiciously at the crate one more time, but obediently ambled over and dropped down, head resting on his front paws, eyes and ears alert. Tye turned and nodded his thanks to the old man who had collected the few loose bags left on shore and was piling them beside the trunks.

"On my blessed mother's grave, you sure said a mouthful there, sir," Amos agreed, and with shaking hands, he hurried to the back of the boat to check the lashings on the coffins and crates.

Chapter Two

Tye Ashmore unfastened the crude hemp rope mooring the small flatboat to the weathered dock and cast off. It wasn't difficult to propel the boat downstream. The river with its gentle current, swollen from incessant late summer rains, offered little resistance. Overhead, the sun spread its amber warmth over the colorful landscape. Pungent green spruce and pine dotted the riverbanks along with various kinds of reeds and scrub brush, thick and tangled, pushing their way down to the shoreline as their roots searched for water. At the back of the boat, Maria was seated atop her trunk with her sister.

The young school teacher's nervousness did not go unnoticed. Surreptitiously, Tye watched her gaze flit over their meager belongings and linger on the coffins, an undisguised fear marring her face. Her hands fidgeted with a corner of her sketchbook. For a moment, he had the urge to give her some words of condolence. For he, too, once knew the fear of leaving familiar surroundings, coming to the West, and he, too, knew the taste of death.

But the death he had known had always haunted him. He had been only fourteen when a group of men had come to their house in Virginia, insisting his father enlist his oldest sons in the Confederate cause. A fight erupted and someone pulled a gun. His mother,

Rebecca, stepped in front of her husband and took the bullet meant for him. Tye and his sister, Betsy, had watched while his older brothers, Flint, Marcus, and Luke took down the five men in a haze of smoke. Their father wasted no time burying his wife and loading their wagons to come west. Thomas Ashmore had wanted no part of the Civil War. He had never owned any slaves. Together, the six of them had set out and traded their lives of eastern farmers for western ranchers.

Tye glanced down and studied his hands. Callused and hardened by long hours in the sun and rain, they were hands of a man who knew how to work horses, cattle, and the land. Sometimes he couldn't believe he had already lived another fourteen years in the West. Next year, the Colorado Territory was hoping for statehood, and he was proud he was going to be part of it. He would be the first to admit he had fallen in love with the rich landscape where everything was wide open and free, and a man could earn a living by sweat, long hours, and honest hard work. And if the days were lengthy, the nights were worth the wait. The heavens above turned as dark as the inside crown of a black felt hat and were strewn with millions and millions of glorious stars.

He shoved his pole into the water and turned to watch Amos lay his pole aside and move between the coffins at the back of the boat, then shuffle over to the crates. The old man was acting fitful, out of sorts. In the last half hour, he had repeated the routine again and again. He reminded Tye of an old trapped barn cat itching to be set free. Each time Amos made his rounds, his wrinkled eyes strayed to Abigail who smiled reassuringly. Maybe he couldn't swim. Maybe he was afraid of water. Or maybe he feared the flatboat would upset and leave them in the same sad shape as the men inside the two coffins. Whatever was eating at the old codger, Tye knew it was eating at him like a consuming fever.

Now the older O'Donnell sister, Tye decided as he stole a quick look at Abigail perched beside Maria on the trunk, was a woman he would have liked to throttle if he were a man who leaned toward violence. Thanks to her brazen enterprising nature, he had lost his chance of gaining possession of the dang mailbag. And it was the sole reason he had gone to Canon City. He needed to get his hands on the U.S. mail headed to Golden. He should have never lingered on the riverbank to stretch his aching leg.

Several miles downstream, his friend, Brett Trumble, was waiting and counting on him to have the bag on board. He swore softly to himself. Tarnation and damnation! Why in heaven's name had he promised he would help him intercept it? Why couldn't he mind his own business? Why couldn't he say no? He removed his hat and wiped the sweat beading on his forehead with the back of his hand. Because Brett was a good friend—and because Brett was in jeopardy of having a record of desertion slapped on his good-looking head along with a humiliating dishonorable discharge which would mar his flawless military career.

Brett's father, Aaron Trumble, would never understand the letter from the U.S. government was a mistake, a misunderstanding. Nor would the town of Golden ever let Captain Brett Trumble have a moment's peace if they thought he was a traitor and deserter. Most of all, Tye owed Brett. They were best friends. In addition, he had saved Tye's life a few years back when they had come upon a rogue band of aggravated Indians with no sense of humor. The Indians had wanted his horse, his hide, and his gun. What they got was some buckshot in their scrawny backsides instead.

His wandering thoughts were interrupted by Abigail. "In all fairness, Mr. Ashmore, there's something I need to tell you." The tone of her voice held an uneasy, apprehensive quality.

Tye jabbed his pole into the muddy river bottom to discourage the boat from drifting toward the right riverbank. They would make better time in the swift, strong current in the middle where the river needed little assistance from him. "What's that?" He turned to face her.

"We're not carrying crystal and bone china."

Tye glanced at the two crates for a second and then met her gaze with a cautious one of his own. Warning bells began to jingle inside his head. What was under the tightly bound crates? Why had Swamp earlier shown distrust of mere china and crystal? "What *are* we toting?"

"Explosives for the Henderson Mining Camp near Cripple Creek." The words slipped out so innocently, so nonchalantly, she sounded as if she was picking her favorite flavor at an ice cream social.

It took barely a second for the words to register. He almost dropped his pole in the water. "Nitroglycerin? We're toting nitroglycerin? On *this* boat?"

Abigail nodded.

"Why? Why in tarnation are we hauling explosives?" It was a strain for him to remain calm.

Now a million thoughts tumbled around in his head at one time. If any one of those bottles had a mind of its own, it would blow them clean out of the water.

He looked over at Amos whose face was as white as fresh Georgia cotton. "Please tell me she's a little possessed and this is a bad dream?"

"Yes, sir, sometimes I think she is, and no, sir, it's not a bad dream. It's a downright frightful one."

Tye moved to the crates, withdrew a sharp knife from his buckskin boot, and carefully sliced through the maze of twine covering one of the crates like a fish net. He peeled back a corner of the stiff canvas cover and lifted the lid high enough to peer inside.

"Confound it! You fool woman! Whatever possessed you to decide to transport explosives?"

He stormed to the back of the boat and grabbed for Abigail, but she was quicker and she stood, defiantly crossing her arms at her chest, eluding his grasp. His voice rose to a shout. "Again, Miss O'Donnell, I'm asking why you agreed to transport explosives?" He stared at her with narrowed eyes. When she didn't respond, he blew out an exhausted breath of air. He turned to Maria and glared at her. "And you, Miss…Miss Schoolmarm, did you know about this, too? A sensible man would heave the lot of you overboard this very minute and let you swim with the fish and river rats!"

Distraught, Maria scrambled off the trunk, her face ashen, her mud brown eyes full of fear. "No. Oh-hh, please, no," she choked out. "I had no idea there were explosives in those crates. Abigail never told me." She laid a trembling hand on his arm. "Please, please don't hurt her! It's not her fault. We have barely a penny to our name. We're poorer than church mice."

"You won't need a penny or a name if this boat blows sky high." He gestured to the coffins. "We'll beat your dear dead cousins on their journey to meet the Almighty!" With lips thinned in anger, he removed his hat and ran his fingers through his hair. Behind him, sensing danger, Swamp rose from his spot and growled low. Tye turned, signaled, and the dog dropped in his place. Moving to the front of the boat, he recovered his pole. He had to think this madness through, and he had to do it quickly. Less than a few miles downstream, Brett Trumble was waiting to hold up the boat and grab the mail. If he fired even one single errant shot, they would all be dead in a bare second.

Tye glanced at Maria. She was still quivering, gnawing on her lower lip. Abigail, however, was cool, aloof, without a sign of fear marring her delicate blonde features. She stood in a defiant stance and was as unremorseful as a fencepost.

"How much money did the fool dispatcher offer you?" He blew out another exhausted breath of air.

"Ten dollars a crate."

"You, Miss O'Donnell, have been sorely hoodwinked. Most river boat operators would have asked twice the amount!"

"I had no choice. I would have taken any price the station master offered, just to get us to Pueblo."

"You certainly don't place much value on our hides, do you?" He scanned the contents heaped on the boat. Somehow, he had to warn Brett about the nitroglycerin. He knew the man all too well. Once he discovered passengers on board, he'd want to make a spectacle of robbing the mail. Brett had a swashbuckling way about him. The last thing Tye needed was for him to announce himself with a flourish, waving a gun, and firing theatrical errant shots like a blithering idiot.

Tye snatched the pole from Amos's hands and turned, confronting both women. "Have either of you a white towel or apron, or perhaps a petticoat stashed in those trunks?"

Maria spoke first, her voice faltering, "No, no, just some old dresses and books."

"What about you?" His eyes came to rest on Abigail.

She shook her head. "Why do we need something white? What are you planning to do?"

He glared at her. "I'm trying to save our hides and keep us alive. We have dangerous cargo. We need to fashion a makeshift flag to alert others to be cautious."

"What on earth for? Why all the fuss?" Abigail didn't try to disguise her annoyance. She flapped both her hands in the air and waved them at the riverbanks. "Do you see even a hint of civilization out here? We're in the wilderness, Mr. Ashmore, for heaven's sake. Stark, uninhabited wilderness. Who are you expecting? A few wild ducks to attack us?"

It took all of Tye's patience not to curse aloud. The last thing he wanted to do was to divulge information about Brett. "There are dozens of scalawags underfoot who ply this river, Miss O'Donnell, just hoping to steal goods and their next meal rather than work for it. This is rough territory out here."

Maria's face blanched even whiter, and she shuddered. She looked like she was about to pass out. "Are we going to sink? Are we going to die?" Her eyes filled with tears as she nervously wrung her hands and stared at him with a desperate hopeless expression.

Aware he had frightened her, Tye felt a pang of regret. He shook his head and lowered his voice. "No, hopefully not, but we need to take precautions."

"You...you can have the petticoat I'm wearing." She plucked at her skirt with her thumb and forefinger.

Tye whirled on Abigail instead. "How generous of your sister, Miss Abigail, don't you think?"

Unflinching, hands on her hips, Abigail stared back at him with equal disdain.

He waved his fingers in a beckoning gesture. "Since Maria came up with the idea, it's only fair you lend a hand and give up *yours* instead—after all, it was *you* who got us into this miserable mishap."

"Now just a second!"

"Come, come, Abigail, we must all learn to sacrifice for the common good."

She snorted, but turned her back, hiked up her skirt, and untied the petticoat ribbons. It fell to her feet in a white heap, and she stepped out of it. Scooping it up, she flung the delicate confection at him. He deftly caught it and tied it to the pole, propping it between the two coffins. It fluttered in the soft autumn breeze.

"You don't honestly believe a person would attack this boat, do you?" Abigail's blue eyes flashed cold like a winter sky. "Who would be crazy enough to want two coffins, two women, or the U.S. mail?"

Tye ignored her. Fool woman. Even without Brett downstream about to launch his ruse, they could be blown to human splinters. He silently prayed whoever packed the bottles, packed them well and spared no straw. One jagged rock or one floating tree limb could jar the boat and excite the unstable liquid inside the bottles. His gaze circled the group. "Many a man, down on his luck, has been known to rob, just to scavenge for any little articles which could net him a decent meal or a bottle of whiskey," he explained. "Now, ladies, sit down, remain seated, and don't move no matter what happens, hear me?"

He took up his pole and dug it into the swirling water. Amos moved forward to stand beside him. "How the devil did you ever get tied up with the likes of those two?" Tye gestured with his head to the back of the boat but kept his eyes keenly trained on the current ahead, looking for any floating debris.

"Their father, sir—"

"Don't call me sir," he snapped, still disgruntled.

"Mister—"

"No mister, either. It's Ashmore or Tye."

"You're a rancher?" Amos asked.

Tye nodded. "I once lived in Virginia on a farm, then came west before the war with my father, three brothers, and a sister. I thought it was the longest, most miserable trek I'd ever experienced in my life. Now I'm only praying I get forty miles to Pueblo in one piece. Hell, I could sure use a stiff drink of whiskey."

The black man stared curiously at him a moment and chuckled lowly. "Maria and Abigail's father was a small storekeeper in New York. When their mother died from pneumonia, he asked me to help him with the household and a small orchard he tended. When he decided to try his hand in Utah, he asked me again to help with the move and his new store. 'Course when the War broke out, the store's profits went downhill fast. Mr. O'Donnell was a kind gent. Much too kind and generous. He let people run up some mighty big bills. Said the War was hurtin' everyone, and he didn't want no starving children on his conscience. God rest his soul! He gave to others and left his two daughters near destitute. When Miss Maria decided to take a job in Golden and convinced her sister to relocate too, the least I could do was accompany them. Not safe for young ladies to travel alone these days."

"And Joshua and Adam?"

"Who?" Amos looked confused. "Oh, yes, Cousins Joshua and Adam. The coffins," he stammered. "Pity them, sir...I mean, Tye. These cousins died unfortunate deaths in a mine accident, but their last wishes were to be laid next to kin."

Tye's forehead wrinkled. "I thought Abigail said they died in a wagon mishap."

The old man's eyes grew round as saucers. "Oh, yes. Yes...you're right."

Tye looked at him curiously. "Well, let's hope we don't accompany them to their resting place."

Both men fell silent, lost in their own thoughts as they watched the shore where aspen grew thick, spilling their leaves into the dark water like floating gold coins. Tye carefully guided the straying boat into the current as they rounded a bend in the river. Despite the pleasant day, Tye was still irritated. He removed his hat and pushed his fingers again through his damp hair. He was sweating enough to raise the river level an extra inch. By now Brett Trumble had checked at the station and inquired about the mail and was probably waiting somewhere along the riverbank downstream. Why, oh why, did he ever agree to Brett's shenanigans? All he wanted was to be left alone, to be a common rancher, to be tending the cattle with his brothers. In peace. But even Brett wouldn't leave him to his dreams. Gently, yet persistently, Brett was hounding him to become a scout for the army, especially since he had a talent for speaking many of the local Indian languages. Tye rubbed his right leg, stiff and sore from being broken when he fell underneath an Indian pony he was trying to break a few months back. Luckily, his brother, Flint, had dragged him away from the bucking bronc or he might be dead, just like the two corpses onboard.

His eyes fell to the mailbag at Abigail's feet. Brett had recently received word the final batch of discharge and war-related papers had been released by the army, and his papers could possibly be inside the bag. But Brett's papers wouldn't read the way he would have liked. Crazy Brett had left his credentials with a Union soldier when he sneaked behind enemy lines in civilian clothes to spy on the Southern ranks. When a Northern detachment finally recaptured the Southern unit and the captain had been caught with them, his papers couldn't be located. The Northern soldier holding his papers had been killed and sent home in a lowly pine box. Brett's papers were never found among his belongings. For almost a decade now, Brett had been petitioning the U.S. government to take him off a list that threatened to mar a flawless military career and list him as a deserter and traitor.

Tye was so absorbed in his thoughts, he neglected to see the small skiff dart out of a stand of scrub oak along the riverbank behind them and glide silently and swiftly to the side of the flatboat.

"Look! A thief!" Maria screamed, jumping up.

Tye whirled about as Brett's small boat plunged

swiftly through the water and drew up beside them.

"Have care," Tye shouted in warning to the masked individual. He could see sunlight flash off the barrel of Brett's drawn gun. "We have women and *explosives* onboard."

"Allow me to board," Brett's muffled voice demanded from behind the bandanna covering his lower face.

Abigail jumped up beside Maria. "You're not going to let him do it," she said with a hiss. "Stop him!"

"May I point out to you the obvious, Miss Abigail—he's holding a gun?" Tye shook his head in disbelief. "Unless you have a monumentally better idea, I would remain seated. One bullet in those crates and we're feeding the catfish. Sit down. Let me handle this!"

Brett Trumble leaped lithely aboard and threw the rope from his skiff around a tie-down along the side of the flatboat. Tye could see his green eyes swing a wide arc around the boat and come to settle on the crates. There was no mistaking his surprise and puzzlement.

Beside Tye, Swamp rose and instead of growling, cocked his head curiously at Brett. Tye motioned to him to sit, but as soon as he obeyed, his tail began thumping wildly on the bottom of the boat. Tye prayed no one noticed the dog's affable behavior.

"You carry unusual cargo, my friend," Brett drawled. "Coffins, a dog, women, and explosives. All worthless when a man needs some quick money." He pointed his pistol at the mailbag. "Perhaps the mail might hold something of more value." He walked to where the women had resumed their seats on the trunk and reached for the bag beside Abigail, but her hand flashed down and clamped onto it.

"No, you can't have it," she said through clenched teeth. "This mail is worthless to you, but people are waiting for these letters with news from loved ones and home. They need to be delivered."

"Give him the bag, Abigail," Tye ordered, his voice low and insistent. "Let's not join your dear cousins."

Abigail's jaw tightened, and she flashed an irritated glance at him. "Whose side are you on? This is worth two dollars if we deliver it to Pueblo."

"Side?" Tye's voice raised an octave. "What the blazes are you thinking? He's holding a gun!"

"Give it to him. Please, Abigail," Maria pleaded. She stood. Her face was the color of newly fallen snow, and her hands trembled as she tugged at her sister's sleeve. "Please, Abigail, don't be difficult."

Tye watched Abigail reluctantly release her grip. Brett quickly scooped up the bag, then turned to survey the flying petticoat. "Yours, miss?" He looked at Abigail.

She blushed. "Sir, you are no gentleman!"

He laughed and hooked a thumb over his shoulder toward the coffins. "Oh, I suppose they were?"

"But, of course. My cousins were gentlemen to the very day they died."

From behind his bandanna, Brett chuckled. "Next you'll be telling me they were men of the cloth."

"No, of course not. The O'Donnells were honorable men who worked the mines and never once stole from others, I might add."

"Irishmen, eh? I knew it!" Brett flapped his hand in front of his concealed face. "Shoot-fire, it seems they died with the best Irish whiskey still on their breaths. My daddy said there are many men who've been known to hit the sauce with one foot in the grave. These miners are living proof."

Tye watched Abigail's eyes widen and her face blanch, and for a brief moment, he swore he could smell whiskey on the gust of wind seeping over them from the north riverbank. He squinted curiously at her, then at the coffins. He hoped Brett would not further enrage her. She had the temperament of a cornered rattler.

Beside Brett, Maria stood, obviously overwhelmed by his ribald humor and the commotion. She took one faltering step and started to speak, then collapsed, crumpling sideways onto the trunk before she rolled onto the worn floorboards of the boat.

"Damn you." Tye lunged at Brett. "Now look what you've done!" He swung his fist, connecting it solidly with Brett's jaw. The blow forced Brett to stagger backwards, and before Tye could grab him, he toppled over into the river with his gun and the mailbag in tow.

"The mail!" Abigail shrieked, jumping up and waving her arms frantically.

"Forget the mail and that blackguard sinner. And stop rocking the boat!" Tye crossed to where Maria lay and stripped off his jacket. He knelt beside the fallen girl. "Help me with your sister." He gathered Maria into his arms, turned her onto her back, then bunched his coat into a ball and settled it beneath her head for a pillow. He was so intent upon tending to the girl, he hardly gave Brett Trumble's escape any conscious thought.

Amos hurried to help him.

"Get me a wet handkerchief, Amos, and my saddlebags. Then untie the skiff before it catches on a rock or collides with something, and we crash right along with it."

"But he's getting away!" Abigail screamed above his head. "He's got the mail. We have to stop him! You're giving him his booooooat?"

Tye glanced up to see Brett slicing through the water in clean long strokes toward the opposite shore.

"Let him go, we've more serious things to worry about." Snapping open his bag, he removed a small muslin bag and waved it under the unconscious girl's nose.

Abigail looked down at them. "What are you doing?" There was even more alarm in her voice. She knelt beside her sister.

"It's rosemary, basil, and mint. The Indians sometimes use piñon pine. After living among the Indians for a few years, I gained a little knowledge of their medicine. These are from my sister, Betsy, who runs the General Store in Golden. Even if doesn't help to arouse those who have passed out or fainted, it sure does make my gear smell good."

Tye held Maria's head gently in his hand as he placed the cold cloth on her forehead and flapped the muslin bag beneath her nose. He could feel the soft silky texture of her dark hair resting in his palm. Her delicate face was pale and flawless. How long had it been since he felt a woman in his arms? How long had it been since he touched the smooth skin of a vibrant beautiful woman such as this? A long time, he admitted to himself.

"She's not fainted from the excitement as much as

from hunger," Abigail admitted, her face growing red. "We haven't eaten since noon yesterday."

"Why on earth didn't you say something?"

The girl moaned beside him. She raised her hand and pushed the bag of herbs away from her face.

He gestured toward the bow of the boat. "I have food in a bag stashed up front. Excellent goat cheese and bread made by my sister-in-law, and some dried beef and apples. There's a ring flask full of clear, cool water, too."

"We're not charity cases," Abigail said.

Tye heaved an exasperated sigh. Beside him, Maria slowly came to her senses, and he gently helped her to sit upright. His hand traveled to her back where he continued to support her. "I'd take it easy for a moment," he cautioned. "Get your bearings before standing."

She tried to smile. "I'm sorry. I'm not generally prone to fainting."

"Empty stomachs have a tendency to cause it. At least now I can be the first to offer you a meal on behalf of Golden's welcoming committee. I'm sure my oldest brother, Flint, would want me to greet you on behalf of the school board, too."

"Oh, no-ooo," Maria groaned and lowered her face into the palms of her hands. "Don't tell me your brother is a member of the *school board*?" She looked up at him, her cheeks taking on a glint of red. "This is embarrassing." She stood with his help and sat on the trunk.

Amos interrupted, handing Tye his saddlebags. "We're obliged for even the slightest bite to take the edge off our hunger."

With the incident behind them, the group ate in relatively peaceful silence while Tye and Amos took turns with their poles guiding the boat. Minutes later, into the lull, the old black man looked over to Abigail still eating an apple. His dark eyes narrowed. "Take heed, missy, and remember what I've told you about apples."

Abigail's mouth fell away from the MacIntosh, and she turned it round in her hand. "Land sakes, Amos, there's at least a dozen more bites left, and I plan to devour all of them."

Curiosity piqued, Tye waited quietly for an explanation.

Abigail laughed, tossed the core into the water, and watched it bob a few times, before it slowly sank below the surface, only to pop upward again.

"Amos is a trifle superstitious," Maria explained. "He was born and raised in the South, but came north as a young man. He believes if an unmarried woman takes the last bite from an apple, she could end up an old maid for the rest of her life."

Tye met her cinnamon-colored eyes with ones as dark as molasses. "You don't sound like a believer. However, at the rate your sister has been making friends, an apple might not have anything to do with her chance for marriage. No offense." He grinned.

Maria smiled. "No offense taken. Abby and I tend to humor Amos and his black magic."

They rounded a leafy bend in the river, and Tye stood and walked to the front of the boat. "Pueblo is straight ahead about a half mile." He pointed to a tiny settlement coming into view. Mismatched structures of all types and sizes, fashioned of wood and stone, lined the steep riverbanks. The sun was beginning to sink on the horizon and color the sky in shades of pink. Behind them, the Rocky Mountains stood tall and proud in varying shades of blues.

"The landing will be to our left." Tye poled the boat to a shallow silt-bottomed area just below a huge wooden station standing high up on the bank like a guardhouse. Minutes later, with the help of Amos, he glided the boat into the docks along a hand-hewn pier and tied off, then helped the women alight.

"Let's give the Henderson Mining Company the pleasure of unloading their wares themselves and just light out of here," Tye suggested.

"No. Please." Maria turned back toward the flatboat. "My trunk. Can you take my trunk? Inside are all my books for teaching. I can't afford to get them wet or lose them."

Reluctantly, Tye limped back to the boat and retrieved the trunk, carrying it up the grassy bank and setting it beneath the canopy of a poplar, bowing down with heavy foliage.

"The coffins, too?" Abigail asked.

"They're already dead." Tye heard Amos give an anxious little cough beside him.

Abigail's voice was insistent. "I can't stand by and allow the dead to be so ill-treated."

Tye gave her an unfriendly lengthy stare, then abruptly turned, whistled to Swamp, and moved toward the small footpath leading up to the inn. "Then I'd suggest you get them yourself." He was glad to be alive. The only thing he really wanted was to get away from the nitroglycerin and these fickle females. He wanted a warm supper, a good stiff drink, and a soft bed.

"They're worth a bottle of pure well-aged corn whiskey," Abigail called out after him.

He spun around. "Another ploy, Miss O'Donnell?"

He looked over at Maria who shook her head. "No, she's telling the truth."

He walked back down to the flatboat. Behind him, both women followed. Minutes later, with everyone's help and a lot of muscle, they managed to drag the heavy coffins up the slippery grass, several yards from the landing under the tree with Maria's trunk.

Panting, Abigail knelt and patted the coffin. "My dear Cousin Adam thanks you, sir."

To Tye's amazement, she fiddled with the coffin's locks and flipped the lid open. The familiar smell of whiskey assailed his nostrils as he stared at the satin-lined coffin where rows upon rows of whiskey bottles were wrapped in cloth and stacked in thick layers of straw.

"Ah-hhh, it looks like we lost only one." Abigail examined the contents, then smiled, removed a bottle, and held it up with its amber liquid toward the fading light. "The best Canada has to offer!" She paused and smiled. "A deal is a deal, Tye Ashmore." She handed it to him.

Tye took the bottle from her outstretched hand and nodded at the other coffin. "And dear Cousin Joshua?"

Abigail walked to the other coffin, knelt, opened the hasps, and flipped the lid. "Only the best imported French wine in the country." She showed him a bottle. "Now all we have to do is get this delivered to Golden and stored properly in the Mule Shed Inn's wine cellar. It took all of my mother's jewelry and what little cash we had to buy out a saloon in Cedar City going belly-up. I bought only the finest from the owner's stock."

"Mule Shed? Your uncle is Henry McNeil?" Tye asked.

"The same," Abigail replied.

Tye whistled lowly under his breath. "Oh, heaven forbid," he said with an exhausted sigh. He bent his head, pondering how he could best tell them his unfortunate news. Finally, he looked up. "I hate to be the one to tell you this—but your uncle, Henry McNeil, was murdered over two weeks ago, stabbed in the chest with a dagger which appeared to be from a vagabond Confederate soldier."

"Murdered?" both women asked simultaneously.

Tye reached out to grab Maria's arm and steady her trembling body.

"Yes," he said softly, "truly, I'm sorry."

Chapter Three

While he and Amos walked the O'Donnell sisters up the path toward the station at Pueblo in silence, Tye wondered if they had any inkling about the sad state of affairs at the Mule Shed in Golden. Henry McNeil was, by all means, a most shrewd proprietor, except for his one weakness—his wife, Emma, a beautiful but strange woman.

Tye also wondered whether he should tell them about the rumors flying about town Emma married Henry for his money. It was said she aggressively pursued the old bachelor after her first husband died and left her in debt. But what purpose would it serve? There was little use in having either niece meet their aunt with a wrong impression. They would hear about it soon enough. There was no shortage of local gossip in Golden.

Now, after the death of Henry McNeil, many had believed she had gone crazy as well. Late at night, she could be seen seated at the spinet before the old front window of the manse, playing the same Southern tune over and over again by the light of an oil lamp.

"How could Uncle Henry have died at the hands of a Southerner?" Maria disrupted the silence. "The War has been over for ten years."

"For some, the War will never be over." Tye heaved a disgruntled sigh. "Tensions die hard. I was told he was found in front of the old graveyard with a knife, forged in North Carolina, in his chest and clutching a button from a Confederate uniform."

She looked at him with troubled, yet puzzled eyes.

"I can't rightly figure it out myself," he admitted. "Henry was a favored man around these parts. It's said he gave food and shelter to all poor and hungry, regardless of their skin or uniform color. The Mule Shed Inn's kitchen was open to everyone, including drifters and vagrants."

They stopped outside the station.

"What do we do now?" Maria wiped a tear running down the side of her face. "It's almost nightfall. We have no place to stay, little money, and we're burdened with two heavy caskets of whiskey and wine. And, Uncle Henry is dead!"

Abigail looked at her with a grim expression. "One thing at a time, Maria. We must find a place to hide the coffins, find a cheap place to stay, rent a wagon, and start out for Golden tomorrow, just as we planned. There's no going back. I'm hoping Aunt Emma is kind enough to agree to take us in, not being blood kin."

A dozen thoughts went through Tye Ashmore's mind as he listened to the women discuss their plight. If he were a smart man, a thinking man, he and Swamp would abandon these females like scared jack rabbits and be on their way, headed out of town with his sister's wagon as he had earlier planned. But he was an Ashmore, and Ashmores were honest, honorable men. And how would he ever explain to his oldest brother he dumped the new schoolmarm on the bank of the Arkansas River to fend for herself? The women needed help. Oh, please give me enough strength, he prayed silently as he looked skyward, to collect these women and their worldly belongings and deposit their pretty backsides in Golden as quickly as possible.

He spoke. "It might be best if we get you a hotel room for the night. Tomorrow I'm headed for Golden with a wagonload of supplies for the General Store. If we rent another wagon, we can take the coffins and head out at daylight. I'm betting a couple of those bottles of whiskey will be more than enough payment for a wagon and team."

"How far is Golden?" Maria looked at him with a sad, sorrowful gaze worse than Swamp when he was being scolded.

"A good five days of travel." Tye saw sadness turn to weariness to apprehension on her face.

"We have no supplies, no food." She told him the obvious.

"I think I can rustle up enough to get us by." He looked at Amos and withdrew some coins from the inside pocket of his buckskin coat. "Take the women to the hotel and make sure they get a room and some food, and meet me back at the livery stable. We need to get those coffins undercover before night closes in." He started to leave, then turned back around. "Oh, and if anyone gives you any problems, tell them you are friends of Betsy Ashmore. My sister is well-known throughout these parts. She now owns the General Store in Golden, has another in Colorado Springs, and does a lot of business here in Pueblo."

Amos nodded, picked up their traveling bags, and herded the cheerless women toward town.

Tye looked at the bottle of whiskey he still held in his hand and smiled ruefully, glad he wouldn't have to drop any money in the saloon later on. He headed in the opposite direction toward the end of town where the livery was located. Maybe he'd uncork it early and have himself a few swigs to calm his jangled nerves. After all, he needed to know how good it might be if he was going to barter for a wagon and a team. And hellfire, he needed something to help him forget the silly notions racing through his head about courting the schoolmarm once they reached Golden.

****

In spite of Tye's earlier trepidation, the trip northward to Golden was uneventful as the group covered ground quickly, stopping only long enough to eat and rest. Both women were silent, almost brooding, never complaining about the dust, hot sun, cold food, uneven trails, or long hours. Tye suspected they were mulling over in their minds the sudden death of their uncle and wondering what might happen with their grieving aunt in charge.

They reached Golden in late afternoon on the fifth day and stopped at the edge of town, outside the huge, three-story inn. The women paused to stare at the monstrous structure before they alighted from the wagon and climbed the wide front steps. Solidly built of weathered gray timbers, the Mule Shed Inn boasted a railed porch on the front and both sides. It was deserted and quiet, obviously shut down since Henry's death. To the left and behind it, several yards away, an expansive, squat stable sat among a stand of towering pine which protected it from the winter snows and shaded it from the summer sun.

Tye followed the women up the steps. They were surprised when they pushed at the thick entrance door to find it unlocked. Maria and Abigail moved silently inside, past the large entrance hall and dining room on the left where rows upon rows of windows, framed with dusty, threadbare curtains, faced Main Street and allowed diners a view of the town's activities. Beyond the dining area, a large office and another lobby guarded one corner of the room while on the right side through an arch, a barroom occupied three quarters the length of the establishment and served whiskey and all varieties of ale from the same two barrels. Between the dining room and barroom, an ornate staircase led to the rooms above. Along the entire back of the Mule Shed, a well-equipped kitchen and pantry opened onto a spacious back porch leading to the outside.

The second floor, just as spacious, was divided into two bedrooms, a Ladies Parlor, an Arbitration Room for settling minor disputes among townsfolk, and a sitting room for the guests of the house. Higher on the third floor, a long hall carved a path in front of a row of sleeping chambers capable of easily accommodating a dozen or more guests. The entire structure was dusty, worn, and in need of paint, wallpaper, and lots of soap.

Maria and Abigail said little as they walked about the quiet, lifeless structure, ending at the main floor again. Finally, Maria sighed and spoke, "Well, it appears we can't stay here. Maybe we can use the little cottage Uncle Henry wrote about in his letters. He said it was located back in the grove, between the manse and the inn's private stables, and would be a perfect place for us to live."

Tye could see the utter disappointment and dismay in the women's faces at the sorry state of the structure. "The War was hard on everyone," he pointed out.

"Brocade drapes were not a priority, and fancy furniture was difficult to come by. Yet, the West and rural areas had the advantage."

Maria stared at him wordlessly and looked confused.

"These were the people who had food," he said quietly and ushered them out back and down a soft slope with Amos trailing behind.

Even before the group reached the front door of the cottage, it was evident they were not about to fare much better. From a distance, the roof was tattered, many of the shingles ripped free by brisk winds. Once a white structure, the blistered cottage had faded to a milky gray. Its tiny porch was rotted and in sad need of repairs. The only beauty amid the decrepit structure was a rambling rose climbing lazily up one side of the rickety porch and spilling over in riotous red blooms.

Abigail was the first to reach the porch, swinging the door open, its rusty hinges whining and complaining. Inside, dust covered the floors and furnishings. Furry occupants had gnawed holes in the upholstered chairs and left evidence of their presence on the floor, fireplace hearth, and table. She moved to the back door, hanging by one hinge, and pushed it open to reveal an overgrown, generous back yard. Once planted with herbs, it was now growing wild and full of weeds. It was an ideal private area, ringed by the dense forest beyond. A small springhouse stood to the left of the backdoor, and at the back of the yard, a large shed with a chicken coop attached to one side fought for space with a lean-to stable barely big enough to shelter a few cows or horses. A small path on the left side of the property wound through a grove of bushes and pines and ended at private stables situated far below the manse.

Tye heard Maria give a disenchanted sigh.

"It can be restored," he said and glanced at Amos whose old eyes widened in dismay. "Well, maybe you had better see if Emma McNeil could keep Abigail and you for a few days. At least until we get the inside in better order."

Maria pushed a tendril of dark hair from her face. "Without money? We have nothing except what the wine and whiskey might bring."

"No, oh no, we're not selling the liquor and wine." Abigail didn't try to keep the sharpness from her voice. "It would bring twice the amount inside the barroom once the inn was reopened."

Leaning on the doorjamb, Tye pursed his lips. "I don't believe your aunt has any plans to reopen the place."

"For heaven's sake, why not?" Maria squinted up at him. "Uncle Henry mentioned it in his letters. He was looking forward to working with Abigail who used to help Papa with his store."

"It would be quite an ambitious undertaking, and I fear Emma doesn't have the business sense your uncle Henry had. Word's out she's looking for a buyer."

"Why, there's a fortune to be made now. Settlers are pouring into the West, and gold and coal are enticing others into the mines," Abigail said.

Tye shrugged. "Maybe your aunt wants no part of the toil and sweat." He gave them a sympathetic smile. "You know, that's what I like about you, Abigail; you can't resist the sound of coins jingling in another man's pockets and not wonder how you might lighten the poor fellow's load." He watched her mouth twitch in amusement, then turned to Maria. There was tenderness in his eyes when he spoke, "I'll wager Golden's school board could give you an advance on your wages if it would help."

Maria shook her head. "No, thank you. Although I can guess which member might vote in my favor."

His answer was merely another smile. "I wouldn't spend time chewing on it; we'll figure it out. The school board does pay for a place for the teacher to stay. This cottage is easily renovated, and my brothers are easy marks for free labor. I'll notify the mining company about the crates at the dock and make certain dear cousins, Joshua and Adam, are laid to rest in the inn's cellar."

His gaze caught hers and held it. She looked fragile, exhausted, and drained. Her eyes were red-rimmed and beneath, dark circles were forming. She had not slept most of the journey northward. At night he heard her move from her bed underneath the wagon and sit with her back against a wheel, knees clasped to her chest as she stared at the stars and wept. But he didn't dare disturb her. He knew from experience all people grieved in their own way. Some openly. Others, silently by themselves.

"You need to get a good night's rest," he said.

"I'll try." She smiled wanly.

He turned, clambered down the rickety porch steps, and started toward the inn before he halted, turning back. "Amos, I could use some help at the ranch, if you're looking for a warm place to spend a few nights."

"I'd be obliged." The old man nodded from the porch.

"Meet me at the Mule Shed once you help the ladies get their baggage up to the manse. I'll deliver my sister's wagon to the General Store." Nodding in farewell, he started back up the slope toward his wagon, his limp growing more pronounced.

****

As soon as Tye headed up the path, Maria hurried to the window and brushed aside the tattered curtains. She watched his tall, dark image fade in the dim light. She scolded herself for feeling attracted to his rugged good looks and quiet strength. He was obviously not a man to shirk his duties. He could have dropped all three of them like a hot potato straight out of the fire, yet now he was talking about helping with the cottage renovations. She wondered if his broad shoulders ever tired of the many burdens he carried.

"Maria, Maria. You know it's bad luck to watch someone walk out of sight," Amos scolded, hurrying to where she stood. His old arthritic hand moved to sweep the curtains back into place.

"Oh, don't be a simpleton, Amos." Abigail rolled her eyes toward the ceiling and sighed. "Look around you. Can our luck get much worse than this? Please see to poor Joshua and Adam's safety. Maria and I can take what we need for the night up to the manse in a carpetbag."

Later, after Amos had left, Maria and Abigail moved out into the yard, following a small worn footpath winding its way past the cottage and stables and up to the huge house perched on a knoll above the town. The door opened before they barely set foot on the flagstone stoop, and a middle-aged woman with iron gray hair timidly greeted them.

"Oh, my, the O'Donnell sisters! I'm Millie Hanson, the housekeeper, pleased to meet you. You're exactly like dear departed Henry described you. I'm so sorry for your loss. Your uncle was a good man." She led them to a badly lit parlor, promising to fetch their aunt and return with tea and cookies.

Maria stared at the dim, almost eerie room and shivered as if an army of tiny spiders were creeping up her back. The parlor was nothing like she had ever imagined. Every shade had been lowered, except for a corner window where a ray of light shed its faint beams onto the furniture, draped with white sheets like ghostly second skins. Only a lone, blue velvet love seat and a cream brocade chair, to the right of a spinet, was bare of any covering.

On one side of the room, a massive stone fireplace inlaid with Dutch tile crawled up a wall covered with a flocked gold wallpaper. Bookcases flanked either side of the fireplace, and above the mantel, a huge gilded frame held a portrait of a man who bore a striking resemblance to the McNeils and their deceased mother with his square high cheekbones and angular jaw. She instantly knew this was her late uncle at a much earlier age. Across the room, hanging from a gold cord, another similar frame held the portrait of a much younger, lusty Aunt Emma, similar to the small daguerreotype their father had once shown them. But in this portrait, she was heavily rouged, and she wore a revealing, low-cut lace-trimmed blouse magnifying her already ample endowments.

Moments later, amid the sound of ruffling taffeta, Aunt Emma swept through the archway and into the room. She was a tall, regal-looking woman with gray blonde hair. It was evident she had taken all precautions to disguise any hint of aging. Her face was generously powdered, and her hair was swept up into a youthful mass of ringlets and curls. A single diamond pendant hung from her slim neck, and matching earrings glittered like ice chips from each ear lobe. Her Venetian lace shawl pulled together with an opal and diamond-studded pin fell elegantly over a black mourning dress.

Maria rose first, extending her hands. "We're so sorry to hear of Uncle Henry's death. It must have been a devastating shock."

Emma grasped them graciously, then removed a delicate linen handkerchief from her sleeve, and dabbed at her eyes. She moved to the portrait of Henry McNeil above the fireplace. "Ah, poor Henry, such a good man…to everyone." She sniffed, then glided silently about the room until she took a seat in a draped armchair, instead of the brocade one. She motioned to the girls to be seated on the love seat across from her.

"Do the authorities have any idea who might have killed Uncle Henry?" Abigail asked.

"Authorities? Heavens, child, there is only one sheriff here, and he's inebriated most of the time!" Emma laughed a high, nervous laugh. "Why, the nearest law is a U.S. marshall who covers almost the entire Colorado Territory." She twisted the gold band on her finger round and round. "No, no one seems to know anything."

"What shall you do now?" Maria's gaze slowly skirted the room, taking in the fine layer of dust on the rich oak floor rimming an expensive Oriental rug beneath their feet. Earlier, she had noticed the spinet in the front window wore a meticulous shine, and the brass oil lamp was polished to a brilliant sheen. A small crystal dish with an elaborate lid sat behind the oil lamp and held a solitary button. She suspected it was the one found at the scene where her uncle was killed.

"I shall have to carry on without dear Henry," Emma lamented with a dramatic sigh. Her hand fluttered to her breast. "Someday, perhaps, when Henry's death is not so heavy on my heart, I may return to my beloved hometown in Georgia to live."

"What about the Mule Shed Inn?" Abigail resettled herself more comfortably on the loveseat.

The woman lifted her thin shoulders into a shrug. "I've given it deep thought these past few days, and I've decided to sell."

"Why?" Abigail sat forward. "Why not let someone manage it for you instead? There are scores of settlers pouring into the West. There's money to be made."

Beside her, Maria cleared her throat. "Maybe Aunt Emma doesn't think respectable women should run inns with a drinking establishment, Abby."

"Penniless ones do."

"Oh, my," Emma said, frowning. "I hardly think it would be fitting."

"For me to manage it?" Abigail glared at her. "I don't plan to be the bar maid. I can hire a bar keeper and help for the inn's barroom."

The housekeeper appeared with a silver tray of cookies and tea. A wane smile crossed her thin lips as she individually served each of them before retreating silently to the kitchen again.

Emma sighed and fingered the lace on her shawl. "Actually, now with Henry gone, I was thinking you might want to rethink your plans. Perhaps you may want to consider returning home to Utah."

"There is no home," Maria rejoined. There was something disturbing about this stiff-backed woman who seemed almost annoyed by their presence. "My father left us little, and what we did have, we spent traveling here. We sold our home in Utah, all our belongings, and my mother's jewelry to cover his debts."

Emma blinked her eyes, and her lips puckered into a scowl.

"Unfortunately, what Maria says is the truth," Abigail said. "It would be impossible to return. Anyhow, Maria has agreed to accept the teaching position Uncle Henry arranged."

Emma McNeil leaned forward and poured them each a cup of tea. "Surely you understand with Henry dead, there's hardly enough cash to feed the mouths I already have on staff." She stared at the portrait of her husband for a moment, then added offhandedly, "Your father's and Henry's generosity to help the destitute at the expense of their surviving relatives seems to run in the family, doesn't it, my dears?"

"Perhaps," Abigail agreed, taking a thin lemon cookie from the plate. "But with a few repairs, some good housekeeping, and a firm hand on the liquor, the inn and its barroom could be back in business. I've never known a man who wouldn't spend a few coins from his hard-earned paycheck on a good drink now and then. We could put it back on its feet in a relatively short time. I used to help Father with the books and inventory, and I'm sure Amos is more than capable of managing and renting rooms."

"Amos?" Emma asked. "Who's Amos?"

"An old black man who used to work for our father and who accompanied us here."

"Free or slave?"

"Aunt Em," Maria said gently, "you forget. They are all free now."

"Yes, of course, my dear. I only meant whether he was from the North or South."

"North," Maria said. "He has been with our family since Mother passed away. He accompanied Father when we moved from New York to Utah. He is highly organized, and his math skills are beyond reproach. He used to help Papa in the store."

Before Emma could say more, Abigail spoke, "We could split the profits, Aunt Emma, and we'd not be underfoot once the cottage was repaired. Uncle Henry had mentioned it in his letters."

Emma stared at her, a look of displeasure etching her sharp features, as she pondered Abigail's proposal. Finally she nodded, relenting. "Well, why not? Of course, you can try. I mean, you must try."

"Oh, thank you!" Abigail jumped up from her seat and excitedly clapped her hands together. "You'll see; you won't be disappointed."

"My dear, everything about Uncle Henry and his passel of penniless friends and sniveling relatives has been a disappointment over the last few years. I don't anticipate things will change."

Later in the evening, as the girls undressed for bed in a front bedroom on the second floor, Maria voiced her thoughts about the latest events. "I do pray Amos is safe and well fed, and I do hope we can get the cottage in order as soon as possible and the inn restored."

"I'm sure Amos is faring well," Abigail said. "Don't fret. Tye Ashmore seemed delighted to have a guest for the night. Once we get the rooms cleaned, Amos will be able to stay at the inn and be close by."

Maria looked around the room with a glum face. "I don't believe I'll miss this drab place." She refolded their meager belongings in their carpetbag.

Abigail combed her long hair before a small dressing table and watched Maria turn down the covers of the bed. "It is rather stark and cold."

"And dreary," Maria said, shuddering. She refused to voice her worries aloud. There was something not quite right about Emma. "Did you notice her portrait was downright scandalous? Hideous!"

"Why do you suppose all her parlor furniture was covered? It looks like wraiths have invaded the sitting room." Abigail frowned.

Maria crawled between the sheets and blankets on the bed and pulled them to her neck. "You keep forgetting the War, Abby. Everyone was forced to be frugal, to try to save his belongings from dust and wear. Now with Uncle Henry's death and no income, I'm sure Aunt Em realizes she must be frugal."

Abigail looked at the door thoughtfully. "I wonder what else is on this floor?"

"More bedrooms, I suppose."

"And the third?"

"An attic? Why do you ask?" Maria yawned and crawled deeper under the counterpane. It felt good to finally sleep in a down-filled bed with a full stomach, even if the outside temperature was warmer than the inside one.

Abigail slipped in beside her. "Just curious, I

guess."

"Oh, please, Abby. Your curiosity is what gets us in a fix all the time. Just go to sleep."

Within the hour, they both fell into a deep slumber, but not before they heard Aunt Emma at the spinet downstairs playing the tune, "Bonnie Blue Flag," over and over again.

Chapter Four

Maria and Abigail met Amos and Tye outside the Mule Shed Inn the next day, long before the sun threw its rays through the lace curtains of their bedroom. The men had arrived with a buckboard, Tye's horse tied behind it, and what looked like a basket filled with food.

"Well, what should we do first?" Abigail was eager to take another look at the inside of the inn. Together with Amos's help, she planned to make a list of only the essential repairs needed to reopen the barroom and dining room.

"I'd like to see the school," Maria suggested eagerly.

Tye Ashmore shrugged. "I've the whole day to myself. I can take Maria to the schoolhouse while you and Amos start planning what needs to be accomplished immediately on the inn and cottage. It should only take us an hour or so."

"Oh, no." Maria shook her head, blushing. "I couldn't ask you to do that."

"Of course, you can." The last thing Abigail wanted to do was spend hours inside a stuffy schoolhouse while Maria poured over musty books and stared at dusty slate boards. "After all, his brother is a member of the school board, so who better to show you?"

Tye motioned to Maria to follow him to the buckboard. "I think your sister is politely trying to tell us she has no interest in the schoolhouse."

After they left, Abigail wandered through the Mule Shed's rooms, making a mental note to locate the local brewery and lumberyard. She would need to refill the wine cellar, and from the amount of damage to the barroom floor and cottage porch, she knew she was going to have to convince the owner of the mill to provide her with lumber on an advance. She doubted she could persuade her aunt to part with a measly coin.

"It'll take a few weeks to get it in shape," Amos said. "It won't be easy. It won't be cheap."

"It withstood over ten years of neglect," Abigail pointed out. "If necessary, it can stand a few more weeks until we realize a profit. Why don't you start a list of what we'll need for the cottage, then go out to the inn's stables and check for damage there as well. Oh, and look for some tools."

When Amos departed, Abigail headed directly to the office where she had earlier seen a pile of ledgers stacked on an old rolltop desk. She sat in the well-worn swivel chair and opened the most recent book where the latest monthly entries had been penned in by her late uncle. It took only moments to check the debit columns before she realized many of the purchases were not inn expenses, but rather entries for expensive yard goods, ribbons, muslin, satins, taffetas, and velvets, obviously purchased for her aunt. Despite the hardship of the last few years, Emma McNeil's extravagant tastes had not waned.

Randomly, she riffled through the pages, making a mental note of the names of persons who had once supplied her uncle with services and goods. She groaned aloud when she discovered the names of farmers, Tye Ashmore included, who had supplied beef and hay. She had completely forgotten about the stables and the need to stock it with grain and fodder for travelers' horses and mules. It would also have to shelter wagons and buggies of visitors and guests. She quickly penned a note to remind herself to speak to Tye Ashmore when he returned with Maria.

In a second leather-bound ledger, she stumbled across the payroll for the inn's hired help. In his familiar, painstakingly neat script, Uncle Henry had listed their wages and any debts they owed him. Much to Abigail's relief, the ledgers had been meticulously kept up-to-date and were a wealth of information for managing the barroom, kitchen, and dining room. Everything she needed was right at her fingertips. All she would have to do was spend a few evenings poring over them, and she'd learn more than anyone could possibly teach her firsthand.

Once, while she worked, she thought she heard a door open but dismissed the thought. The mind could play tricks with anyone in an old deserted building, and thanks to Aunt Emma and her odd welcome, she found herself becoming a nervous Nelly. Even Maria had admitted there was something disturbing about their aunt and her behavior. Instead of being overjoyed at seeing them, the woman had seemed almost uncomfortably irritated with their presence. Or was it just her grief which made her appear so? Whatever the reason, Abigail knew she couldn't give it further thought. There simply was too much to worry about with the inn itself without adding the complications of an eccentric old widow—a woman with expensive tastes and a love for Southern songs.

****

Brett Trumble propped his body against the doorjamb and crossed his arms, watching the blue-eyed girl before him, poring over the ledgers as if she had discovered a magical potion. Unaware of his presence, she flipped the pages of the ledgers with her agile, slim fingers and traced entry upon entry, taking only a split second to push away a stray tendril of blonde hair when it tumbled into her line of vision. She wore a simple blue gingham dress, the plainness of which only served to contrast and heighten the color of her periwinkle eyes.

Brett considered himself an ambitious man with a keen business insight. He had worked the lumber mill with his father until the war broke out, and with the profits he made, he had bought up land around the area, knowing the value placed on timber. But it was his arrogance and stubbornness that got him in the fix he was in. The North had needed spies to go behind enemy lines, secure weapon tallies, and assess enemy strength. Living in the backwoods of the Colorado Territory, he had been a natural for the job. But he never figured the government he had served so loyally would turn its back on him.

Brett stared at the girl. Actually, she was the source of all his trouble at the moment, even though he had been secretly hoping to meet her again. When Tye come sailing down the river, he had never once thought he'd arrive with anything but a bag of U.S. mail as planned. Now things were complicated, thanks to his good friend's willingness to come to the aid of the defenseless duo. If either of the O'Donnell sisters recognized him, they might turn him in for a thief. It was a chance he couldn't take and a worry he didn't want. The humiliation alone would destroy his father.

He cleared his throat, and Abigail's head shot up. She jumped, spilling a pile of ledgers heaped on her lap.

"I didn't mean to frighten you." Brett started forward to help collect the scattered books. He squatted at her feet and peered up at her. "You must be Henry McNeil's niece."

"Abigail O'Donnell."

"I'm Brett Trumble."

"What can I do for you, Mr. Trumble?"

Brett could see there was a curious look on her face as she eyed him with reserved caution. He rose and piled the ledgers on the desk. "I guess I owe you a dollar."

"A bar debt?" She raised a delicate eyebrow.

He grimaced and let out a long, audible breath. "No, for your help in delivering the mail."

"You!" she shrieked as recognition dawned on her face. "You stole the mail!"

This time, he laughed, his green eyes sparkling like pieces of emeralds. It was a delightful, fun-filled, bubbling laugh.

"You. You're a thief. A no-good thief!"

"No, Miss O'Donnell, I merely borrowed it. I've never stolen anything in my life." He extracted a silver dollar, flipped it into the air, and deftly caught it in his palm. "I removed the letter I was looking for and returned the rest to the stage office in Pueblo to be distributed to all those poor dear friends and relatives awaiting news of their loved ones from back home."

She glared at him, ignoring his attempt at sarcasm. "It's a federal offense."

"The federal government has offended me by insisting I'm a Northern deserter and traitor because I misplaced my army papers. The only reason I'm coming to you is so my thievery won't be disclosed should you stumble across me in town and recognize me."

"Hah, what makes you think I'd remain silent?" she challenged.

Brett gave her an indulgent smile. My, she was a feisty one, just as Tye had warned. "Because your uncle owes me two hundred dollars." He picked up the most recent ledger she had been reading and deftly leafed through the pages.

"Now, see here, just a minute. You can't go poking around in someone's personal accounts!" She jumped up and reached for the ledger.

"Now, now." He held the book over his head, out of her reach. "And what were you doing, but poking in them as well?" He lowered the ledger and flipped through the pages until he found the date and entry he wanted. "Look here." He shoved it toward her. "It was just a small gambling debt Henry owed me."

"Gambling?" She looked at the figure with knitted brows. "Two hundred dollars? My uncle was never one to play games of chance."

"Cards, Miss O'Donnell, cards. There's always the first time, and he wasn't very good at it." He watched her face redden in anger.

"What makes you think one indiscriminate act by my uncle will keep me from disclosing your lawless brazen act?"

"Oh, come, Miss O'Donnell, this is a small town. You don't strike me as a person who'd want to blacken your deceased uncle's reputation, nor your aunt's, not if you're even considering opening the inn and barroom. And think of your sister. What would the townspeople and school board think if they thought the schoolmarm's late uncle was less than an upstanding citizen?"

"That's blackmail!" Abigail's hands flew up in the air.

Brett grabbed one of her flying hands, opened her palm, and dropped the silver dollar into it.

"Keep it," she said, shoving it toward him. "You shall have your money as soon as the inn is reopened and on its feet again. I assure you, you'll be the first to be paid."

He laughed softly but refused to take the coin. "You really do have a temper, Miss O'Donnell. I think it would be best if I stopped by when we both have more time to spare, and we can discuss this further." He spun on his heels, and before she could utter another word, he walked to the door. He stopped, his hand resting on the knob, and grew serious. "I'm pretty fair at keeping books myself. If you need any help deciphering your uncle's ledgers, I'd be willing to lend a hand. You can find me down at the lumberyard." He stepped through the door, closing it solidly behind him, whistling as he walked out onto the porch.

****

Tye had promised himself two women and two crates of nitroglycerin were enough excitement to last a lifetime. But when Amos needed a place to stay, he couldn't refuse. He had never abandoned any man down on his luck, and lately, the farmhouse was far too lonely and quiet at times to suit him.

His oldest brother, Flint, had married Julia Gast, a red-haired potter, seven years ago and moved onto her neighboring place along Cherry Creek, and his other brother, Marcus, had married a Swedish gal who worked with Julia. Marcus and Anna had built a small ranch house several miles away from Flint and Julia's homestead. His sister, Betsy, still preferred to spend most of her time in town overseeing the General Store, which she now owned. And his brother who was a U.S marshall spent most of his time up north, trying to keep law and order in the Territory.

The evening had proven to be more entertaining than he had ever imagined. The superstitious old man had lifted a second bottle of whiskey from Cousin Adam's casket, rationalizing if they were both fool enough to be willing to be blown to bits and fed to the fish, they deserved to properly celebrate the escapade at the expense of the O'Donnell sisters. They had almost tied on a good one when Brett arrived as cranky as a polecat, rubbing his sore jaw. The rest of the evening was a ribald string of war stories sprinkled with tales and antics of the two O'Donnell sisters, provided by Amos.

Now, as he rode with Maria to the schoolhouse, with Swamp trotting along beside them, Tye wondered whether he was as transparent as a two-way mirror. He was becoming enamored with the young woman's quiet, gentle ways. Her beauty was exquisite, almost fragile, from her perfect oval face to her dusty rose-colored cheeks.

He pulled the buggy to a stop just outside town

where the old granite cemetery was situated along a chokecherry-lined road leading to the school. The sun shining through the leafy foliage turned the roadway into speckled scene of shadows and light.

"My uncle, is he buried here?" Maria asked.

He nodded and helped her down from the buggy, wordlessly guiding her through the wrought iron gates at the entrance until they arrived at a recent burial plot near the far back. Fresh fall flowers, marigolds and asters, adorned the earthen mound of Henry McNeil where a marker had yet to be placed. Tye quietly walked back to the front of the cemetery, aware of her need for solitary reflection.

She said nothing when she returned several minutes later, and he helped her into the buggy. Instead, they rode in thoughtful silence until they reached the school. It was a little white rectangular building with a row of windows on each side, and a cast iron bell beside a cherry bright red door. A well with a pitcher pump was barely a few feet to the right of the door.

"Now don't get your hopes up," he warned. "It's only a little rural dwelling and hasn't been touched since school let out for summer. I understand the school board has money for renovations, books, and supplies, but they were waiting to see what your priorities might be." He secured the horse and buggy to a hitching rail to the front left side of the structure.

Undaunted, she smiled. "I'm sure it's charming. I'm used to far worse conditions than you might imagine. The school I taught in had a faulty chimney, and more often than not, was cold or filled with smoke."

"Well, ours has been known to do the same, though

I doubt it was from a malfunctioning chimney." He chuckled. "Some of our creative troublemakers have been known to crawl up on the roof and stuff the chimney with everything from clothes to dried grass, even books, in hopes of smoking up the classroom and buying themselves some time from their studies."

"I'll remember." She laughed. "I'll try to keep a stern hand on their antics and keep them away from the roof."

Her soft rippling laugh was the first Tye had heard since she learned of her uncle's death six days ago. Together, they entered the building, and he sensed her pleasure as soon as she stepped inside. The one-room interior held three rows of seven oak desks with benches marching up the room to end before a raised platform with a teacher's desk. Behind it, a huge piece of slate hung on the back wall with bookshelves on both sides, and to the right, a shiny potbellied stove stood with a wood box and bin for coal. Trunks below the platform kept books and supplies safe from dampness and dust.

"The windows, oh my," she said, sweeping her hand to the left and right. "There's so much light."

"Yes, you'll have the warmth of the morning sun and a view of all the students who arrive, using the main path. The curtains have been taken down to be washed, and I understand there are heavier ones for the cold weather to help trap the heat inside. "

"It's...it's...it's delightful!" She twirled in the dusty sunlight like a young school girl herself. Then she stopped, blushed, and straightened her dress. "Forgive me, I'm so enchanted, I lost myself in the joyful moment. How many children will I have?"

Elbows crossed, his back against the back wall, he watched her with an appreciative eye, pleased by her response, pleased just to be able to look at her. "I believe the school board said there would be about nineteen pupils ranging in ages from six to fourteen. Why don't you check out the books?"

She crossed the room to the trunks, knelt, and opened a lid on one of them, lifting out a primer. She nimbly leafed through the pages, no stranger to the book's contents.

He came to stand above her. "All of my family are avid readers. It was a habit passed down from my mother and father. We have an extensive library at the ranch if you need more books. I can take you out there sometime to look through them."

"It's kind of you to offer." She rose, swiping her palms together to dislodge any dust. She looked at him and smiled. "I understand my uncle was also fond of reading."

"Yes, he was."

"And do you have any favorite authors?"

She was standing so close to him he could smell her rose perfume. "I've read most of Cooper's and Irving's works. Winters can be long here." Her nearness kindled feelings of fire and desire. He met her gentle gaze with one almost as intimate as a kiss. They stared at each other from several seconds, mud brown eyes with cinnamon brown ones, before he broke the spell and silence. "However, before we start getting the school house in order, I think it's best if we make the cottage as clean and comfortable as possible."

She must have felt the heat, too, because she took a step back. Her cheeks turned a darker shade of rose.

She cleared her throat. "Tell me, Mr. Ashmore, how closely did my aunt follow the war?"

"Call me Tye," he said softly, then shrugged. "If you mean was she a professed Southern sympathizer, I can't rightly say. She never openly admitted she was, although it's no secret she originally came from Georgia. Now, your uncle, he made it pretty well known he supported the Union cause. Why do you ask?"

Maria sighed. "Oh, nothing, it's just my aunt seems to have a great admiration for Southern songs. Already, just after one night, I've had enough of the "Bonnie Blue Flag" to last a lifetime."

Chapter Five

The next few days passed in a whir of activity for the O'Donnell sisters. The cottage was moving toward restoration with the help of a volunteer work party organized by Betsy and Tye Ashmore. Somehow, Tye had secured lumber, supplies, and shingles free of charge. Abigail and Maria were amazed at the esteem the Ashmore family held in the eyes of the entire community. In fact, it seemed the family name was known throughout the entire territory.

Abigail and Amos immediately set to work on the barroom and rehired the old stable master, Will Singer, as a handy man and to help haul lumber from a nearby mill. Abigail was adamant they should avoid Brett Trumble's establishment. The last thing she wanted to do was be further indebted to him. On the insistence of Aunt Emma, she hired a thin, pale-looking man to help with the stables who called himself Lanky Red, but whose given name was Lang Redford.

Now, as she watched Amos, Lang, and Will tear up the old splintered floor in the barroom and replace it with cherry planks, she darted about, inspecting every inch as it progressed.

"Miss Abby, do you know the meaning of skedaddle?" Amos spit out a nail he held between his lips. He knelt and snugly positioned another floor board. "Maybe Maria could use your help at the cottage?"

"No, she sent me here," Abigail confessed. "Anyhow, Tye has more parents and volunteers from the school board than tools."

"Maybe the group of church ladies I hired to start on the rooms upstairs could use your assistance?"

"I tried, but after two minutes they shooed me away and were less than gentle when they suggested it might be better if we didn't work together. They sent me down here."

Amos shook his head wearily and rose. He ambled to the kitchen and returned swinging a small, tin bucket in his hand. "We could use a few late berries for a cobbler or pie. Why don't you take a walk and scour the berry patches along the woods near the stables?"

"Amos, I do believe you're trying to be rid of me, just like Maria and those church ladies." Abigail faked a pout and crossed her arms at her chest.

"Miss Abby, I do believe your constant motion and unbridled eagerness is beginning to set everyone's teeth on edge." He pushed the bucket into her hands and nudged her toward the door. "Stay out long enough to get a bucketful, and please stay out of trouble! Watch out for snakes. Tye tells me there are rattlesnakes underfoot in these parts."

Minutes later, Abigail found herself climbing the steep slope behind the stables where a small footpath, used by deer and wild game, wound its way upward among briars which held a few late black berries still undiscovered by hungry birds. At the crest of the slope, she looked down upon Cherry Creek flowing joyfully along, held fast to its course by its green, grassy banks. She easily picked out the Mule Shed Inn towering over the town like a German castle on the Rhine. Onward, she trudged until she wandered into a clearing at the edge of the dense woods where late blooming berry bushes bowed down with overripe fruit sending off a sweet delicious scent into the air. Careful of the thorns, she began to pick the berries, sampling as many as she put into her bucket. She moved quickly around the perimeter of the patch, careful to watch where she stepped, remembering Amos's warning about snakes.

But the threat came from above. A deep-throated snarl split the air before she had time to react. High on a pine limb above her head, a full-grown lynx peered at her from a crouched position. Abigail froze, dropping her bucket as her heart leaped to her throat. The mottled gray brown face with its hazel eyes stared menacingly at her. It was a magnificent beast, its body sleek, streaked with shades of chestnut and grays. Tufts of hair beside its ears and the ruff beside its face made it appear like an old unshaven man.

"Back away slowly, gal," a gravelly voice sang out from somewhere behind her. "Don't scream. Don't talk. Just stare the critter right in the eye, and give it some breathing room. Given a choice, he'd probably enjoy eating a rabbit instead of tangling with you."

Feeling helpless, Abigail stepped backward and heard a twig snap beneath her shoes. "Some more," the voice coaxed. She backed up again, almost stumbling, but she caught herself. Her heart thumped wildly in her chest. The lynx slowly raised itself from its crouched position and stood, snarling, revealing sharp long teeth.

"Go on, be gone with you, you old varmint. Git!" the voice ordered, and before Abigail could react, a hatchet whizzed past her right ear and landed in a limb beneath the lynx, shaking the tree. Startled, the beast turned and leaped into the air, gliding into the soft needles beneath the pine and disappearing into the forest.

"You can move now, gal. He ain't gonna bother you none. Got to give you credit, you're not one of those weeping, fainting kind of females."

Abigail turned on shaky legs and found herself looking into the face of a filthy, middle-aged man dressed in sweat-stained lumberman's clothes. She heaved a sigh of relief. "I think, sir, you saved my life."

"Maybe I did, maybe I didn't. I reckon that old bugger might have wandered off by himself, given enough time. Heaven knows you weren't about to." The man laughed in his raspy voice.

"My name's Abigail. Abigail O'Donnell, and I'm certainly pleased to meet you."

"Folks call me River Roy," he replied, "although they might not rightly be too fond of making my acquaintance. Over yonder is my son, Lenny."

A young boy, as unkempt as his father, ducked out from among the nearby bushes. Abigail guessed he was close to ten or eleven years old. He had suntanned skin and dark hair and eyes. His coveralls were a tad too small and as filthy as his father's. His hair looked like it had been cut with an axe.

"Hello, Lenny," she said. "Your pa is mighty skilled with that hatchet." When the boy hung his head bashfully, she turned to the man. "Do you live around here?"

"In a cabin in the woods way up over the next rise."

"I'm new here. My sister is the new school teacher

in town. You'll probably meet her once school starts." When the remark brought no reply except a quiet, blank stare, she asked instead, "Are you a lumberman?"

"Yep, lumberman and sometimes miner. My eldest son and I used to work the woods for the local paper mill," he said, "until the fool kid went off to war and got himself killed. Now it's just me and Lenny."

"I'm sorry." Abigail hesitated, unsure of what to say.

"No use in being sorry, gal. He marched away with the best of them, rifles thrown over their shoulders—all of them like eager beavers, ready to beat them Rebs. Only Walt weren't so lucky, not like that Trumble kid. Walt came home ridin' in a box."

Abigail felt the bitterness radiate from the man. Beside him, the young boy merely hung his head and remained silent. "I wish I had something to offer you for your help." She reached down and retrieved her bucket containing the few berries she hadn't spilled. "You're welcome to what I have." She held out the bucket.

The young boy moved beside her, knelt, picked up a few berries from the ground and popped them in his mouth.

"Keep 'em." River Roy walked to the tree and retrieved his hatchet. "There's plenty more where they came from." He chuckled. "And you left us plenty on the ground."

Abigail stepped toward the footpath. "If you ever need anything, stop by the Mule Shed Inn. I'd be pleased to offer you a drink on the house."

The scruffy man cackled. "I just may take you up on that. Not often anyone's ever bought me a free drink or anything free for that matter."

"I'll do one better." Abigail smiled. "I'll save the best bottle of Canadian whiskey and have it reserved just for you. The entire bottle is yours."

"The *whole* bottle?"

She nodded and started down the path.

"Hey, girl!" River Roy hurried after her. "You're not the new gal the whole town's talkin' about, are you? You the one who's planning to reopen the inn and barroom?"

"Yes." Abigail turned toward him. "Yes, I am."

"Where you come from? You ain't from around here."

"Utah by way of New York. The state."

"Well, I'll be darned! I thought you'd be much older—to run a barroom, I mean." With a bemused gaze, he gave her a once over as he hitched up his pants to sit more securely around his waist.

Abigail grimaced in good humor. "Well, thanks to you, I just might have that chance now—to grow older. And, I'm planning to manage the inn and hire someone to bar keep."

"You met Emma yet?" He squinted and rubbed his whiskered face with a dirty knuckle. "Be careful of that one. She's more than a few shots short of a full bottle." He turned to leave, but thought better of it and added, "And if I were you, gal, I'd shy away from trees along the path, unless I was carrying a gun. There are other varmints in the trees beside lynx, and there are snakes in the ferns along the path."

Nodding her appreciation, Abigail left, walking briskly down the mountain until she arrived at the cottage. Breathless, she found Maria, dust-covered and laughing, as she helped Tye who stood on the seat of a chair, trying to hang some curtains in the small parlor window. He looked like there were a thousand jobs he would rather be doing at the moment.

Maria whirled abruptly when Abigail entered. "Oh, Abby, everyone thinks we might be able to move in tomorrow! The remaining repairs to the outside can be made after we move in. While they fix the front porch, we'll use the back door. The bedrooms, kitchen, and living area have been cleaned and set up. People have been so generous. They've brought furniture and curtains, and they've offered to help paint—" She stopped abruptly, peering at her sister's ashen face. "Why, Abby, what's happened? You look like you've seen a ghost!"

"I met the lynx that owns the mountain."

Tye jumped off the chair. "Are you hurt? I forgot to warn you about the four-legged wildlife around here."

"Aren't you a little late with that piece of advice?" She offered him a wane smile.

"You need to learn to shoot, and you both need a gun."

Through the doorway, Amos appeared with Brett close on his heels. It was obvious the old black man heard the conversation because he wore an expression of sheer terror. "Might be best to wear onions and garlic in your socks next time you go on a jaunt up the mountain," he said. "The smell just might discourage them critters."

"We'll do no such thing." Maria frowned. "The smell would discourage any hopes of enticing business for the barroom as well as travelers who planned to spend a night. And what would my students think if I showed up smelling like that?"

"Tye's right. I think a pistol would offer far more protection than a smelly sock." Abigail glanced at Maria. "And it would be best if we *both* learned how to handle one."

"Oh, no." Maria's eyes widened, and her face filled with fear. "I couldn't pull the trigger even on a foul old skunk."

"Then you'd better become acquainted with a hatchet like old River Roy. If it wasn't for the old man, I'd be sitting on the mountain still trying to stare down that lynx."

"You've met River Roy?" Tye's eyebrows raised in amazement.

"And his son, Lenny." She looked at her sister. "You'll probably have him in school."

"I doubt it," Brett spoke up, thumbing back his hat. "He doesn't believe in sending the child to school. They keep to themselves up there and rarely come into town, except to buy supplies. I don't even think either of them can write their names. Lenny is half-Indian, his mother was an Arapaho, I believe. River Roy lost his wife when Lenny was only a few years old, then lost his oldest son in the war."

Wide-eyed, Abigail pointed to Brett. "What's he doing here?"

"Hush, Miss Abby. Mind your manners." Amos put a calming hand on Abigail's shoulder. "Why, Brett, here has been generous enough to supply all the lumber and shingles for the cottage porch and roof."

"What?" A soft gasp escaped from Abigail's lips as she whirled on Brett. "Is this some sort of a joke?"

He rewarded her with a cocky grin. It sent her pulse racing and her temper rising.

"Now, now, Abby," Tye said. His voice was gentle, but firm. "The school board asked for his assistance. You can't rightly turn away those eager to put a roof over your sister's head so our young-uns might have an education. Brett's father is on the school board along with my brother."

Brett pushed himself from the wall he was leaning against. "Ah, yes, my friend, my sentiments exactly. You couldn't have put it more eloquently." He touched a finger to his hat. "If you'll excuse me, I'll get the wagon unloaded. I've a business to attend to." He stared at Abigail a moment, daring her to challenge him. When she only glared at him, he merely winked and strolled insolently out the door.

"That man is a cad." She huffed.

"He's a very generous man," Maria countered.

"And my friend," Tye added.

Abigail's mouth fell open. "You knew all along he was the mail thief? You were in cahoots with his devious little plan?"

Tye nodded.

"Who else knows about this?"

Amos, Maria, and Tye shifted uncomfortably in their stances, peering guiltily at the floor.

"You all know?" Abigail shot them an incredulous look.

"And we need to keep it a secret," Tye said. "Gossip flows around here like the water in Cherry Creek."

"Well, good luck with that," Abigail said and flounced out the door.

Later that day, when Abigail told her aunt about the incident with the lynx she was surprised by Emma's reaction. The woman nodded indulgently, then suddenly broke out into a long, hysterical ripple of laughter. "I told you to go back to Utah, if you know what's good for you."

It was only when Maria mentioned the fresh flowers on their uncle's grave that the woman stiffened and grew sober, staring at her in confusion before her eyes glazed over in hostile fury. And much earlier in the evening than before, and later into the next day, they were tormented by the same plaintive and repetitious sound of the spinet.

Chapter Six

Abigail hesitated in the entranceway of the Mule Shed Inn inhaling the sweet smell of newly sawed wood and the tangy odor of linseed and shellac. It had been three weeks to the day since she and Maria had arrived in Golden and settled into their cottage. To her relief, Maria spent every minute of every day caught up in arrangements for opening the school, which left Abigail a free hand with the inn.

Under the skilled direction of Amos, the shabby-looking structure had come alive like a pauper putting on a suit of fine clothes. Abigail had decided immediately the Mule Shed should be perceived as a new establishment and under new management. She wanted it to be a place where a gentleman could take a lady to dine, an establishment where a man could play cards and imbibe in good whiskey, a place of entertainment, and center of activity for the local town folks.

Inside the barroom, she tore down all the undesirable pictures of robust, scantily-clad women and replaced the back wall behind the bar with an array of mirrors and gas lights. Later, once she had some profits to spare, she would have murals painted along the room's expansive, newly painted walls. For now, the only portrait adorning the room was a large oil painting of her grandmother she had discovered while sifting through the dust and junk stored in the attic of the cottage. It showed a vivacious young woman, seated demurely atop an open wagon, pulled by a team of four, gray, stout-shouldered mules. In the Arbitration Room, she hung a series of pictures depicting lumbering operations she had stumbled across in her uncle's office.

Under Amos's meticulous directions, all the bedrooms on the third floor were cleaned, disinfected, aired, and ready for patrons. Abigail closed down all but six, pilfering the best furniture from each room and redistributing them among the others. The largest room, at the very head of the stairs on the second floor, she relegated to Amos, despite his protests for something smaller, less fancy.

With the help of Will Singer, she rehired the cook and two serving girls for the kitchen and dining room. On the advice of Tye, she located a crusty old lumberman, Charlie Haney, who had injured his back in the woods and was looking for less strenuous work as a bar keeper. Noted best for his ability to make lively conversation, Haney was also an expert at distinguishing good whiskey and ale from the smell alone, and it was through him, she was able to engage the services of a piano player and two Irish sisters whose voices were as light as mockingbirds. Big Jake was the last to be added to her staff. At two hundred pounds, the robust trapper could break a man in half with his well-muscled arms. Abigail hoped his looks alone would keep the peace, but she cautioned him to remove anyone from the premises who started the slightest disturbance including any gentleman who entered the guest parlor without a calling card or a good reason.

Yet, despite her frugal maneuvering, she still needed new draperies, carpeting, and some much-needed paint for the dining room. Although she hated the thought of being indebted to anyone, she realized there was only one way she'd ever be able to complete the room and open the inn—borrow the money. She approached Emma the same afternoon.

"If we make the place as presentable as possible," she told her aunt, "we have a better chance of enticing people to return."

"I know, my dear, but the object of allowing you to manage the Mule Shed was to make money, not for you to spend it," Emma replied curtly, standing like a queen in the center of her furniture-shrouded parlor.

"Have you been down to see it?" Abigail swallowed, trying hard not to disguise her irritation.

Emma shook her head. "Why on earth would I want to go down there and *see* the pitiful place that did little more than take up hours and hours of your uncle's time?"

"It's really coming along. Sometimes you have to invest time, money, and effort before you get to reap the rewards. A few hundred dollars would go a long way to help the time and effort."

"Oh, my. Really, my dear." A shadow of annoyance crossed Emma's face. "Whatever makes you think I'd risk my money on Henry's old, dusty, flea-bitten place?"

"But you're more than willing to take half the profits if I succeed?"

Emma threw back her head and let out a frightful peal of laughter setting Abigail's nerves on edge.

"What an ungrateful thing for a penniless waif to say! In view of your situation, I shall overlook your boldness."

Abigial felt her cheeks grow hot. It took every ounce of energy to swallow her fury and pride. She wanted to shout at the old biddy. "I apologize, Aunt Emma, but we do need to secure the money. If I can't get any help from you, I'll be forced to ask for a loan from the bank. Certainly Uncle Henry was well-known in town and his credit was excellent."

Emma's brutal look was almost too much to bear. "Don't be a silly, silly fool, my dear girl! You'll not get a penny from the bank in this town. They're a tight-fisted lot who would sell their mother's souls before they would loosen their grip on a handful of cash."

Abigail heaved a weary sigh. "I'll have to try, nonetheless." She rose, walking stiffly toward the door. "Should I succeed, Aunt Em, I'll be forced to deduct half the amount of the loan from your share of the profits. It's only fair."

"Fair?" Emma spit back at her. "You'll shortly learn what's fair and what's not fair in this town, once you visit the bank!"

Later in the afternoon, seated in the plush office of Golden's National Bank, Abigail forced herself to smile at the paunchy, balding bank president, Patrick Marsh, before coming directly to the point.

"I need a loan," she admitted, "to cover a few expenses at the Mule Shed. Paint. Draperies. Things for renovation."

March leaned back in his chair, crossing his fleshy hands on his protruding stomach. "Collateral?" he asked.

Abigail shook her head. "None, except for a few cases of Canadian whiskey and some French wine. My aunt still owns the inn. I've agreed to manage it and divide the profits with her. Eventually, I hope to buy her out."

"Sorry, that won't do, Miss O'Donnell."

Abigail straightened and raised an eyebrow. "Your bank doesn't believe in speculating?"

"On the contrary. We take risks and chances all the time. You must understand, you are new to our area. We would need someone to attest to your character."

"My late uncle's reputation is not enough?"

The banker blushed. "Yes, yes of course. You misunderstand me. Your uncle was an honest man, but I fear your aunt's reputation is—" He cleared his throat nervously. "Well, suffice it to say, a little questionable. Emma has been known to run up outrageous bills about town."

With as much dignity as she could muster, Abigail rose. "I see. Thank you for your time." Weak-kneed she carried herself to the door, halting on the sidewalk to catch her breath and steady the heaviness she felt in her chest. Her disappointment settled in her stomach like a painful knot. She was helpless to halt her embarrassment. Tears began to form, and she wiped them away quickly with the back of her hand.

A voice called out to her.

She looked up to see Brett sauntering up, a crooked grin on his face. "Lovely day, Miss O'Donnell." He stopped and gave her a thoughtful stare. "But the look on your face tells me we might be in for some rain."

Abigail sighed a disheartened sigh and swiped at her cheek again. Of all the people she had to run into,

Brett Trumble was the last person she hoped to see. It was humiliating to have to admit she had been rejected for a loan by the local bank. "It seems Golden's bank doesn't back people willing to give a good day's work to make an honest living. Holding up a flatboat with goods is beginning to appear like a sound idea to raise some cash."

Brett winced. "You are not going to let go of our misfortunate encounter, are you?" He shoved his hands deep into his pockets. "You know, there are secrets to loosening the grip on those stiff-necked old weasels inside."

"I'll not have a thief telling me how to swindle a banker." She sniffed and dug into her reticule, but before she could withdraw a handkerchief, Brett shoved his into her hands and pulled her close to him to shield her from the curiosity of people passing by.

"Ah, but you see, thieves and weasels understand each other, Miss O'Donnell," he whispered near her ear.

She felt the warmth of his body as he shielded her from onlookers, and she wanted to hide there forever. He waited until she composed herself and dried her eyes, then gently turned her by her shoulders and nudged her toward the door of the bank.

"I'm not going back in there," she murmured, shaking her head, digging in her heels. "It was embarrassing."

"Oh, yes, you are. You never let the weasel win, Abigail."

Once inside, he ushered her straight toward the teller's window where he demanded to see Patrick March.

The old banker appeared almost instantly, scuttling across the floor like a crab. "This is a surprise, Captain Trumble. Is there something I can do for you?" He looked uncomfortable as soon as he noticed Abigail standing beside Brett.

Around them, Abigail felt the heavy silence as the teller and bank personnel ceased their tasks, watching the display.

"Now, now, Marsh," Brett said in a lazy tone as his gaze circled the bank and landed on each employee. "You know I never discuss business anyplace other than behind closed doors, away from prying eyes." Heads dropped on cue, and paper rustled as employees scuttled about looking busy.

"But...but of course," Marsh stammered. "My office. This way, please."

Inside the office once again, Abigail took a seat Brett held for her before he lowered him to one on her right, propping his booted calf casually atop the other knee. Patrick Marsh eyed Abigail suspiciously, then glanced at Brett.

"Is there something I can do for you, Captain Trumble?"

"Actually, there is something you can do for Miss O'Donnell here." Brett smiled an easy smile that Abigail was becoming accustomed to. "I don't believe you know Abigail's dear cousins, Joshua and Adam, fought valiantly beside me in the cause."

When Abigail started to protest, Brett reached out and laid a restraining hand on her arm. "And Miss O'Donnell, noble to the end, has spent her last penny trying to bring these brave soldiers to their final resting place beside their beloved uncle. Now she yearns to get her uncle's inn on solid financial ground and reopen it, and all she needs is a loan, but I understand she was refused. How terribly unsympathetic and unpatriotic of you."

Abigail watched red heat creep up Patrick Marsh's neck and settle about his ears. Clearing his throat, he asked, "How much does the young lady wish?"

"Three hundred dollars," Abigail spoke up. She dug her nails into the palms of her hands. Brett Trumble was shameless. She almost hoped the banker would refuse her request. Instead, he merely nodded and said, "I shall draw a draft this afternoon, and she shall have her money tomorrow morning. Will that be acceptable?" He pulled uncomfortably at his cravat as if it was choking him. "I didn't know you were familiar with Miss O'Donnell, Captain Trumble. She never mentioned she knew anyone in Golden."

"Know her?" Brett grinned and gave the banker a conspiratorial wink. "Why Mr. Marsh, I was so smitten by Miss O'Donnell the first time I met her I felt like I was falling overboard into the depths of the Arkansas River! Of course, I know her."

Later, back out on the street, Abigail threw him a vexed look. "Besides a thief, you're also a very talented liar."

Brett threw back his head and roared with laughter. He pulled her around the side of the building, yanked her to him, and kissed her soundly. When he released her, she stepped back dazed and regarded him.

He held up a hand palm up. "Just add amorous rogue to my list of qualities, if you must," he said. "And I'm enormously pleased you're keeping one!" Then he turned and sauntered away, hands in his pockets and whistling softly to himself.

"And a scoundrel," Abigail called out after him. Her hand went to touch her lips as she watched his back disappear from view. "A pompous one, too," she added in a whisper.

Chapter Seven

Tye Ashmore stopped outside the General Store and stared at all the goods in the window, but especially the black lace scarf his sister had thrown over the shoulders of a mannequin dressed in a yellow satin gown. The black color reminded him of Maria's thick raven locks, and the jewels sewn into the lace sparkled as bright as her hair in sunlight.

"Are you checking to see if Betsy has any new guns for sale?" a scratchy voice said behind him. He turned and looked down at old Theofila Sarowski, mother of the town's blacksmith, and whom everyone called Theo. She leaned on her cane with a face wrinkled worse than a dried apple. Her eyes were like tiny black beads, and her hair was as gray as the color of flagstone. She reminded him of a baby possum, small and wizened. Betsy had often described her as being as old as dirt, as sharp as the best knife in her store, and as odd as a two-headed snake.

He touched the brim of his hat and smiled. "Actually, I purchased a new gun, but today I'm picking up a school bag for the new school teacher and checking on the delivery of a petticoat. I was also looking at the shawl." He held the door for her. "I was wondering whether it would be appropriate as a birthday present for a lovely woman."

Mrs. Sarowski clutched her hands to her chest and

faked a swoon. "Ah, Tydall Ashmore, if I were only ten years younger I'd be chasing after you—good-looking fellow that you are—with or without a present of a shawl. I'm surprised no gal has caught you yet. You have to stop sidestepping so fast." She grunted. "But it's a mighty fine shawl, young man. And far be it from me to refuse any kind of petticoat you selected, though I tend to like those new imported ones the best—with fancy French lace!"

Tye laughed. Old Mrs. Sarowski was at least eighty years old, and he'd bet his last dollar at seventy she probably could have given any man a fair run for his money. She had raised ten kids and now lived alone on the outskirts of town where she took care of a few milk cows and goats. She was an avid reader, canned all her vegetables, often exchanged books and recipes with his sister, Betsy, and made the best cheese in the Territory.

Betsy raised her head as they entered the store, obviously having heard their conversation. "Tye's brothers and I believe if we can get him out of those buckskins he's so fond of, we might be able to find him a wife, Mrs. Sarowski."

"And what about you, missy?" she asked. "How about a husband for you?"

Tye leaned his hands on the counter and raised any eyebrow as much as to say, "Now look what you've started, sister."

"So tell me, Tydall," the old woman continued, "are you courting this young lady?"

"I'm hoping to, but she seems to be the independent sort. Like some other women I know." His gaze skidded from Theo to his sister.

"Now, young man, you need to give her some time

to get settled in and to get to know the town and its people. Don't push the river, it will flow on its own accord."

"This may be a case when I'm in the river rowing with one oar," Tye said sourly. He twirled his finger to indicate he was rowing in circles and getting nowhere.

Both women laughed. Beside them, the bell tingled over the door, and Emma McNeil swept in. She wore a black mourning dress of the finest taffeta. When she saw Tye and Theo Sarowski, she stepped around them to reach the counter. "I need some yard goods and supplies," she said. "Immediately. I've other places to visit today."

"As soon as I finish with Mrs. Sarowski, I'll be able to help you." Betsy smiled.

Emma McNeil's face turned from calm to disgust in a bare second.

"No, no," Theo spoke up. "Please wait on Mrs. McNeil first. I want to browse the merchandise and jaw a bit with you young'uns. This petticoat thing is scratching at my curiosity with a vengeance.

"I would say stepping aside would be a wise thing to do," Emma replied tartly. "After all, it's evident who buys more goods in this town."

Theo chuckled. "True. True. So don't forget to put a pound of sugar on your account." She turned and started to the back of the store, her cane tap, tap, tapping on the wooden floor.

"Why on earth would I need sugar?"

"Crabby old biddies need every means possible to sweeten their dispositions," the old woman said, her voice fading as she proceeded up the aisle.

Unbridled anger raged in Emma's eyes. "Why I

never have spoken with anyone so ill-bred and ill-mannered in my life!" She spit the words out for everyone in the store to hear.

"Bull! Have you listened to yourself lately?" Theo rejoined from somewhere in the back of the store.

With a huff, Emma slapped her list onto the counter. "Just deliver these supplies to the manse by nightfall. I refuse to be in the same room with that crazy woman!" She sniffed in disdain and stomped to the door.

Tye winked and looked at his sister who was doing everything possible to suppress a smile. The door slammed shut with a bang.

"Yes!" they said in unison and exchanged relieved glances.

The bell tingled again, and Frank Norwell stepped inside. He tipped his hat and gave Betsy a warm smile. Norwell was a prosperous, white-haired rancher with land adjacent to theirs. "I just passed Emma McNeil on my way in, and it looks like she's been eating something sour."

"See, I told you," Theo mumbled, coming to stand beside the front counter.

Norwell raised a quizzical eyebrow, then turned to Tye. "I saw your horse outside and was hoping to talk with you." He leaned against the counter and pushed his hat up. "I heard you helped the O'Donnell sisters to find their way to Golden."

Tye nodded and regarded Norwell with somber curiosity.

"I'm told the youngest is a teacher."

"Yes, she is," Tye confirmed. "Her name is Maria."

"Well, I'm in need of Miss Maria O'Donnell's skills." He tapped his fingertips lightly on the counter. "I have this young man working for me who's a natural with the horses and livestock and has a mind for figures as sharp as a razor. He could make a good foreman some day. Problem is, he can't read very well."

"Send him back to school," Betsy suggested.

Norwell shook his head. "No, Eli would be too embarrassed and never agree to it. He's seventeen. You know most of those boys drop out by thirteen or so. I was thinking maybe Maria would be willing to spend some time tutoring him. I'd be willing to pay whatever she might charge for an hour or two a week." He looked at Tye. "Of course I plan to ask her personally, but I was wondering whether you'd run it past Flint when you see him. I need to know if the school board would have any objections."

"I don't see why they would," Tye said. "They have no restrictions on her free time, but I'll ask Flint and have him get word to you. The women are strapped for money. Maria just finished remaking an old dress of Emma's for Abigail to wear to the opening night of the Mule Shed. She's hoping she can get hers finished in time."

Frank Norwell raised his head. His eyes met Betsy's in an unspoken look of mutual understanding as if they both shared an old aching wound. Tye knew they were both thinking about the town's celebration twelve years ago when Golden became the Territory's capital and Norwell's wife was still alive. Betsy had been only sixteen years old, and they had been in Golden only two years. Virginia Norwell had taken Betsy under her wing and made sure she was dressed properly.

"I just got a new stock of dresses in the back," Betsy said. "Let me see what I can do."

"Put it on my account." Frank Norwell reset his hat.

"No, I'll pay for it," Tye spoke up.

"No, you won't, young man," Norwell said crisply. "A gentleman never wants it to appear like he's trying to buy a woman's affections. This young lady is no trollop from down at the saloon. If my wife were living, God rest her soul, she would have insisted she be dressed properly. If you're looking for something to do while you're courting Maria O'Donnell, how about peddling the litter of five pups your mongrel dog sired with mine to some of these hapless souls around town? Eeegads, man, I'd pay someone to take them off my hands! They're driving my men insane getting underfoot and tumbling around the barn stalls and irritating the horses."

"I'll see what I can do," Tye said biting back a snicker.

"Appreciate it." Norwell turned to leave, then thought better of it, and faced them again. He scowled. "Oh, I don't know if those young women know Lang Redford hired two drifters to help him with Emma's stables. I have no idea why. Even an idiot can see that Emma has only a handful of horses to tend." His eyes grew serious. "They're no accounts who can't be trusted. Drifters. I fired them both. Jebb Masters for stealing and Pat Wenson for a knife fight. Though Wenson is known for all kinds of fights—fists, guns, words, and knives. That lowlife isn't particular. You might want to warn those young ladies to keep their eyes open and their doors locked...and to shy clear of Emma's stables when the men are around."

Theo Sarowski who had remained silent during much of the discourse spoke, "Is Jebb Masters the tall, sullen-looking blond who wears a black shirt and black leather vest?"

Norwell nodded.

"I saw him down at the bakery a few days ago. Funny thing, I was sure he had a wallet identical to the one Henry McNeil used. The only reason I noticed was Henry often came out to my ranch to buy freshly made goat's cheese for the inn. He showed me his wallet once and was so proud of it. He said it was hand-tooled leather, sent as a Christmas present from his brother-in-law in Utah and was specially designed by a saddlemaker down in Texas. Right pretty work."

Tye and Norwell stared wordlessly at each other. Finally Tye asked, "Do you think it's a coincidence?"

"I think one of us should have a little talk with the sheriff," Norwell replied.

****

Later in afternoon, while Maria and Abigail waited at the cottage for Tye Ashmore to take them on a picnic and to see the countryside, Maria presented her sister with a blue satin dress she had secretly remade from an old one of Aunt Emma's to wear to the opening night of the Mule Shed Inn. But it was the new petticoat Tye Ashmore gave to Abby when he arrived that sent them into a fit of delightful giggles.

"It's beautiful," Abigail said, holding the delicate, sheer undergarment in front of her. "The lace is so fragile and delicate. Your taste is excellent."

Tye blushed, his face turning as bright as an

evening sunset. "Actually, my sister picked it out and had it shipped here once she found out about my little exploit with the flag on the boat."

From the steps of the cottage, he picked up a picnic basket, quilt, and Maria's sketchbook and put them in the two-seat buckboard beside the house. After everyone was seated, he drove the wagon to a grassy knoll east of his ranch where Cherry Creek meandered south and bubbled over rocks and wound its way into a patch of dense hemlock.

As he unhitched the team, Maria and Abigail spread out the quilt and began to unload the picnic basket and piles of food they had prepared. They had barely finished when the sound of an approaching horse interrupted the peaceful silence around them. Brett drew up and slipped off, just at the edge of the quilt. He tied his horse to a nearby laurel bush and flopped down on the quilt beside Abigail.

"Perfect day for an outing, darlin'."

"It *was*, Captain Trumble," Abigail corrected him.

"Good to see you, old man." Tye clapped him on the back before dropping down beside him.

"How long have you known each other?" Maria asked, smiling.

Tye's mud brown eyes twinkled. "Brett and I go a long way back. Fourteen years. We've chased a few Indians in our lives and outran even more of them."

"Chased a few women, too," Brett added with a smirk.

"And ran from even more of them." Tye grinned. "Did you get your gun dried out?"

"I don't see how you can laugh about it, Tydall Ashmore." Abigail fumed, her hands on her hips, a scowl on her face. "You were abetting someone committing a federal crime."

Maria spoke, coming to Tye's defense. "Because Brett is innocent, Abigail." Maria didn't think Tye did anything more underhanded or dangerous by trying to help Brett clear his name than her sister did by smuggling a load of explosives on board, although she hesitated to voice it aloud.

Abigail glared at her sister.

"Come, come, ladies, let's not quibble." Tye's lips melted into a smile only enhancing his rugged, suntanned face. "I have a present from the school board for Maria, and I want her to open it." He handed her a large wrapped package, tied with a blue velvet bow.

Eagerly, Maria unwrapped the paper and took out a brocade bag with delicate gold threads woven through it. "Oh, my. For my school books and papers," she exclaimed. "Thank you!"

"Open the bag," Tye coaxed.

Maria unfastened the buckle and pulled out a copy of Longfellow's *Tales of a Wayside Inn*. Tenderly, she held the book of poems before her and opened the book's cover, leafing through it.

"It's wonderful," she whispered, clasping it to her chest. "Thank you, again."

"I'm glad you like it." From under his coat, he pulled out a small pistol. "Now this may be another story. You need to learn how to use a gun. It's also a gift."

"Oh, no." Maria jumped up and took a step backwards from the group.

****

Not surprised by her response, Tye stood and

watched her with cautious eyes. "Listen, Maria, it isn't wise for two women to be alone near those woods without the knowledge of how to handle a weapon. You're situated at the edge of town, and during the winter hungry bobcats are known to wander close. Even wolves check out local doorsteps, and I don't want to even discuss snakes." There was an awkward silence as they stared at each other. "You walk to the schoolhouse each day along a footpath with the possibility of harboring any type of creatures with two legs or four," he added. He held out his hand. "Come, I'll show you how," he coaxed and urged her forward, down the knoll to a cleared area where he placed a few rocks on a stump. Standing beside her, he guided her through the loading of the weapon. When, at last he convinced her to try it, she hesitated, shaking her head.

"I can't," she said biting her lip.

Tye turned her gently and pulled her in front of him as he wrapped her hand around the gun's grip and steadied her trembling hands. Together they fired a round at the rock.

"Try it by yourself," he whispered gently near her ear and stepped back.

"I can't." She was almost in tears and lowered the gun. "The only animals I've ever encountered were deer coming into our orchard in New York to swipe a few apples each fall."

"Listen to me, Maria." When she looked at him with somber cinnamon-colored eyes, he said with complete honesty, "Handling a firearm out here is like breathing. I understand your trepidation at not wanting to aim a loaded pistol at anyone, even an animal, but it's a skill you have to learn to survive out here. You don't have to be an excellent shot, like my brothers or sister, but you have to have enough courage to at least point and fire at your target. If nothing else, you might scare an intruder away."

"I...I just could never point a gun at anyone," she whispered.

He heaved a sigh and shook his head, a hopeless look on his face.

"She's afraid." Abigail lifted her skirts and stepped carefully down the rock-strewn knoll. "We never grew up with firearms in our home. We never grew up among violent people or dangerous animals."

"Give it a try, Abby." Brett walked over to stand beside her.

Tye handed Brett the pistol. He deftly unloaded it, loaded it again as Abigail watched, then handed to her. He took his place again behind her. "Use both hands. Line up the sights and squeeze the trigger. Take your time. Remember, you have the advantage, you're holding the gun."

Abigail grinned. "I'll think of the rock as your head, Captain Trumble." With that, she squeezed the trigger and sent the rock flying off the log. Five more tries sent Brett searching for five more rocks for targets.

"I think we've had enough for today," he said, wincing. He took the pistol from her. "I'd hate to see you get too good at this."

Chapter Eight

After a hearty lunch of bread, meat, and cheese, Tye and Maria wandered off to take a walk in the woods and locate a grassy spot along Cherry Creek to relax and allow Maria some time to draw. Tye wanted more than anything to have some time alone with her. Ever since he laid eyes on her at the landing in Canon City Landing, his attraction to her was like an appetite he couldn't satisfy, and he yearned for the hours when they could be together. He found himself making all types of excuses to spend more and more time away from his ranch and at the cottage and schoolhouse instead. He wondered whether she felt the same.

Together, they followed a narrow path leading to the stream and passed a series of high ledges where industrious miners had prospected for coal seams, leaving cave-like indentations into the mountainside. Maria looked up at a mine's entrance, yawning like the mouth of an old bear. "Oh, wouldn't it be fun to climb up the spoil pile and see what's inside?"

Tye shook his head, a shadow of alarm marring his face. "Some of those hollowed out old mines aren't very stable and have been known to cave in without warning." He had no desire to admit that he had never liked small, dark places even as a child. In fact, he never liked any cave, unless he could see light streaming in from its entrance. Growing up, his brothers had often teased him about his claustrophobic nature, but he had great respect for miners, especially the Territory's local bituminous coal miners who went hundreds of feet down into shafts to bring out the ore.

He touched her back and urged her forward. "Come, Maria, you are not dressed for exploring caves. Let's go down to the stream where it's cool. You can sketch and maybe I can catch a nap." He was relieved when she agreed, and they continued onward down a narrow path shaded by pine where they seated themselves on the grassy bank in the shade.

Maria opened her sketchbook. A strand of sleek black hair came undone from the rest tied at the back of her neck and fell into her eyes. She pushed it aside, and it fell back again.

Just as she was about to raise her hand again, Tye reached over and tenderly tucked it behind her ear. They looked at each other for several moments, unable to tear their gazes away. "You are a beautiful desirable woman, Maria," he whispered and watched as a flush of red crept up her neck onto her cheeks. He stared longingly at her.

She nervously looked away. "I thought you wanted to take a nap," she stammered.

"I did." Removing his hat, he stretched out on his back beside her and placed it over his eyes, content to give her some space, content to listen to the sounds of the forest. The sights and sounds of the outdoors always made him feel life was good. Above them, birds warbled, and the wind rustled through the tops of the pine trees. Around them, insects droned and crickets chirped. Below them, the stream sang a merry tune as it gurgled over rocks on its way to bigger waters.

Twenty minutes later, he sat up, interrupting Maria's concentration. He could see she had already sketched a picture of the stream and forest beyond. She had paid careful attention to a nearby bush where a butterfly flitted above the leaves of milkweed plants lining the opposite riverbank. He was just about to speak, when in his side vision he caught sight of a scruffy head with two dark eyes peering out from behind a nearby cottonwood. He had no idea how long the boy had been watching. It was obvious he was curious about Maria's artwork.

"You know, Miss O'Donnell," he said in a whisper, "I have had the urge to kiss you for the last ten minutes. No, to be truthful, for the last ten days."

Surprised, Maria looked up at him and gasped. "Why, Tye! I thought you were asleep all this while—"

"—but unfortunately my wishful thinking will have to wait." He sighed and motioned to the large cottonwood behind them. "It appears we have company, and the boy seems to be curious about what the school teacher is doing instead of my sleep habits or amorous advances."

Maria swiveled to face the tree. The child had ducked back behind the trunk. She smiled and called out, "You'd better come down here if you want to see the picture."

The boy cautiously revealed himself and crept forward a few steps. He was wearing a faded plaid shirt much too big and a pair of dirty, suspender overalls much too small. His small inquisitive face was as dirty as his bare feet.

"Closer. Right here." Maria waved her sketchbook in the air and patted the ground beside her.

Tye turned to the boy. "It's all right, Lenny. This is Miss O'Donnell, the town's new teacher. You and your pa met her sister, Abigail, the other day. You know, the gal your pa saved from the lynx sitting in the tree? The gal who was picking blackberries?"

The boy nodded and edged closer, craning his neck to get a glimpse of Maria's sketch pad. Finally, he knelt beside her, and she handed it to him.

"My, that's right purty," he whispered in awe. He ran his finger over the picture as if he was caressing it and committing it to memory. "I like the butterfly."

"It's actually not good," she admitted. "Some artists can capture every little detail. I just draw for fun."

"Can you teach me?"

"I could show you a little about it, but you start by selecting something you like and then you try to draw your picture as close to the real thing as possible."

"Whatcha going to do with your picture?"

"Nothing. You may have it, if you like."

Lenny's whole face split into a wide smile.

"In fact, you can have the sketchbook and pencil." Maria rose and dusted off her skirt. "I have another at home and one at school."

The boy shook his head vehemently. "No, it wouldn't be right."

"Yes, it's fine." Maria thrust the book and pencil at him. "There's only a few sheets left anyhow. You see, I tear out and burn all those sheets of objects I've attempted to draw and don't like. Think of it as a present for your father taking care of Abigail the other day when she encountered the ornery lynx. Go on, give it a try."

Lenny took the sketch pad and pencil she offered. "Thank you, ma'am." He nodded politely, then without another word, scampered up the bank and between the trees. They heard Lenny give an excited hoot as he galloped through the bushes. "I'm gonna capture me a picture of a red squirrel on this here paper!"

Tye stood. "I believe you made the kid's day, Maria."

A smile played at the corners of her mouth as she surveyed the ground at her feet. "My talents as an artist aren't spectacular. Often I just waste precious time when I should be doing other more worthwhile things." When she looked up, Tye Ashmore's face was just inches from hers.

"Then let's not waste any more precious time, and let's do something worthwhile." He placed his hand gently on her shoulders and drew her toward him.

"Tye, this isn't such a good idea," she whispered and pressed her hands against his solid chest. "I could lose my job. Most school boards prefer unattached, unmarried women."

"As do I," he said as his lips descended slowly to meet hers.

"Tye, no." She tried to shy away, but he held her firmly.

"Just one, Maria," he said. "Just one to remember me."

She felt his lips touch hers. The kiss was light and gentle like a summer breeze. And when he pulled away and looked into her eyes with a covetous gaze, she realized this man was going to be a complication she had not counted on.

****

Although Abigail was pleased Maria and Tye had taken some time to be alone, she didn't like the idea of having to suffer through the afternoon with Brett. She suspected Maria had already grown fond of the quiet mannered, sometimes brooding rancher ever since the day on the flatboat when she fainted. And Abigail also knew unsupervised time together could only help to further their relationship, even though Maria had been adamant she would not jeopardize her teaching position. She started to repack the picnic basket and was surprised when Brett rose to help her before he sat down beside her to relax and stare at the cloud formations in the sky.

"Why doesn't Tye want to work for the army?" she asked. "I heard he was offered a good job to scout for them."

Brett removed his hat, ran his fingers though his hair, and reset it. He leaned back on his elbows. His long booted legs spilled out onto the grass.

"Tydall is a rancher at heart, even though he's one of the best scouts around the Territory. He soaks up Indian languages like a dry desert in a rainstorm, and he can speak or understand Ute, Arapaho, and a little Apache. He can sign as well and can speak half-decent Spanish. He came here with his family when he was fourteen and took to the hills and backlands, often taking off for days to explore the woods and land. He's trapped, hunted, and crossed paths with numerous bands of wandering Indians who befriended him. Often he'd spend time in their villages just learning their habits and enjoying their friendship while they taught him their skills." Brett laughed. "His brothers often joke how you don't get Tye mad when he's handling a knife.

I guess I was lucky I only have a sore jaw from the escapade on the flatboat."

"The Indians didn't try to kill him?" Abigail asked.

"Growing up, he was wild and more Indian than White. It didn't hurt that the Ashmores would turn a blind eye to bands in the area, letting them drink from their wells, and loot a calf or two from their herds to fill their hungry stomachs."

"I'll bet the army was far from pleased," she said in a pointed tone.

"Well, you have to understand the Ashmores were originally from Virginia and came west to avoid the Civil War. Tom Ashmore, their father, was a peaceful man and never believed in killing as a way to settle any argument. But his boys, although thoughtful and respectful of their pa's position, never shied away from a fight when it came to them."

An easy smile played at the corners of Brett's mouth. "Then there's Julia Gast, Flint Ashmore wife, who's a potter. She even worked with a renegade, Two Bears, who helped her gather wild horses to sell to the army when she arrived in the Territory and needed cash. The family's ties to the Indian tribes are knotted pretty tight, and Tye won't ever try to undo those knots or sever the rope." He stared over at her, and she could feel his warm gaze travel from her face down to her tips of her feet. She felt a tingling in the pit of her stomach.

Abigail stammered, "Charlie...Charlie Haney who works at the inn said Tye is often called on by the army when they need an interpreter or help when they cross paths with errant bands passing through the area."

Brett removed his hat, reclined on the quilt, propped his hands under his head, and closed his eyes, enjoying the feel of the late summer sun on his face. "It's the only time he won't refuse to help—when children and families are involved." He snorted out a laugh. "The last time he interceded for the army and helped a band pass safely through the area headed for Utah, he found his doorstep at the ranch heaped with wild game, a new buckskin shirt and pants, moccasins, a string of Indian ponies, and a ton of other gifts. Indians admire loyalty, and word travels quickly from tribe to tribe."

He opened his eyes, sat up, and turned to her. "So how's the inn coming along? Tye tells me he's taking Maria to dinner there on Friday night to celebrate the re-opening. I can't wait to see him get out of those buckskins."

"It's coming along wonderfully." There was exuberance in her voice. "We've redone the barroom and renamed the dining room to the Lantern Room when we ran out of money for more gas lights and had to hang rows of miners' lanterns along the walls instead."

"I heard you tore down those ugly curtains."

"Yes, they were hiding the view of the town," she said. "We put up some sheer curtains we could tie back and lined the sills with vases of wild flowers. I've hired two sisters to sing for the diners before they perform later in the bar. Uncle Henry would be surprised if he could see it now."

"No doubt. He helped a lot of men in his days."

"Did you know him?" she asked. "What was he like?"

"He was an honest man. A man of his word. He never turned down anyone who was destitute. Loaned people money."

"Then why would someone want to kill him?"

Brett shrugged. "For his money, I imagine. Supposedly his wallet was missing."

"Why would my uncle be in the cemetery in the evening?"

He shook his head and balanced his elbows on his knees. "I don't know. Did you have a chance to look at all his ledgers?"

"Yes, but not in great detail. What can you tell me about Aunt Emma?"

"Emma was a charmer in her younger days, I hear. Beautiful, but people say she was crafty, for whatever it's worth."

Nodding, Maria asked, "Were they happy?"

Brett pursed her lips and sighed. "Hmm…why wouldn't a woman be happy when a man gives her everything she wants? From the looks of things, Henry paid her debts, dressed her in the finest clothes, and built her a mansion."

"I see." But she really didn't. He had never once said anything about love. She thought about the upcoming re-opening of the Mule Shed Inn. She hoped there would be a large gathering of people so as not to diminish all the work she and her help had accomplished. Brett Trumble interrupted her wandering thoughts.

"And who will be escorting you on Friday, Miss O'Donnell?"

"I have no escort. I plan to dine with Tye and Maria."

"Oh, no. That will never do. I'd be pleased to escort you."

"Thank you, but no," she said in a determined voice. "I'll be too busy to even eat."

"I insist."

"Absolutely not!"

"A two hundred dollar debt says I will, Abby." His voice was low and insistent.

"You'll get your money and whatever it cost for the lumber for our cottage." Abigail rose from the quilt, stalked to a nearby tree, and stared out over the landscape. Brett walked up behind her and propped a hand on the trunk of the tree, just above her head. She felt his shirt brush against her back.

He heaved a sigh, his breath warm on the back of her neck. "Your temper's like the nitroglycerin you hauled down from Canon City Landing—prone to explode when you get rattled."

"And your manners are like an old mule, despicable, deplorable, and obstinate!"

Brett spun her around and pulled her toward him, bending his head and covering her mouth with his. He kissed her soundly, lifting his face a moment, before he plundered her lips again. When he released her, she stepped backwards, away from him. He reached out to caress her cheek, but she turned her head sharply away.

"You'd better leave," she ground out in a low voice, refusing to look up.

"I'll pick you up at six on Friday."

"Don't bother. I have to leave early and be there at five." There was fire in her voice.

"Look at me, Abigail." She turned and gazed at him. "Now who's the one being obstinate? I'll pick you up at five. You shouldn't go unescorted." Without another word, he touched two fingers to the brim of his hat and walked to his black stallion, a magnificent beast wearing a hand-tooled saddle. He slipped up easily on his mount, turned the stallion toward town, and rode away.

Chapter Nine

It was the first day of school, and Maria was fighting with her tangled hair and rattled nerves.

"I look like a plucked turkey," she wailed, studying her reflection in a small mirror propped against a stack of books on the cottage's nicked kitchen table. She had combed her hair a dozen times until her scalp hurt. Finally, she had pulled the tresses back into a tight matronly bun at the nape of her neck. Her ears stuck out on both sides like handles on a buttermilk urn.

Abigail turned from the breakfast dishes she was washing at the sink and looked at her sister in mild amusement. She wiped her sudsy hands on a towel and snatched Maria's hairbrush from the table. With quick, efficient motions, she plucked the pins from her sister's bun and vigorously brushed out the snarls from her hair cascading down her back.

"You're a school teacher, not an old maid, for goodness sake," Abigail scolded, parting Maria's sleek hair down the middle, smoothing it gently over her ears and pulling it back into a loose bunch of curls to fall down her back. She tied them firmly in place with a white ribbon to match the starched white collar on Maria's brown dress. "Now shoo, or the teacher is going to be late for her first day of school. How embarrassing would that be?"

Maria grabbed the new bag, her shawl, and a small

picnic basket with her lunch and a plate full of cookies she had baked the night before as a treat for her new students. She set off at a fast pace on a path lined with end-of-the season buttercups and daisies leading to the schoolhouse on the opposite end of town. She was so nervous, she hardly noticed the morning unfold in front of her as chipmunks darted over the dew-laden grass collecting dried seeds and birds high in the trees sang their early morning melodies. But she was thrilled to discover she was not late. She hung her shawl on a hook in the cloakroom and eyed the room critically.

Desks of various sizes, the largest in the back, marched up the room in three rows and were scrubbed clean. The slate chalkboard behind her desk shone with an ebony brilliance. Even the beeswax on the furniture and floors emitted a familiar, clean scent heralding the start of a new school year. Early morning light sparkled through the newly washed windows and covered her desktop in a soft yellow glow. But it was only when she approached the desk to deposit her book bag and basket, she noticed the white sheets of paper lying there.

Maria frowned as soon as she recognized her familiar old sketchbook and pencil she had given Lenny. She picked up the book, pleased to see he had kept her butterfly picture. She lifted the cover. There, underneath, was a delicate sketch of a red squirrel perched high on a tree limb, with its head cocked as if it detected danger nearby. Lenny had not missed a single detail and had perfected it right down to the clusters of pinecones amid sharp, spiny pine needles.

Tears welled in Maria's eyes as she stared at the picture. The child was talented way beyond normal children his age. The work was exceptional. She frowned, realizing his father must have demanded he return the drawing materials. She slipped it into the top drawer of her desk as the children began to file in, and she made a mental note to remember to ask Tye or Abigail to take her to see River Roy. She now knew the child would not be in school as Brett had earlier predicted.

The remainder of Maria's first day flew by smoothly. Besides a few braid pulling and spit ball incidents, and one scraped knee during tree tag at recess, all nineteen children were well-mannered and eager learners. It took Maria the entire day to determine where each child should be placed for reading and math as she challenged each one with reading passages and math problems until she settled upon a level to match their skills. Exhausted, she was glad when the hour of dismissal drew near, and they each had a cookie and sang a parting song together. She decided to give them the freedom of no homework for their first day, aware many of them still had fall chores awaiting them at home. Blissfully happy, but tired, she stood at the window and watched as they boisterously scattered in all directions, lunch pails slapping against their legs, poking and prodding each other as they raced away. She couldn't help smiling. The day had been glorious, and the children seemed to have no trouble relating to her and her set of firm but fair classroom rules.

Minutes later, when she left the building, she found Tye Ashmore outside, sitting on the ground, his back against a large cedar at the corner of the lot. His hat was pulled over his eyes as if he was dozing. His horse, tied to a nearby sapling, pulled on grass not trampled by her students' feet. Swamp was dozing right beside his master, his head on his thigh. He raised his head, ears alert, as soon as she approached.

****

"Looks like the little rascals have done in the schoolmarm on her first day," Tye drawled and pushed his hat up to reveal his dark eyes. Errant strands of her thick dark hair had come undone from the ribbon at the back of her neck, and her fingers were covered in chalk dust. Her once crisp dress was wrinkled at the waist from leaning over student desks and was smudged with chalk as well. But her beaming smile was not lost on him either.

"Today was wonderful, simply superb, if exhausting. However, I fear many of the children have not progressed at the rate I had been expecting for their ages. The milliner's daughter, Jodie Watson, could read only half of the primer, and she's an exceptionally bright child."

"You haven't heard about our former teacher, Whiskey Will." Tye smirked, pushing his rangy body up. "His real name was William Wate. He was said to have a heavy hand with discipline, but an even heavier one on the bottle he kept in the bottom drawer of his desk. It's really quite amazing children learned anything useful last year. The school board had to dismiss him despite his professed fine education and sheepskins."

"Well, you just explained the confusion I saw in the children's eyes." Maria shook her head, her eyes clouded with disappointment. "Lenny didn't come to school, but he left me this picture with my sketchbook and pencil." She held up the picture for Tye to see.

"Would you take me to his cabin on the mountain after school on Friday?"

Tye shrugged noncommittally. "I don't see what good it would do. The boy's old man is one bullheaded badger. You'll never talk him into allowing the child to attend school. And it's a long way up the mountain, Maria."

"Please, Tye."

He looked into her cinnamon-colored, earnest eyes and knew it was useless to argue. This fine-looking school teacher had made up her mind, and nothing he would say was going to change it. He had to admire her quiet determination. From the picture alone, he could see the boy was bright and talented. This was a child who should be in school. He looked up at the sun and scratched his chin, making one last attempt. "You know, Miss O'Donnell, some things are deemed hopeless before they're even attempted."

"Mr. Ashmore," she rejoined with an impish smile, "hope is what makes us live today as if tomorrow was yesterday."

He sighed. She was going to hang on to the idea like a hungry dog with a ham bone. "Can you ride?"

"Yes. My father taught Abby and me how to ride when we were children."

Tye nodded appreciatively. He had no desire to walk up the mountain, although he knew there were paths so narrow where they'd have to dismount and lead their horses. Beside him, Swamp whined a low, soft sound and looked at Maria. "Looks like my partner here wants to make friends with you."

Maria held out her hand for the dog to sniff it, then patted him affectionately on his head, and scratched him behind his ears. The dog groaned in appreciation. "He looks like an Australian cattle dog."

"Well, I'm convinced he has some blue heeler blood in him because he's the best cattle dog I've ever seen. He's also a top notch watch dog."

"Why do you call him Swamp?" she asked, her forehead furrowed.

"Long story. I'll tell you someday when we have lots of time to spare." A soft smile lingered on his lips. Without warning, he bent and brushed his mouth gently against hers. She smelled like roses and sunshine and tasted like sugar cookies. When she didn't protest, he kissed her more insistently and caressed the side of her neck with his hands.

After a moment, she stopped and pushed on his chest. She hung her head. He knew her heart was racing as fast as his own. "Tye, I've told you, this is not a good idea," she said in a low voice. "My contract with the school board frowns on romantic relationships and entanglements."

He took her face in both of his rough, callused hands and stared into her eyes. "We're going to have to find a way to work around it, Maria, 'cause I'm not about to give up or go away. I'll meet you on Friday, right after school. Be dressed and be ready to ride. We'll need all the daylight we can get." Releasing her, he whistled for Swamp, mounted, and rode toward town.

Four days later, he sat under the same cedar at the far corner of the school's play yard, patiently waiting again for school to be dismissed. He was not surprised when Maria came flying out the door as if she was being chased by a swarm of bees. She wore a gray split riding skirt and brown leather vest over a simple white blouse. She had her teacher's bag slung over her shoulder, and it bulged with what looked like books and materials. Tucked under her other arm was a large bundle of men's clothing tied with twine.

She beamed as she approached him. "I met Betsy, the other day. What a precious sister you have! She stopped at the cottage and gave me all these second-hand clothes to give to Lenny."

"You have no idea what we've had to endure while we were growing up with precious Betsy," he replied with a poker straight face. "She knows how to pickpocket, can shoot better than most men, and has no qualms about voicing her opinion, whether it's right or wrong or close to insane. Oh, and she's wicked with a broom in her hands."

Maria peered down at him with joy still bubbling up and washing over her face. "Sounds like Abigail. Both seem to be rather assertive in their approach to life."

"That's a diplomatic way of putting it." Tye rose and took time to survey her from head to toe. No woman, he decided, should look that good in riding clothes and boots. No woman's laughter should make him feel so helplessly smitten. No woman, especially one so beautiful, should have him lassoed so tightly it hurt to breathe. He had horses to break and chores to do, and yet, here he was once again, succumbing to the will of the new schoolmarm even though he knew the trip would be futile. His brother, Marcus, had laughed like a hyena when he told him where he was headed, then had said mountain climbing was, by far, a most novel, but unusual way to court a young lady.

Marcus was the jokester of the family and now a father of two small children, a girl and boy. He had married a Danish gal who had opened a bakery in town. When she wasn't baking the best pastries in a hundred mile radius, she helped with his sister-in-law's pottery business. More and more Scandinavians were flooding into the area, and Anna's bakery was doing a brisk business, selling out every day before nightfall. In fact, he had specifically requested Anna to save him some bear claws and donuts and had tucked them away in his saddlebag as a treat for both Maria and himself, and for Lenny and River Roy.

He heard Maria speak, breaking his reverie.

"And I had the opportunity to visit your sister's General Store and purchase a few things."

"So I've been told. Oh, that reminds me." From around his saddle horn, he removed a charcoal gray Stetson. "She forgot to add this to your outfit." He set the hat on her head, making sure the strings fell forward under her chin. His eyes never left hers while he worked. When he went to adjust the cord under her chin, he felt her soft hands cover his and send a jolt clear down to his toes. "Don't, Tye. I can do it. I'm not helpless."

"Sorry, I never thought you were," he said in a smooth undertone and held his hands up in defeat. He moved away to tie the bundle of clothes to his saddle and her book bag to her mount, a sleek, little brown cow pony. He could feel the tension radiate into the air around them and was certain she felt it, too.

She walked to the front side of her mount and stroked the mare's neck affectionately, then moved to her head and blew a few soft puffs into her nostrils.

"Hey, gal. How are you doing today?" The horse tossed her head, snorted an impatient response, and sidestepped. Laughing softly, Maria said to Tye, "I have to look for saddle horses for Abigail and me. Aunt Emma only has carriage horses in the barn, although Lang Redford said two others are saddle broke. I know Uncle Henry used to ride."

Tye glanced over his shoulder at her and was glad she changed the subject to relieve the tension. "I don't believe I've ever seen Emma ride a horse. I don't know if she's ever handled a buggy by herself, now that you mention it." When he was finished, he gave the cow pony a few reassuring pats as well. A flicker of amusement lighted up his face. "I bought this little mare from Flint who picked her up awhile back for his wife, Julia, to ride, not knowing she had her eyes set on a quarter horse down in Colorado Springs. You'll like this sure-footed filly. She responds well to the slightest commands. However, if you dismount, keep hold of the reins; I'm not certain she is trained to be ground tied or how loyal she might be. I've only had her for a few weeks."

Maria's gaze circled the yard. "Where's Swamp?"

"Working back at the ranch. My men are moving some cattle closer to water." He saw disappointment in her eyes and cursed beneath his breath. The darn dog had a better chance of winning her affections and courting her than he did. "You've taken a shine to him, I see."

"Don't be jealous, Tydall." She laughed gently, taking the reins from him. They mounted and set off toward the west at a brisk pace with a warm breeze fanning their faces. The ride up the mountain was a leisurely one. Around them, Maria paid strict attention to keeping her mount in line behind Tye's whenever the path grew too narrow for two horses. Above them, the birds chattered in the trees and the overcast, colorless sky was a welcome relief from the earlier heat of the day.

Minutes later, when they were riding side by side once again, Maria asked, "What do you know about Aunt Emma? Besides she doesn't ride a horse."

Tye Ashmore shrugged. "I know Emma came from Georgia and married a miller, who was not the best businessman around. When he died from drowning, he left Emma with a slew of debts. She was a beautiful woman, and it didn't take long for Emma to pursue your uncle. He fell in love, paid off her debts, and married her. People around town always said she was a strange one, not especially friendly, but then, you must remember gossip in a small town has a way of spreading like wildfire in dry grass. Emma never socialized much with the other womenfolk. Maybe she felt uncomfortable mingling with those who had less. She always dressed in expensive, beautiful clothes and I'm told, even by my sister, she ran up enormous bills about town which your uncle paid. Betsy once remarked no one would ever want to get on the wrong side of Emma McNeil."

At one point when the path became so narrow, they were forced to slip off their horses and lead them. Behind him, Tye heard Maria ask, "Why doesn't Lenny's dad believe in educating his son?"

Tye motioned for her to catch up to him as the path widened enough to walk side by side. "Oh, I don't rightly know. I suppose he does, but he's just distrustful of people. He's led a hard life, Maria."

"I know. I heard he lost his son in the war."

"Yes, Walt." He frowned. "The old man's life has been one heartache after another. He acquired the rights to a rich coal vein and requested access from the adjacent land where it was safer to mine. Denied, he built an entrance from his property, tunneling beneath a soft area supported with only props and wooden beams. One night six years ago, his wife brought him dinner, going deep into the mine to find him. The tunnel collapsed, and she was killed. River Roy closed up the mine shaft and buried her where she fell. The cave-in was her grave."

She took a quick, sharp breath. "Oh, how horrible."

"And if it was tough having to see his son abandon him and march off to war, can you imagine his pain when he learned the son was killed? Ironically, Walt and Brett became good friends, drawn together being from the same area of the country. It was Walt who Brett left his army papers with before he went to spy on Southern lines. After he was killed, no one was able to locate Brett's papers. They just disappeared."

"Did Brett ever question River Roy about them?"

"Of course, but he swears he only received his son's corpse in a pine coffin."

"Could he have a reason to lie?"

"None I know of. The man may be bitter, but he isn't known to be vindictive."

"How will Brett ever clear his name?" They stopped beneath a huge pine tree just before the path widened to catch their breath. Maria removed her hat to let the breeze cool her head, then reset it, letting it fall onto her back by its strings.

"Right now, Brett is collecting testimony as to his allegiance to the North. I've even written a letter for him. But it doesn't look good because he was in civilian clothes and found far from the Northern prisoners in the splendid company of Southern officers."

Maria's face tightened. There was sarcasm in her voice when she spoke, "Why would any man whose mission was to spy and gather information on the enemy hang around with his fellow Northern soldiers being held prisoner? The Southern officers would have more information about troop movement."

Tye shrugged. They mounted again and rode in comfortable silence until they reached the top of the mountain where they traveled deep into the forest and arrived at a dilapidated one-room cabin with a patched roof and a front porch with a broken railing. It sat before a small, bubbling stream winding its way even farther into the dense, leafy undergrowth. On the right side of the cabin was a lean-to, stacked full of rows of firewood, and on the left, a larger lean-to held four robust mules in stables. Frayed and shabby gray curtains hung limply in the cabin's two front, flyspecked windows both badly in need of soap and water.

"Ease up, Maria." Tye stopped his mount several yards from the cabin. "Sometimes folks aren't too friendly when strangers approach." He called out, "River Roy! It's Tye Ashmore. Can you spare a moment to talk?"

River Roy ambled out on the weather-beaten porch with a shotgun under his arm and Lenny peering out from behind him. "Talk's cheap, Ashmore. I reckon I can. Who you got there?"

"This is the new school teacher, Maria O'Donnell. You met her sister, Abigail, the other day." Tye stepped down from his horse and held the reins to Maria's horse while she dismounted. He reached into his saddlebag, pulled out a cloth sack, and spoke. "Anna sent some donuts and bear claws. She told me she made too many the other day and didn't want them to go to waste." It was a lie, but River Roy's pride would never allow for charity. He motioned to Lenny. "Here take these indoors, away from the heat, flies, and critters."

The boy jumped at the chance, scrambling down the uneven steps. He snatched the bag, opened it, peered in, and grinned. "Thank you!" He looked back at his father. "Pa, can I have one?"

"We don't take hand-outs, Ashmore," River Roy snapped.

"No, and I don't waste food, nor do I insult my generous sister-in-law."

The two men faced each other, and a silent standoff ensued. A minute later, River Roy let out a low chuckle and propped his shotgun against the outside doorjamb. "You Ashmores are a difficult lot to argue with. Yes, son, you can have one."

"We don't like to argue at all." Tye took off his hat and wiped his forehead with the back of his hand. "I can do enough sparring with my cantankerous brothers and my sometimes loco sister…and it's too hot today to be clever enough to outwit you."

****

Maria listened to the conversation between the two men, amazed how easily Tye could diffuse a prickly situation.

She stepped forward and spoke, "I never once

meant for the sketch paper and pencil to be a hand-out for Lenny. It was a present. Your son has an extraordinary talent. You can see he's a very bright boy from the detail in puts into his drawing. I was only trying to help. My sister was thankful you came along when she encountered the lynx."

"The boy don't need to be playing with no paper and pencil. We've work to do in the woods between chores here at the cabin and huntin' for food." River Roy rubbed the side of his bearded face with his hand.

"If Lenny could go to school and learn to read and write, he could have a chance at doing something different than logging." Maria tried to keep her voice level so she didn't sound insulting.

"I need him here."

Tye interrupted, "I agree."

Startled, Maria looked at him with a shocked expression, but he continued, pushing his hat back slightly and squinting up at River Roy leaning against a rough wooden post on the porch. "The lumbering business is moving forward with new ways and new-fangled machinery to do the work, Roy. You know how the paper mill has taken off. They're paying good wages in town, and it would be a shame for Lenny to work the woods when he could be making three times the amount at the mill. He's good with his hands, his drawings are proof."

"Then we'll go back to the mines if there's no job for us in the woods."

"But Lenny can have both," Tye said calmly. "Send him to school a couple days a week, and have him work the woods with you for the rest."

River Roy grunted. "He ain't got any clothes for

going to school, and I don't aim for my son to be laughed at."

When Maria started for his saddle, Tye stopped her with a warning look. "Betsy sent a whole bundle of clothes that no longer fit my brothers. She wanted you to distribute them to the other loggers' children in the area. Have Lenny pick out a shirt and pants from the bundle."

"We ain't charity, Ashmore."

Tye sighed. "Dang! *Now* you want to insult my sister, Betsy, helpful soul that she is? You know River Roy, I'd shoot you right here and now and end this conversation and my misery, but you wouldn't be worth the effort. And I'd be putting Maria here in the uncomfortable position of being a party to the crime as well as being a witness. Just send Lenny as he is. Tarnation! It makes little difference to me."

Maria looked over to where the rows and rows of wood were stacked along the cabin. "We could do a little bartering," she offered hopefully. She gestured to the woodpile. Her forehead wrinkled; she gave him a quizzical gaze. "By the way, what *is* your last name? I'm not used to addressing people with odd nicknames."

"Sanderson." He spit a stream of tobacco juice in the dirt below him and smiled.

"Mr. Sanderson," she said, starting over, "I need wood to take the chill off the classroom on fall mornings. If you can deliver me a few bundles, I'll give Betsy a few coins for the used clothes."

"And she'll be putting the wrath of God on her head when she does," Tye said with a cold edge of irony in his voice. "Betsy will not be pleased. Next time you go to the store for supplies, you can deal with her and her fussy disposition. Maybe *she'll* shoot you."

River Roy laughed. "Your sister is one mule-headed woman when riled."

"Then it's a deal?" Maria asked. "I'll take my chances with Betsy Ashmore."

"I'll tell you what." River Roy pushed off the post to stand straight. "Lenny can come two days a week, and we'll see how it works out."

It was a begrudging compromise, and Maria knew it took a lot for him to make. She walked over to her horse and pulled out a book, a sketchbook, and a pencil while Tye took the bundle of clothes from the back of his saddle and threw it up on the porch.

"Lenny's first assignment, before he arrives, is to learn to write his name." Maria quickly and clearly printed, Lenny Sanderson, at the top. "And I want him to draw something that makes *you* happy, Mr. Sanderson."

"Me? Nothin' makes me happy, Miss O'Donnell," River Roy muttered, his tone harsh. "When I lost my wife and then my oldest son to the War, I realized happiness is not meant for everyone."

"If you say so," she agreed and gave him a pointed stare, "but you better think on it and find something so the boy can properly do his homework." She handed Lenny the book and smiled. "This is for you to look through. There are some colorful pictures on the pages. You'll like them. The book is about animals." She walked over to her horse and mounted. "I will expect Lenny on Tuesdays and Thursdays, but you may bring my wood whenever it pleases you."

Together they turned their horses and headed

toward the trail winding back down the mountain. Neither of them spoke. Minutes later, Tye pulled up under a stand of hickory trees, reached behind him, opened a sack from his saddlebag, and offered Maria a bear claw. "Nice work up there. You have a stern side to match the quiet reserved one." He pulled out a donut for himself.

Maria bit into the bear claw. It was fresh, and the richness of cinnamon and sugar melted against her tongue with a delicious sweet sensation. "I have you to thank. I never thought a man could be so stubborn. Though I must admit, I feel sorry—"

Suddenly, a shot rang out and a bullet landed with a soft thud in the trunk of a tree beside them. Before Maria could react, Tye leaped from his horse, threw himself at her, and knocked them both to the ground. He rolled off her, grabbed her by her upper arm, and half-yanked and half-pushed her toward a large outcropping of rock sprinkled with briars. She stumbled and fell down, landing on her knees and forearms, but righted herself, oblivious to the scrapes and scrambled onward. Together, they crouched behind a boulder, peering out at the vacant trail before them. Maria watched the flying tails of both horses as they cantered down the rocky mountain path. Around them, the forest grew eerily quiet in the fading light.

Chapter Ten

Crouching beside Tye, Maria looked at his grim face with wide, frightened eyes. "Do you think it was a stray bullet from a hunter's rifle? Surely no one would shoot at us on purpose."

Tye peered out from the rock formation, turned, slumped down on the ground, and checked his pistol. His rifle and water had galloped away with the horses. "A bullet lands that close, and you think it was an errant shot?" He stared at her with narrowed eyes. Her face was still white, and she was trying to keep her hands from shaking.

She rubbed her knees where she had fallen on the ground, rolled her sleeve up, and inspected her brush-burned arm. "If not errant, then obviously it was meant for either you or me since no other shots were fired, and we're the only ones in the vicinity."

"Looks that way." He took off his hat, wiped his forehead, and blew out a disgruntled breath of air. "You just got here, so I don't reckon you've had enough time to make any enemies. Are you hurt?"

"It's nothing. Just a few scrapes. I'm fine." She waved him away.

He nodded, pondering the situation. It was too risky to try walking down the mountain trail until darkness fell. Whoever shot at them would pick them off like ducks on an open lake. If he only had his rifle.

He was certain his horse would eventually return, unless the stallion got his reins tangled in the dense brush. He hated to leave Maria without a firearm, but if he could slip through the tangled undergrowth lining the path, he just might find his horse, his rifle, and his ring flask with water. He swore softly under his breath.

"Why are you angry?" Maria asked.

Staring at her, he slumped down farther, scratching his chin and tipping his head backward to rest against the rock behind them. He closed his eyes and let out a low grunt. "Tarnation, I was just starting to enjoy the dang donut! Now here we sit—one gun, no water, and our food lying yonder out of reach and feeding an army of ants. It's a fine pickle we're in." He closed his eyes and sighed. "I wish I'd brought Swamp. He would have alerted us if someone was near."

"So do I."

"I knew it! I'm competing with a four-legged mongrel for your affections." An arresting smile softened his face.

"You never did tell me how he got his name."

He reached over and lightly fingered a loose tendril of hair on her cheek, then pulled his hand away to rest on his knee. "I was fishing down by the creek when I heard this pup whimpering and slogging through the mud, making his way up from the river through the nearby swamp. He came out a muddy-looking mess and scampered right up, shaking mud and water all over me."

"How did he get in the swamp?"

Tye raised an eyebrow. "It's more like—how did he make it *out* of the creek?"

Maria's eyes widened. "Oh, no. Don't tell me

someone tried to drown him."

"When settlers are moving onward, it's quite common to drop off litters of pups or kittens near the ranches around here or…" He paused. "…find a burlap sack and a nearby body of water."

He rolled up into a crouch, reset his hat, and faced her.

"Listen, I have an idea. I'm going to take you farther back into the forest, hide you, and then I'm going down the mountain a bit in search of my horse."

"You're going to *abandon* me, Tydall Ashmore?"

He winced, his expression was almost apologetic. "No, I'm going to leave you for a few minutes. I promise I'll return."

"No, take me with you. *Please*." Icy fear glistened in her eyes.

He raised his hand and caressed the side of her face with his knuckles. "You have to trust me, Maria, if we're going to get back down this mountain." He gestured toward the dense woods behind them. "Come, let me find a place farther from the path where it's safe and secure. I promise I'll be back to get you."

Minutes later, when he turned to leave, she grabbed him by his upper arm. "Wait," she said, her voice faltering, her gaze fearful. "Please be careful."

He felt the electricity of her touch, and for a moment they stared at each other, unable to tear their attention away. He left her then on the perimeter of the small clearing, but not before softly touching his lips above her eyebrow and whispering near her ear, "Trust me. You have to trust me, Maria. I'll come back for you."

****

Under the cool shadows of a tall pine tree, Maria sat with her back against the rough bark of the trunk and peered out into the snarled undergrowth surrounding her. Around her, the woods smelled of earth, drying leaves, and sweet blackberries. Soon the sun would be going down, and she would be alone in the dark as the air grew colder. She removed her hat and nervously weaved the strings between her fingers while she waited for Tye's return. She silently berated herself for pestering him to take her up the mountain to see River Roy. They could easily have made the trip on Saturday when they had the entire day. She was so engrossed in her thoughts she missed seeing the Indian who emerged from the brush a few feet beside her with two rifles under one arm and eating a donut with the other hand.

"You look worried, white woman," the Indian mumbled, his mouth full.

Startled, Maria looked up as a wave of apprehension swept over her, and her stomach felt like she jumped off a cliff. An Indian. He stood tall and proud, his greasy black hair tied back with a rawhide string, and he was missing his two front teeth. On closer look between the opening in his dirty leather vest, she noticed his chest was covered in a mass of scars. Her heart thudded in her chest. She pulled her knees to her chest and inched her body farther against the tree until the bark bit into her back.

"Are you the school teeee-cher? Or are you white woman who owns the whiskey everyone is talking about?" The Indian had a ring of powdered sugar around his mouth as he devoured the last of the donut, then wiped his mouth with the back of his hand.

"The…the school teacher," Maria stuttered. "Maria O'Donnell."

The Indian grunted and tapped his chest. "Me Two Bears. Too bad you don't own the whiskey. Two Bears likes good whiskey."

Maria eyed the Indian warily and stuttered again. "I…I...I can get you whiskey."

Two Bears grunted and laid the rifles down carefully on a bed of pine needles. He approached her, squatting and studying her carefully, tilting his head to the left and right. "Do not be afraid. I am friends with the Ashmores. Are you Tye Ashmore's woman?"

"Tye Ashmore is my friend. He's coming any…any minute," she managed to blurt out. "He left to get his horse and his rifle." She rubbed her elbow and lower arm which had started to sting.

Two Bears snorted and nodded toward the rifles. "Two Bears has his rifle. I came to give it to him." He eyed her carefully, then reached out his hand and grabbed her by the top of her injured arm.

"Leave me alone," she ground out and tried to pull her arm free, but he held fast. He pushed her sleeve up higher and looked at the scraped skin on her elbow and underneath her forearm. He grunted a disapproving sound then stared at her with dark penetrating eyes before rising and heading back through the trees. He returned with a small tin and handed it to her.

"Put this on your wound," he ordered.

"What is it?"

"Bear grease," he replied solemnly. "Good for cuts and scrapes."

Maria wrinkled her nose and shoved the tin toward him. "No, no, thank you. I'm fine."

Two Bears snorted. "Go ahead. It will help. It smells like horse dung, but it works."

Maria shook her head vehemently. "No. Thank you, but no. I don't need it."

Two Bears walked to a nearby pine and sat down opposite her, stretching his feet out, still silently studying her. "Read the tin, white woman teacher."

Maria looked at the tin more carefully. It was petroleum jelly. She opened it and smelled it cautiously, and heard him chuckle. "Where did you get this?"

"Betsy Ashmore."

She shrugged and applied some jelly to her stinging elbow and arm, still warily watching him.

Finally he asked, "How long has Ashmore been gone?"

"At least ten minutes."

He nodded. "It will take him a few more minutes." He crossed his hands at his chest and stared at her. "Can you teach a man to read and write, Ma-reee-a?"

Baffled, she looked at him. "What do you mean? Learning to read and write is the same whether you teach a grown man, woman, or child. You start with the letters and then string the letters into words."

"I have seen these letters and words you speak of. Two Bears would like to read and write the white man's language. Can you teach Two Bears?"

Teach him? A multitude of thoughts flew through Maria's head. What would the school board think if they discovered she was teaching an Indian? What would the townsfolk think? What would anyone think of her right now, sitting in a forest with an Indian? Hesitating, Maria continued to gaze at him, torn by conflicting emotions as she weighed each question. But before she could answer, Tye walked into the small cleared area. He held a ring flask in his hands.

The Indian rose and grinned. "At last. You are back. I have your rifle, Ashmore. And your sack of donuts. And your woman. Tell Anna the donuts are good. Very good. You may have your woman and your rifle. Two Bears keeps the donuts."

Tye sighed with relief. Eyes narrowed, he said, "Besides finding Maria, I'm sure there's a story about how you managed to get the rifle and donuts."

Two Bears grinned and shook his head. "No. No story. I took them. Not so hard when you leave horse with its reins caught in the bushes."

"I didn't leave my horse on purpose. It was scared off when someone shot at me, and I jumped off to save my hide and Maria's. The rifle, water, and donuts went with it." Tye threw him a cold look that could freeze running water in a summer sun.

"And a sorry hide yours is, Ashmore. You are getting careless. You leave woman with hair the color of mink all alone. You lose horse, rifle, donuts, and water. And you do not take dog with you."

"If you keep insulting me, Two Bears, I'm going to take my rifle and wrap it around your greasy neck. Why didn't you bring my horse?"

"Why didn't you?" Two Bears asked. His mouth was tight and grim. "If I had moved the horse, anyone watching would know to follow me back to you or your woman. This way, they do not know if you are on the mountain or not."

Tye nodded. "I figured the same. I decided we'd walk down to get it when it gets dark."

Maria rose and stepped between them. She was

scared, she was weary, and she wanted to get home, take a bath, and soak her skinned arm and injured knee. "Why can't we just start now?"

"Your woman is not happy." Two Bears grunted. "An angry squaw can make sunny days seem like rainy ones."

Maria glared at him.

"Maybe we're both not happy since you're eating our food," Tye countered.

Two Bears thumped his chest and grinned. "I even ate the ones you dropped on the trail. Before any varmints could get to them. Come, I know another path to your horse. By the time we arrive, it will be dark, and you can take your woman and go the rest of the way safely."

"I am not *his woman*," Maria snapped. "I am not a piece of property. Stop saying that!"

Two Bears jumped back, away from her. "If you say so." He looked at Tye with wide eyes. "Hair like a mink. Temper like a badger."

****

A mile down the trail as darkness descended, they found Tye's horse and parted with Two Bears who silently disappeared into the underbrush with the agility of a bobcat. The dampness in the approaching night air caused Marie to shiver. Tye untied his buckskin coat from the back of his saddle, handed it to her to wear, and mounted his horse, but not before he checked his rifle and returned it to his scabbard. He held out a hand, taking hers and pulling her up behind him.

"I doubt anyone will be crazy enough to wait half the evening to try to shoot me in the dark," he said in a low, rueful voice.

With her arms wrapped around his waist, Maria felt the heat of his back radiate clean through the coat, and she felt warm and safe as they started back down the mountain. "What will happen to my horse and my school bag?"

"Your horse has probably returned to my ranch or to Flint's, and Amos, your sister, and Betsy are probably crazy with worry by now."

"Tell me about Two Bears."

"That fool-hardy Indian is a Ute renegade whom my sister-in-law befriended when she first came to Golden and needed some wild horses to sell to the army for money. At the time her pottery business was just getting started."

"What does he do?"

"Besides driving our family crazy?"

She laughed. "I mean, how does he live?"

"He has a simple life gathering wild ponies for locals to sell to the army. He lives alone since his wife and children were killed in a raid by white men when he was younger. The claw marks on his chest are from a time when he tangled with two grizzlies who are now in animal heaven."

When they reached the bottom of the mountain, Maria could see the tiny speck of light peeking out from between the mullions in the front window and could smell the wood smoke from the fireplace long before they reached the cottage door. Around them the songs of night insects filled the air. Abigail and Betsy came flying out of the cottage when they rode into the yard.

"It's about time!" Abigail said in a harsh, haughty voice. She stood with her hands on her hips. "Do you realize, Maria, it's way past dark? Do you realize how this will look to the entire population of Golden?"

Maria slid off Tye's mount and stumbled, but not before Betsy grabbed her by the arm. She flinched, and Betsy could see she was injured. "Why don't you help get Maria cleaned up and ready for bed?" She pushed them both gently toward the cottage and looked at her brother's weary face as he dismounted.

"Maria's horse came back to the ranch an hour ago," she said. "When yours didn't, Flint decided we should wait until morning to go looking for you. He's at the Mule Shed Inn getting a party of men together for a morning search. Marcus is with him."

Tye spoke. "Someone shot at us while we were coming back down the mountain."

"Do you have any idea who was behind the rifle sights?" She laid a gentle hand on his tired shoulder. Around them, thunder rumbled.

Tye grunted derisively. "Someone who wants to see me dead?"

Betsy pried the reins from his grip. "Well, at least you haven't lost your sense of humor. I'll take your horse to the General Store and bed him down with mine. You'd better go to the inn and let Flint and Marcus know you and Maria are safe. I'll leave the door open, and you can have the spare room tonight. No sense in riding all the way back to the ranch in the dark." She threw him a pointed look and her unspoken message—she didn't want him riding around in the dark or the rain—was not lost on him.

"Don't wait up for me, Betsy. I think this would be a good night to imbibe in some good Canadian whiskey." He removed his hat and ran his hand through his unruly hair.

Betsy smiled. "Especially if you can get your brothers to sympathize with your plight and throw down some coins for the rounds."

He looked toward the cabin. "I should check on Maria and apologize or explain to Abigail. This whole situation doesn't look good with both of us out so late. She's a single woman and new teacher, to boot. Gossip has a way of settling itself over the town like a dust storm."

Betsy shook her head and looked up at the ominous black sky which had opened up and was spitting huge raindrops. "Abigail hasn't been in the best of moods for the last two hours. I'd wait until tomorrow when everyone is rested to sort it out." She hugged him. "Everything always looks better in the light of a new day, Tydall."

Still hatless, he nodded and allowed his breath to seep out in a long, relieved sigh, then trudged wearily up the path toward the Mule Shed Inn. He hated to be on the wrong side of a gun. He hated when he wasn't in control of any situation. He looked at the sky and felt a large raindrop hit him squarely in his left eye. Come to think of it, he even hated rain.

Chapter Eleven

It wasn't the aroma of coffee, bacon, and hotcakes that finally roused Tye from sleep the next day. It was Swamp whining in his ear and nudging him awake with his cold nose. He threw back the quilt, sat up, and realized he had made it no further than his sister's plush settee in the parlor when he returned from the Mule Shed Inn's barroom yesterday evening.

Groaning, he reached out and patted the dog on his head. "You know, ol' boy, there are kinder ways to get a man up after a night bellied up to the bar." He looked around the new living quarters his sister had added on to the General Store after she had purchased it from old man Finley, the former owner. She had decorated in soft blue and green velvets and satins with pictures of pastoral scenes on the walls. Before the additions, she only had a small kitchen, sleeping cot, and eating area. Now she had two bedrooms, an ample parlor, a large kitchen with pantry, and a dining area big enough to handle all four brothers who regularly stopped in to see her. Although she still kept a few possessions at their ranch along Cherry Creek, she preferred living in the noise, hustle, and confusion of a frontier town. Since her move, Tye sorely missed her and her vivacious personality much more so, he suspected, than she missed him with his taciturn disposition.

It was well known Betsy had been adopted by his

mother and father when she was an infant and was left in a basket in their barn in Virginia. Their mother had just given birth to him and had immediately decided the little girl—which she considered a gift from God after four boys—would be raised by them and would be the girl they never had. It was also no secret Betsy inherited a great deal of money via a will after her real mother died and her identity was revealed.

Tye smiled. Upon meeting her, no one would ever guess his sister was a wealthy woman. She wore her favorite cotton dresses and multi-pocketed store aprons and preferred to wear her hair in one long blonde braid falling down her back. She also chose to work in the General Store as many hours as possible. She loved being busy, and she loved the town and the people of Golden. Tye and his brothers often joked she must have been a peddler in another life because she enjoyed bartering, buying, and selling goods.

Bootless, Tye rose and heard the riotous laughter of his brothers. He groaned. Now he would have to face their ribbing about last night, and his head felt like someone had hit him with a sledge hammer. He walked out into the eating area where Betsy was heaping hotcakes and eggs on Marcus's and Flint's plates. She looked up as he slid into a seat at the table. Swamp followed loyally, falling down beside his chair, his head on his paws.

"Your muddy boots are behind the back door," she said. "Good thing your brothers had the foresight to take them off before they deposited you onto my new settee. I guess they couldn't find the spare bedroom." She glared at all of them.

Tye squinted at her and held up a cup.

"Unceremoniously dumped, you mean."

Betsy took the coffeepot off the back of the stove and poured him a cup. "Food?"

He winced and shook his throbbing head.

Flint, his mouth stuffed with food, swallowed, then chuckled. "Can't hold the liquor, little brother?"

"He can't seem to hold onto the little school teacher either," Marcus piped up. "I heard she and her sister have their noses a tad out of joint. Of course, if I were shot at and dragged across a pile of rocks, I'd be a little peeved as well. I told you the mountain was no place to court a young lady."

Hands on hips, Betsy surveyed the men. "You all have absolutely nothing to chuckle about. If someone is out to shoot an Ashmore, we have more trouble than I care to think about at the moment."

Flint looked at her, his gray eyes thoughtful and serious. "She's right. Why would someone be gunning for Tye?"

"Considering I have more friends than all of you put together," Tye mumbled and rubbed his head, "and considering I haven't even been in town for the past two weeks to make any enemies, it doesn't make sense."

"Maybe the shooter wanted to steal his clothes," Marcus said. "Was that a new pair of buckskins you were wearing to impress the schoolmarm?"

"Maybe the shooter mistook Tye for someone else," Betsy said.

"Yeah, Wild Bill Hickok." Marcus snorted.

"Not a chance," Flint said. "Hickok's better looking."

"True. And we can count on our right hands the

number of men around here who wear duds like his and none of them resemble this ugly pole cat." Marcus laughed. "Maybe Maria has a disgruntled student."

"Or maybe someone out for revenge mistook Maria for her feisty sister who has all drunken sots tossed out on their ears. She has certainly cleaned up the barroom and turned it into a respectable place," Flint added.

"Do you think our little brother finally enraged one of his Indian friends?" Marcus asked through a mouthful of food.

Tye stood and groaned. "If you're all going to make fun of me, I'm leaving."

"No! No, they're not." Betsy picked up a nearby broom and stamped her foot to stop the ribald laughter. "I've had enough! If I hear another word from any of you, I'll be using this broom alongside your thick heads—and you, *my dear brothers*, will be using this broom to sweep the sidewalk out front for me. Now get out of here and take your pitiful humor with you." She waved the broom toward a side door leading into the store and out onto the front walk. "I have a store to run and now, thanks to you all, I have a kitchen to clean."

Two chairs scraped on the floor as the brothers scrambled up and headed for the side door while Tye wearily rose and headed for the parlor and the back door for his boots. The last thing anyone ever wanted to do was rile Betsy Ashmore.

****

Later in the morning, while Betsy worked in the back of the store repositioning some of the new glassware shipped in from the east coast, she was surprised to see Emma McNeil sail through the door. In her usual haughty manner, Emma marched up to the front counter and tapped on the brass call bell as if she was beating a war drum.

"I'll be right there," Betsy called out and set the two cups she was holding on a nearby shelf only to hear Emma impatiently rap the bell again, then seconds later, again. Heaving a sigh, Betsy headed down an aisle to the front of the store.

"What can I do for you today, Mrs. McNeil?" She slid around to the back of the counter where behind her bolts of colorful yard goods were stacked on shelves along with spools of thread and drawers of buttons.

"Well, first, you could at least respond to the bell a little faster when you have a customer." Emma snorted out her disgust. "I need some ribbon to match the satin dress I plan to wear tonight to the reopening of the Mule Shed. A burgundy color, like this." She withdrew a small piece of material and shoved it toward Betsy. "And lace. I'd like to see some lace about an inch wide. You'll need to hurry yourself along, too, since I have other errands to run. After all, I am the owner of the Mule Shed, and it's imperative I attend the event this evening and be seen in proper attire." She looked at Betsy as if she were a speck of sawdust beneath her feet and would have liked nothing better than to grind her under her shoe.

Undaunted, Betsy withdrew several spools of lace and ribbons in satins and grosgrain.

Emma bent her head, peered at the spools, and fingered the ribbons and delicate lace. "Is this all you have?" Her voice was close to a whine.

"Yes, it is." Betsy smiled, thinking about the evening ahead. Everyone in town and in the surrounding area was excited about the reopening of the

Mule Shed Inn, and she was certain Abigail would attract a crowd of people curious to see all the renovations. "Tye plans to escort Maria tonight. I'm anxious to see them all dressed up. They're both such beautiful women."

Emma's head snapped up and her beady eyes narrowed. "Those pitiful waifs? Why would anyone care what they might be wearing? Furthermore, I have no idea what Maria sees in that hooligan who's running about town in those wretched buckskins. Your brother was always a wild thing. Your father should have used a heavier hand on him or for that matter, on all the others." Emma shoved two spools toward Betsy and continued in a clipped voice, "I'll take a yard of the ribbon and three yards of the lace. I find it reprehensible Tye put Maria in so much danger yesterday when he dragged her up the mountain to see that filthy lumberman."

Betsy Ashmore stared at the woman, unblinking. Long ago, she had discovered it took a lot of stamina when dealing with unpleasant customers. "Well, I only hope Maria is feeling better and isn't angry with Tye. My brother would never deliberately put anyone in harm's way. I hope to see them both tonight."

"Better?" Emma asked with knitted brows.

Betsy took a yardstick and measured the lace. "I mean, I hope she's fine from all the excitement. She had a few scrapes and scratches when Tye pushed her off her horse." She wrapped the ribbon and lace in paper and handed it to Emma. "The total is a dollar."

Emma sniffed and lifted her chin in an arrogant manner. "Put it on my account."

"Yes, Mrs. McNeil, and I will need you to put

some money on your account sometime soon." This was the part of owning a business Betsy hated the most. She could overlook the poor who needed more time to pay, but she had no tolerance for people like Emma who bought things they didn't need, had the money to pay, and just neglected their obligations.

"What a rude little girl, you are." Emma huffed. "My husband not yet cold in the ground, and you're begging for money?"

Willing herself to remain calm, Betsy drew in a deep breath and let it out slowly. The old biddy's husband wasn't even cold in the ground, yet she had plans to attend the opening of the Mule Shed as if she was the belle of the ball? "I'm not begging for money, Mrs. McNeil. I'm requesting payment on an account three months overdue. It rightfully needs to be paid."

"Why you miserable, ill-mannered girl," Emma snapped. "I'll be sure to let the whole town folk know how disrespectful you are!"

Betsy watched Emma's straight back stomp toward the door. "You do that, Mrs. McNeil," she muttered under her breath. "Have a nice day," she said aloud.

The bang of the door was Emma's response.

****

It was late afternoon and Abigail was nervous. She paced the floor of the cottage after the noon meal, chewing on her finger and mumbling to herself as she re-examined her list of notes she compiled for the inn's re-opening. Table cloths were starched, pressed, and placed on all the tables. Candles and fresh flowers were in vases, and new coat pegs were attached to the walls just inside the main entrance. Logs were placed in the fireplace and barroom stove and were ready to be lit to chase away the evening's chill. Those who had chosen to dine were expected to arrive at six o'clock, and then the inn and barroom would open at seven for everyone else who wanted to see the renovations, imbibe in the various small treats, ales, and liquor—and join in the festivities of song and dance.

The whisky, wine, and ale were all stocked and ready to be served. Charlie Haney, her bartender, had suggested ale at five cents a glass was reasonable, but whiskey at twelve cents was too steep. Good whiskey was hard to come by, Abigail countered, and Charlie had agreed Abigail's Canadian whiskey was the best he'd ever tasted. Abigail wondered how her father could have left them so penniless. Here she was, agonizing over a few cents. She remembered the long trip from Utah, the boat ride on the river, and wagon journey northward with Cousins Joshua and Adam and decided to keep the price as she originally intended.

She looked down at the blue dress Maria had sewn for her. It was exquisite, even if was remade from a cast-off of Emma's, and it made her blue eyes sparkle even more brilliantly. She stopped and looked toward the manse on the hill. Aunt Emma! She had forgotten she had asked Aunt Emma to dine with them. She also had not made any arrangements to get Emma an escort or to have her delivered to the inn.

At first, Emma had adamantly said she couldn't attend the reopening, what with Henry's funeral but a mere month and a half ago. Abigail had insisted her presence would be a tribute to her late uncle, and of course, as owner in the business, Emma would be expected to attend. Abigail assured her if she were properly dressed in mourning black, everyone would be delighted to see her. It had taken little convincing for her aunt to reconsider.

As Abigail paced the room, she decided to let Tye and Maria take care of queer Aunt Emma. She looked at her notes again and remembered she had planned to borrow two matching ribbons from Maria to lend to the two girls who were singing for the guests before the dinner hour. In her haste to get to Maria's hair ribbons in the bedroom, she stumbled over a stool and caught herself, but not before she also caught the edge of her gown on the wood box and ripped the hem. She pulled it away carefully and groaned, just as Maria entered through the back door in time to see the disaster.

"Slow down, Abigail!" Maria set aside the book she was holding and reached for her sewing box. "Sit down, please. You will be in pieces before the evening has started!" She pulled out a chair and proceeded to guide her sister to it. Then she pulled out another, seated herself across from her, and began to repair the damage.

Amos walked in, holding a huge box, and stared at the two women, one with a mouth full of pins, quietly stitching the gown of the other, who looked like she was going to jump out of the chair.

"Bad luck, Miss Maria," he said and shook his head, "to sew a garment while someone is wearing it. And we don't need bad luck tonight."

Maria mumbled around the pins in her mouth. "Bad luck, Amos, is having a fidgeting sister flopping around like a fish out of water. Is there something I can help you with?"

"Come to deliver a package and to get Abigail. Charlie thinks we should haul the piano into the dining room for the singers, but I won't let him until Miss Abby agrees."

Maria stood and took the box Amos held out to her. "It was sent up from the General Store."

Maria placed the box on the table, removed the cover, and lifted out the most beautiful green silk dress she'd ever seen. Its bodice was covered with bead work and rich imported lace was sewn into the sleeves. "Oh, my!" she said. "Oh, my goodness. How stunning!"

Beside her, Abigail spoke, "And just when I planned to throttle Tye Ashmore for the antics of the other night, his sister redeems him with this exquisite creation."

Maria shook her head. "No, the note just says *from a friend.*"

"Well, it must be Betsy or Tye. Who else could it be?" Abigail asked. "Come, Amos, let's go and resolve the problems at the inn."

"What about my hair?" Maria's hands flew up in the air.

"You have an entire hour to get ready," Abby replied.

"What about Brett?"

"If he shows, bring him along with Emma."

"We're taking Aunt Emma, too?" Maria looked at her sister with a sorrowful grimace.

"Yes, see you at six." Abigail dashed out the door, ending any further discussion of the issue.

Moments later, despite her earlier worries, the Mule Shed Inn looked splendid, ready for guests and well-wishers. The dining room was set with dishes, pure white napkins, and sparkling silverware. Brass fixtures in the rooms were polished to a shine, and the office was dusted, although Abigail insisted it was to remain closed. The delicate odor of roast beef and potatoes cooking in the kitchen drifted into the dining room. The bar had been well-stocked, and all the glasses shimmered in the late sunlight streaming in the windows.

"If you want the piano in the dining room, Miss Abby, we'd better get it moved now," Charlie said behind her back.

"Then how do we gracefully haul it back through a crowd when our singers are finished?" Amos asked.

All three sets of eyes darted from one to another.

"Very simply put, you need another piano." Brett strolled through the back door. In his hand, he dangled two pink ribbons. "Miss Abigail O'Donnell, we need to talk."

Abigail stared wordlessly at the handsomely dressed Brett. He appeared relatively civil, but concealed anger brewed beneath his stoic appearance. He was a remarkably imposing figure, tall and muscular, with an angular face that would make the Greek gods jealous. A chilly silence surrounded them as black as the suit he was wearing. She saw a flash of controlled ire in his green eyes. "Now, *Miss O'Donnell.*"

"Let's go to my office, *Captain Trumble*," she managed to stammer. Her stomach did a quick somersault. With her back straight and stiff, she walked toward the back corner of the inn.

Chapter Twelve

Inside the office, Abigail moved to her desk and turned toward Brett, who held out his hand and dropped the pink ribbons into her palm. "You forgot these, and you obviously forgot I was escorting you, Abigail."

"There were problems at the inn, and I decided to come early." She laid the ribbons aside on the desk. "I walked up with Amos."

He sighed. "I don't know what I'm going to do with you." He stepped toward her, and in the blur of a moment, his face turned from irritation to charming. He smiled, reached out, and ran the back of his hand lightly down her forearm. "I would kiss you, but it would only rile you more, and this is no time to have Miss Abigail O'Donnell, manager of the Mule Shed Inn, irritated. Not on opening night." He reached up and caressed the side of her face. He was so close she could smell the bay rum he used and feel heat radiate from his body.

"For once, you're right." She tried hard not to react but was unsuccessful. "And if you would like to keep your trigger finger intact, I'd suggest you remove it from my face." Together their gazes met, merry green eyes with sky blue ones, and they stared at each other for a moment before both of them smiled.

"I have a piano problem. If I want it in the dining room, I'd better get it moved now." She backed away as his hand fell away from her, and she pressed her fingers to her temples.

"And how will you gracefully haul it back to the barroom with over half the town milling about? I thought you wanted the Irish gals to sing there later in the evening."

"I do."

"Then we need another piano."

"Now? Don't be daft, Brett, where would I get another piano?"

Brett pursed his lips, looking skyward for a moment. His gaze fell and met hers. "There's a blacksmith, Joe Sarowski, at the edge of town with a slew of daughters. All four of them played the piano as well as the accordion. They're grown now and married. I can see if Joseph would be willing to lend his piano this evening. We would need six stout backs and a wagon, and we could bring it in around back, through the kitchen, to avoid the front steps."

Abigail sighed. She hated being indebted to anyone. Now she'd be indebted to Brett as well as someone she'd never met. She looked up and found him still studying her. His nearness was overwhelming, and she could feel his energy and power. And did the man ever have charm! She'd bet a gold eagle he could lure the piano from poor Sarowski within five minutes. She waved her hand toward the office door. "Go! Go! See if you can weasel a piano off the poor, unsuspecting fellow." Disconcerted, she shook her head, then called after him, "Please be sure to personally invite both Mr. Sarowski and his wife to dinner at the inn tonight. I'll be sure a special table is reserved for them. Please tell them their meals and drinks are on the house. But hurry, we only have an hour before dinner guests start arriving."

Three quarters of an hour later, Brett came whistling through the door followed by Amos, Charlie, Lang Redford, Will Singer, Big Jake, and Joseph Sarowski lugging a small upright piano. They placed it in the corner of the dining room.

"Your diners are just minutes behind us." Brett grinned and straightened his black silk tie while the staff scurried back to their places and Joe Sarowski took his leave.

And come the townsfolk did.

Abigail was surprised to see all the people who flooded into the Mule Shed, including town councilmen, school board members, the sheriff, the banker, the undertaker and of course, the blacksmith and his wife. With Brett Trumble beside her, her nervousness began to wane as he introduced her to everyone who came through the door.

She was so caught up in the activities of meeting and welcoming her guests, she forgot about Maria and Tye until they were standing in front of her a half hour later. Maria was wearing the green silk dress and around her slim shoulders was a very expensive, black, Irish lace shawl.

"Look, Abby." She rushed up to her sister. "Tye gave me a new shawl for my birthday to wear with my dress. Isn't it beautiful?" She twirled, displaying the exquisite beadwork.

Abigail smiled. Maria looked like a princess. Her hair was caught up on her head in a mass of dark curls, and she wore their mother's single pearl necklace at her throat.

"You look beautiful." Abigail smiled. "Oh, Maria,

everything is turning out better than I ever expected." She paused a moment and surveyed the room. The barroom was jammed with people, and in the dining room, every table was taken except the one she had reserved for Aunt Emma, Maria, herself, and their escorts. The fragrant smell of beef, vegetables, and spices wafted from the kitchen along with the yeasty smell of ale from the taps in the barroom. Around her, the low murmur of pleasant conversation and laughter blended with the tinkling of glass and silverware.

"Where's Aunt Emma?" Abigail looked behind them.

"Emma sent Millie Hanson down to the cottage to tell us she'd arranged to come by herself, and we were to leave without her." Tye grinned. "It appears we are both fortunate and blessed."

Behind her, Brett spoke. "Come, Abby, let's sit with Tye and Maria." He took her elbow and escorted her to their table near the kitchen. "From the turnout tonight, it appears your business may be very successful."

"Oh, I hope so." She spoke in a low voice as they wove their way among the tables. "This is either going to make or break me financially." She said a silent prayer she would make enough money to allow her to pay off her bank loan and cover operating expenses for a few more weeks.

Once seated, the two Irish sisters, Peg and Polly, began their first number, a playful old ballad called, "Gently Down the Stream." They weren't two stanzas into the song when Emma McNeil, dressed in a fashionable, but low-cut, burgundy taffeta dress, sashayed into the dining room on the arm of Lang

Redford. All heads turned to watch the widow. Her hair was piled on her head and pinned with elaborate combs. Her face was covered with layers of powder, rouge, and lip coloring so thick they looked like they had been shoveled on. Even the piano player and singers stopped to stare.

Tye Ashmore leaned in and met Brett Tumble's befuddled green eyes with an equally baffled gaze. "I'm getting a bad feeling about this."

Abigail merely stared at her aunt, tongue-tied. If Aunt Emma had planned to attend in proper widow weeds as she had earlier suggested, she was wearing anything but discreet black. A huge diamond pendant encircled her neck and nestled itself between the two mounds of her bosom like a raindrop falling between two plump peaches. Lang Redford, lanky and clean-shaven, sauntered between the tables wearing a dark, worsted suit, a white shirt with a starched pointed collar, and a grin as wide as the Colorado River in flood season.

Both Tye Ashmore and Brett Trumble had the good sense and courtesy to stumble up and greet Emma as Abigail choked out, "Why, good evening, Aunt Emma and Mr. Redford." She nodded to the singers to begin again as the couple slipped into their seats to the right of Maria and Tye.

Emma patted her hair, preening. "Why, my dear nieces, I'm impressed by the grand turnout. However did you manage to contact so many distinguished people so quickly?" She smiled and glanced about the room, aware everyone was observing them.

Across the table, Abigail looked at Maria who was wide-eyed and speechless. "Actually, Aunt Emma, it was Brett and Tye who helped us collect names for a guest list, and Maria and I wrote personal invitations to each." She glanced at Brett who had leaned back in his chair and was now sipping on a glass of wine and enjoying the entire spectacle.

Emma wasted no time in scrutinizing both her nieces with open jealousy. She turned to Abby first. "Well, I see you're looking like Cinderella at the ball, Abigail. I'd love to know who you use for your seamstress. Her work is exquisite even if it's lost on your broomstick figure. No one would ever guess you're wearing one of my old cast-offs." She laughed lightly like a cackling hen. "If you should have need of any more hand-me-downs, I've several trunks in the attic you're welcome to rummage through."

"And you, my dear, Maria," she continued, turning, "my, my, your shawl must have cost a fortune. I doubt a school teacher's wages are hardly sufficient for such finery, or are those little confections on my account at the store?"

Maria's face turned crimson with embarrassment, but it was not as livid with anger as Tye Ashmore's was. Maria laid a hand on his forearm to try to quell his seething rage. "The shawl is a gift for my birthday from Tye," she managed to say with a calmness she hardly felt, "but the dress—"

Tye cut her off sharply. "Quite frankly, Mrs. McNeil, I'm a bit confused why a relative who has so much would care so little about her nieces."

Emma's lips thinned with anger. She stared at him, then recovering, laughed a high-pitched haughty laugh. "I'm appalled by your words and bold behavior, sir."

"As I am by yours, *ma'am*," he said, his gaze

steady, his face dangerously calm.

Across from him, Brett inhaled and held his breath. Lang Redford leaned forward about to intervene but thought otherwise when Tye glared at him, daring him to make a move. Lang eased his body back into his chair unsure of how to gauge the escalating ominous atmosphere.

A serving girl appeared, bringing bowls of steaming, rich soup to set before them. She was followed shortly after by another server bearing plates of beef, potatoes, and candied carrots. The rest of the meal was eaten without conversation, each person lost in his thoughts, and Abigail was glad she had commissioned the Irish sisters to perform and cover the awkwardness at the table.

"The kitchen staff has outdone themselves," Emma finally said in a dramatic voice and clasped her hands to her bosom as the main course was finished. "I wonder what they will serve for dessert."

"Apple pie, I imagine," Brett said. Devilish humor flashed across his face. He swiveled and smiled. "Both Maria and Abigail have voracious cravings for apple dishes." He openly winked at Abigail. "I saw a farmer unloading six dozen bushels of apples at the kitchen yesterday."

"Yes, but it's Swedish apple pie," Maria corrected him. "Abby hired Anna Ashmore to come over and supervise the kitchen staff in making one of her famous desserts from her bakery. It was always a favorite of ours when my father owned apple orchards in New York."

****

When the singers ended their repertoire of songs,

Emma rose from the table and took a spoon, tapping loudly on her crystal water glass to get the attention of the diners. "I wish to say a few words to my guests," she announced to everyone at the table and in the room.

Brett lightly poked Abigail with his elbow, then glanced at Tye, a smirk on his lips. He mouthed the words, "What the—"

Tye shook his head and glanced toward the ceiling. It was going to be a long night. Emma McNeil was about to steal the show.

The room grew quiet as Emma looked over the crowd, clasping her hands to her ample bosom in dramatic fashion and throwing them outward to the crowd. "Welcome! Welcome. I think it's only proper I should say a few words as owner of the Mule Shed Inn. I'm so pleased to be here and so happy to see everyone turn out for the reopening of it, despite the recent and unfortunate death of my dear husband, Henry, God rest his soul. When I devised the idea of hiring Abigail to manage the inn, I had no idea she was so capable. Her uncle would be proud to see she's now using her God-given talents, doing the same work he loved. I'm sure as you look around, you can see the many changes we've made." She paused. "And, of course, I would like to thank the town council, school board, and everyone in the town for providing a teaching position for Maria as well. As you all know, my two nieces came here penniless, like paupers, looking for a better life than the one in Utah where their poor, destitute father died."

In both shock and embarrassment, Abigail and Maria sat frozen to their chairs.

Tye rose to his feet as if someone ignited a bottle

of nitroglycerin under his chair. He tapped his water glass so harshly with the first utensil he could find, a large serving spoon, and was amazed it didn't shatter. He rounded the table and pushed Emma unceremoniously down into her seat.

"Just a second," Emma sputtered, "I'm not finished—"

"Oh, yes. Yes, you are," Tye whispered in a dangerously low voice. "Don't test my patience, you old witch. It's not beneath me to have you gagged, trussed up like a turkey, and carted out of here."

He picked up his wine glass and took a deep breath. "As you know, I'm the Ashmore who's not much of a talker." The crowd chuckled. "But tonight we toast Miss Abigail O'Donnell for the wonderful evening and reopening of the Mule Shed Inn and its barroom. Lots of work went into the reopening, and she deserves everyone's admiration. She and her staff have worked hard over the last few weeks." He raised his glass to Abigail, still recovering from the sting of Emma. She forced out her brightest smile as the room filled with applause. "And tonight both Captain Brett Trumble and I wanted to do something very special for Abigail and her sister, Maria, our new teacher, who will be twenty-two next week." He motioned to one of the serving girls standing in the kitchen doorway, then nodded to the piano player in the corner of the room.

As a lively Irish song was played, two of the kitchen help rolled out a wooden cart with two cakes, each splendidly done up with layers of gold frosting. Atop one, a replica of a book was fashioned in icing, and on the other was the outline of the inn, done by the artistic hand of someone in the kitchen.

Maria gasped, and Abigail leaned over, gave her a quick hug, and spoke over the din of the piano, "Happy Birthday! If Amos hadn't reminded me, I might have forgotten. We've been so busy lately. You with your school and lessons, and me with the inn's renovations. Let's celebrate together."

When the song ended, Brett rose and said to Abigail, "I'll see to the clearing of a space for some dancing and have the kitchen staff serve the cake and apple pie." They both glanced at Emma whose face was livid. It was taking every ounce of her willpower to remain seated and keep her temper in check. The tension at the table grew like a wild fire out of control.

"I see Dr. Wade is in town," Brett said casually, once he was seated. "I haven't seen him since we served in the war together." He turned to Abigail, "You'll have to excuse me for just a few minutes this evening while I buy him a shot of your good Canadian whisky in the barroom. I'm sure Tye would like to join me as well since Flint and Dr. Wade know each other."

"Cullen Wade?" Emma asked, breaking her icy silence. "The doctor? What's Dr. Wade doing in Golden?"

"Who's Cullen Wade?" Abigail looked confused.

"He's a doctor from Virginia who Flint knew from childhood." Tye pushed away from the table and stood. "Even though he was wearing a different colored uniform during the war, he did a most remarkable job of helping wounded soldiers of both the North and South. I hear he's looking to move west and find a small town where he can relocate and practice."

"Wouldn't it be grand if he chose to come here?" Maria asked. "Our town needs another doctor. Doc

Silverstone is getting up there in years."

Without warning, Emma rose suddenly, jostling the table. Silverware and dishes rattled. "I want to go home." She held a handkerchief dramatically to her temple. "I feel a headache coming on."

"But you haven't even had an opportunity to dance or mingle with the guests." Abigail stood. "Why don't you sip some water or go outside and get some fresh air?"

"I want to go home *now*," Emma whined in a shrill, waspish voice. "I don't need to mingle with dirt farmers, annoying ranchers, and silly lumbermen. And I don't need to mingle with odious young people who have no manners." Her gaze swept the table and landed on Lang. "Get the carriage immediately!" She brushed past Abigail and stormed toward the entrance door. Behind her, Lang Redford scrambled to his feet and followed on her heels like a dog cowering to his master. Amos was standing just inside the entrance when she flounced by and snapped, "My shawl!" She ripped it from his grip as soon as he handed it to her. Within minutes, she was gone.

Tye's eyes narrowed, watching Emma's display. He wondered why the mention of Cullen Wade sent Emma into a despicable rant and hasty departure. There was something not quite right about the old biddy. And there was something troubling about Lang Redford who had spent most of the night in restrained, sullen silence. He reminded himself to wire his brother, Luke, who was marshalling up north and ask him some questions.

With a multitude of thoughts still tumbling in his head, Tye rose from the table and held out his hand to Maria. She looked perplexed, distraught, and downright miserable. "Come, let's have a dance in celebration of your birthday, Maria." She nodded and stood, and he saw the tears brimming in her eyes. "On second thought, let's get some fresh air." Gently, he steered her toward the kitchen and back door.

Once outside, they walked around to the side of the inn where the path led to the cottage and farther beyond to a road winding its way up to the manse on the hill. They could see a lone light shine from two front windows like cat's eyes. Behind them, Amos had lit all the lanterns and gaslights, and a warm glow spilled out from all the Mule Shed's windows along with the infectious sound of music from the fiddlers, banjo, and piano players.

"Why does she act so superior?" Tears began to splash down Maria's cheeks. "Why is she so nasty and hurtful? Why does she have a need to shame everyone?"

Tye heaved a sigh and pulled her to him as she silently wept on his chest. He could smell the sweet scent of roses in her hair. "Maria," he said gently next to her ear, "some people are born with a mean streak. Emma has never been a happy woman. My pa used to tell us happiness is the result of being too busy to be miserable."

"Tell me, does the wretched woman have *any* redeeming qualities?" She began to cry all over again. "All I ever wanted was a warm home, a dependable teaching position, an orchard…and some chickens."

"Orchard? Chickens?" Now where did all this suddenly come from? Tye stroked the back of her hair with his hand. It felt sleek and soft, like the fur of a baby kitten. "You want apples and *chickens*?"

Between bursts of weeping, Maria blurted out, "Yes, chickens. Don't you dare laugh, Tydall Ashmore. Don't you like custard pie? A good breakfast? You know, all those foods you make with eggs? Abby and I used to raise them back in Utah."

Custard pie? Breakfast? He was still unsure of how to sort it all out. His sister, Betsy, had once told him weeping women don't make a hill of sense. Just go with the flow of tears and agree with them. "Yes," he said. "Of course I like custard pie."

"And why does that old shrew berate everyone?" Maria's voice was muffled by his jacket.

"Well, at least two men have escaped the old gal's rage, God rest their souls," he murmured into her hair and pulled her even closer to him. "Her first husband and your uncle. And I'm guessing both of them aren't in line to lay out a bed of lilies when it's her turn to meet the Almighty."

Maria choked out a small laugh and followed it with a hiccup.

He rubbed her back gently as if he was soothing a small child. "Listen, Maria, the Indians have an expression about people like Emma who want to have power over you and your thoughts. They say, don't let your enemy set up a teepee in your head. I'd probably say, don't let the old biddy camp out in your mind."

"Thank you, Tye," she said sniffling. "I'm sorry for ruining your evening. Tell me, who is responsible for buying this lovely dress? Was it your sister? I'm willing to pay for it. I don't want to feel like I'm a beggar."

Tye sighed. "Actually, it's a gift from Frank Norwell, and the only reason I'm telling you is so you won't badger me 'til all *my* cows come home. It was supposed to be anonymous. Norwell's wife, Virginia, once gave Betsy a dress to wear when we first moved here, and now both Betsy and Frank, each wealthy in their own right, make it a point to carry forth her generosity whenever possible as a silent tribute to her. She passed away many years ago."

"She must have been a very generous person."

"Yes, she was. Emma might have learned a lot from Virginia Norwell had she lived."

"Do you think I'm a coward for not standing up to her?" She pulled away and searched his face.

He shook his head. "No, no, I don't. I think it takes far more stamina to be silent." He chuckled.

"What's so funny?" She took the handkerchief he handed her and dried her eyes.

"I was thinking if Emma were *my* aunt, I would have hogtied her, dumped her ugly carcass at the foot of the mountain, and let the lynx have a go at her."

Chapter Thirteen

As the night wore on, Maria was glad to see the crowd was gradually dwindling. Husbands began to escort their wives home, stopping to peer into the crowded barroom where Charlie and Amos were dispensing whiskey and ale with flying hands.

Abigail walked the town mayor and his wife to the door and into the twilight and stood in the center of the wide, three-sided porch, watching the carriages pull up in front of the steps to gather their guests. Her mind scrambled with thoughts, she made her way to a side door leading into the office. Once inside the room, she found the office lit with a single oil lamp on a side table, giving off a rosy glow, and she remembered Amos had told her he planned to have a light in every window of the inn to chase away the evening shadows and welcome the entire town. She slipped back outside and looked at the structure's massive front and smiled. Warm yellow light spilled out every window and made the building glow like a huge beacon. She made a mental note to thank Amos and the entire staff for all their long hours and hard work.

Inside again, her thoughts strayed to her aunt and her bizarre behavior. What had caused Emma to act so maliciously and to leave so suddenly? As she pulled the shade down on the window for more privacy, she paused and looked toward the manse on the hill. An almost full moon lit the sky. Clouds scudding across the night sky and past the moon shed an eerie light bouncing off the slate roof as if goblins were dancing atop it.

She sat at her uncle's rolltop desk and noticed Amos had neatly stacked all the inn's bills for the evening's event in a corner of the desktop. Rummaging through the bottom right drawer, she searched for some blank paper for ciphering but discovered instead a small black book she had overlooked in her early perusal of the desk and its contents. It was a ledger of sorts, dog-eared and tucked beneath piles of assorted bills and papers. Leafing through it, she realized it was a collection book instead with columns and entries of people who had given her uncle money over the last few years. She noticed the name, Aeron O'Donnell on the fifth page. Her father! She hurriedly riffled through the remaining pages until she found more entries where her father paid as little as twenty-five dollars and as much as two hundred dollars to her uncle over the last ten years. The only explanation for the payments was a simple entry, "for Irene M" written beside each entry.

Abigail stared at the pages, horrified, as an ache began in the pit of her stomach. Why had her father sent Uncle Henry money? And who was Irene M? It was preposterous to think her father had a mistress or illegitimate child. Or was it? With shaking hands and her stomach twisting itself in knots, she slammed the ledger shut and shoved it back into the drawer. Discouraged, she laid her head on her forearms on the desk and closed her eyes, exhausted from the day's events.

The gentle tapping on the outside door startled her,

and she bolted upright in her chair.

****

Brett sauntered in holding a glass of whiskey. He closed the door quietly behind him. "Almost everyone in the dining room has left. Only the crowd at the bar remains." He looked at her tired, ashen face. "What's wrong?"

"It's nothing," she lied and stood. "I'm just weary and out of sorts. It has been a long night."

"Sit down, Abigail, we need to talk." He was surprised to see her knees buckle under her as she slumped back down into her chair. Tears welled up between her eyelashes, and she buried her face in her hands.

"That seems to be your favorite line," she mumbled.

"Have you been drinking?" He watched her shake her head. "Are you ill?"

She shook her head again.

"Come, come. Tell me. What is it, Abby?"

She waved her hand in the air and looked at him with tears rolling down her cheeks. "I don't know. Nothing, Everything! The inn. Aunt Emma. It's plain as the nose on my face Maria and I don't belong here. We're not even *wanted* here."

He sighed and ran a hand through his hair. Pulling out a chair from the corner of the room, he dragged it beside her and handed her his handkerchief. They sat in silence for a few minutes while he sipped his whiskey and waited for her to compose herself. He knew better than to try to touch her in such a fragile but agitated state.

At last, he broke the silence. "You do belong here."

He leaned forward and dangled his drink and hand between his knees. "Your uncle had a lot of friends here. Here! In the area. He also had many investments. He, your father, and I invested in the mines up near Black Hawk with the understanding all the land rights we collectively purchased for your father were to be signed over to him after the war. We'd each have a one-third share." He glanced at Abigail who was drying her eyes as she listened. "Only Henry didn't figure on getting himself killed or your father dying. He even planned to have your father move here with you and Maria to help with the business and mines."

"Why are you telling me this? What does it have to do with me?"

"More than you can imagine, Abby. Do you know if your father ever gave Henry any large sums of money?"

Abigail thought about the ledgers she'd just looked at. "No," she said, "unless it was to a lady called Irene M." She rummaged through the bottom drawer, withdrew the small ledger, and held it out to him.

Setting his drink aside, he quickly paged though it, then tossed it on her desk, and chuckled.

"Irene M is the Irene Maiden Mine, the first one we invested in together."

"She's not a person?"

"No, she's going to be one of the richest gold sites west of Denver once we get her opened."

Abigail looked at him confused. "I don't understand."

"The problem is Emma. The Irene M, bought with Henry's, your father's, and my money is in Henry's name. Your father and I were blind partners. I was off in the war and Aeron was in Utah when we formed the business venture. Now, with his death, it can easily be claimed by her unless we can find the deed or have the courts uphold Henry's intentions."

Abigail's mouth fell open. "You mean Aunt Emma is in control?"

"Not yet. At least not until she finds out."

"But she could go to the mining office and find out! Do you think she'd actually cheat me and Maria from a mine that is legally ours?"

Brett raised an arched eyebrow and sipped his whiskey again. "Let's not be naïve. Emma? The Emma who wore the diamonds and burgundy mourning dress while her niece wore a hand-me-down? I doubt she would pass up a chance to become a wealthy woman. Why do you think she allowed you to reopen the inn? She needs money for her rich tastes."

Brett stood and sighed. "You'd better go to your staff and check to see everything is in order before closing. Why don't you give me the ledger? We don't want it to get into the wrong hands."

"How do I know I can trust you?" There was a wary look in her red, swollen eyes.

"You don't, but your chances with old crotchety Aunt Emma aren't much better."

Reluctantly, she handed it to him. "What if we have to go to court with only this as evidence and we fail?"

Brett bent and kissed her softly on the forehead. "Don't worry. The worst possible thing that could happen is you'd have to prove your uncle's intent to form a partnership with me."

"And how will I do that?"

"Marry me?"

****

Brett, Tye, Marcus, and Flint sat in Betsy's kitchen the next morning with long, gloomy faces looking like a bedraggled bunch on a weeklong binge. Although Betsy knew they imbibed for a while in the barroom, she was certain excessive alcohol wasn't the problem. She stood with a plate full of scrambled eggs and surveyed the group.

"My, my," she said, "you all looked a whole lot better last night at the Mule Shed's grand reopening. You know how I love to see a good-looking man dressed in a suit now and then."

"Yeah." Tye groaned. "We all looked so good we could have taken in a funeral on the side."

"With the spawn of Satan at our table, I thought we were at one." Brett squinted through bloodshot eyes.

"I wonder what triggered Emma McNeil to decide to make a grand entrance?" Betsy was proud of her brother for quelling what could have been an embarrassing situation.

"I wonder why Emma acts the bizarre way she does?" Flint pointed to his plate, and Betsy spooned some eggs on it.

"Besides being dropped on her head in infancy?" Marcus shrugged. "She simply has a disposition like a rabid weasel."

Tye rose and took the coffee pot off the back of the stove and poured himself a cup. "Don't insult weasels, Marcus."

Betsy smiled. "Emma's always been a crabby critical woman since the day she arrived. Remember what Ma used to say. A man who blows out the other fellow's candle won't make his own shine any brighter."

"Well, the Good Lord knows Emma was snuffing out a lot of candles last night." Brett rubbed his eyes with his hands. "I'll take some coffee."

Tye poured him a cup, then he looked at the pathetic group. Every face was either glum or tired-looking. "It was near disastrous. Brett had Abigail weeping in her office, and I was mopping up Maria's tears outside. She was crying about her aunt, apple orchards, custard pie, and chickens. If anyone ever suggests we get together with Emma McNeil again, just hit me alongside the head with an iron fry pan."

Marcus's fork stopped halfway to his mouth and grinned. "Deal!"

Betsy finished serving the eggs and toast, and slid into a seat next to Flint with a cup of coffee. "We need to think this through," she said, her tone serious. "No one has been able to find out who killed Henry McNeil or why." She looked around at their somber faces. "And we have no idea who tried to shoot Tye or if the incident is related."

"What do we know?" Flint pushed his chair away from the table to stretch his long legs. He was the oldest and serious one of the group.

"We know Emma is not pleased her nieces came to Golden," Betsy said. "But we don't know why."

"We know Henry McNeil had no enemies," Tye added.

"Only until his death. There's someone out there now," Brett said.

"We need to find out why Emma doesn't like Cullen Wade." Tye took a sip of coffee.

"Emma doesn't like *anyone*." Marcus snorted. "I can't believe you called her an old witch to her face."

Brett grinned and rubbed his chin. "I don't believe Emma can either—which only emphasizes why I try hard not to get Tydall riled."

"I think we need to ask more questions from some of the hired help at the Mule Shed." Flint's eyes circled the group. "Maybe they know something we're not aware of."

Betsy stood. "Everyone has secrets and reasons for them. All we can hope is in time they'll be discovered. Now, who's going to help me clean up this mess?"

There was the thunderous noise of chair legs scraping against the floor as the four men scrambled up and made a beeline for the door.

"Just as I thought." Hands on her hips, Betsy watched them all scatter like buckshot from a shotgun.

****

Maria was glad that school on Monday went without any disturbances. After a long weekend, all the students were weary. Rains sweeping in during the past few days were chilling, adding to the gloomy atmosphere. With her class dismissed for the day, she sat at her desk, grading spelling tests and waiting for the shower to subside. She was pleased with the progress her students were making and with their attentiveness to her teaching methods. They were soaking up knowledge like water splashed on dry sand. She was so engrossed in the task she never heard the door open or anyone enter.

"I see, Ma-ree-a, you are still hard at work," the deep voice said.

Maria looked up to see Two Bears standing inside

the door. He was dripping wet from his stringy black hair down to his knee-high leather moccasins.

"Oh, heavens, Two Bears!" Maria felt her heart thump. "What are you doing sneaking up on people? You scared me."

"This is the way Two Bears always walks."

She stood. "Of course, you're right. I'm used to noisy children stomping around." She came around her desk and stopped. "You look cold. Here. Come by the stove and get warm." She went to the small nook in the corner of the room and removed some old cloths she had planned to use for cleaning. "Use these to dry off," she instructed. "I have water boiling for a cup of tea. Would you like some? I have honey, too." She pulled a small bench away from her desk where she placed unruly students and dragged it to the stove. "I assume you're trying to get out of the rain." The kettle hissed and whistled, and she took it from the top of the stove and poured boiling water into a small teapot on her desk. From a drawer she withdrew two porcelain cups and put them beside the pot.

"I came to see you."

Maria's gaze locked with his and she stared suspiciously at him.

"How is your arm?"

"Much better, thank you."

Two Bears' dark penetrating eyes surveyed her. "I wish to learn to read and write."

She sighed. "Oh, Two Bears. No."

"Why not? Two Bears is quick at learning." He finished drying himself and laid the cloths beside him on the bench. "You do not want to teach me?"

"Two Bears, it's not that I don't want to teach you,

but I fear it's not safe."

"No one has to know except you and Two Bears."
He pointed at her and thumped his chest. "I can pay.
What do you need, teee-cher? I see you have no horse
and must ride horse of Tye Ashmore."

Maria poured the tea into the cups and added a
teaspoon of honey, stirring it with the only spoon she
had. From her desk, she withdrew a tin and took out a
biscuit. She handed the hot liquid to Two Bears along
with a biscuit. "Careful, it's hot."

She leaned against the edge of her desk and gave
him a challenging look. "What if the townspeople find
out?" She blew on the hot liquid in her cup. "And I
can't take anything from you, but if you're wondering,
my fondest wish is to have some chickens someday.
Imagine, fresh eggs for breakfast every morning or a
fried egg sandwich at night."

Two Bears grunted and chewed on the biscuit.
"The people in your town do not need to know. I can
come to a place where we would be safe. After school,
here. Or behind your house and shed. Or in the forest."

"I fear it wouldn't work," she said.

"Fear? Are you afraid of me?"

"I'm afraid *for us*." Setting her cup aside, she
crossed her arms at her chest and paced the room. "I
don't want to be fired out...from my job."

"Fire?" he asked curiously. "What kind of fire?"

"Fired out. Sacked."

"What is this fire in the sack?" He looked at her
still puzzled.

"Get the boot."

"Boot?" He was getting agitated now.

Maria looked at him, stopped, and burst out

laughing. It was going to be a long autumn, if she agreed to his request. "All those words mean to be dismissed. To be let go. Told to leave. I would not have a job here."

He stared at her a minute, then brightened. "Then you'll do it?" His grin, with two front teeth missing, was wide like a jack-o-lantern's. He slurped his tea.

She rolled her eyes and shook her head. "As God is my witness, I have no idea why, Two Bears. Let's meet behind the shed after school two times a week. There's a few flat rocks surrounded by sumac and briars and close to the woods where no one can see. If it gets too cold, we'll have to find another place. We'll meet next week unless it rains."

"Leave a water bucket outside the back door if you can't meet me," Two Bears suggested, grinning. "Leave a dipper in the water bucket if you can meet me in the afternoon."

She nodded, went to her desk drawer, and withdrew a sketchpad and pencil. "Here's your first assignment." She wrote his name at the top of the paper and the first thirteen letters of the alphabet. "Now practice writing these." She sounded out all the letters three times, pausing to point to the corresponding letter on the paper. On the fourth attempt, she encouraged him to say them and was amazed when he repeated them all perfectly.

"Well, I can see you'll be a quick learner." She ripped off the page, folded it, and handed it to him with a pencil.

He handed the pencil back. "I will practice these over and over with a stick in the soft earth by the riverbank." He handed her his teacup. "Your tea is good, Ma-ree-a. Your biscuit is good. Did you make it?"

"No, Anna Ashmore makes them."

"Anna Ashmore bakes for your whole village. She is a hard worker. She would be welcome in Indian villages."

Maria smiled. "Yes, she is a hard worker and a good woman."

"You are a good woman, too."

Maria shook her head in exasperation, went to a peg by the door, and removed her cape. She opened the door and peered out. The sun was starting to peek though the rain-soaked trees. "I will see you soon." She threw her cape around her shoulders.

"You think about what you might need, Ma-ree-a," Two Bears said and slipped silently out the door.

Chapter Fourteen

The sun was not even up on Saturday when Maria planted her feet on the cold floor, opened her sister's bedroom door, and shook her awake. "Let's get up, sunshine," she coaxed as Abigail groaned and yanked the covers over her head. "I want to go up to the manse and see what dresses Aunt Emma may be willing to give us. We've been wearing the same four dresses for the last month. Surely there are clothes of Emma's in her attic I can remake for both of us. With the money we save from not purchasing yard goods, we might be able to buy a few chickens. Oh, how I long for fresh eggs for breakfast every morning."

Abigail yawned. "She'll probably chase us away, the wretched crone. I wouldn't be surprised if she tried to cast a spell on us. She probably doesn't remember offering the clothes."

Maria laughed. "Oh, hush, Abby. Of course, she'll remember, or we'll remind her."

Later, as they walked through the early morning fog and up the hill toward the manse, they met Millie Hanson coming toward the barn and carriage house, located at the bottom of the hill. An empty milk pail in her hand swayed in rhythm to her steps. Tye had told Maria that as soon as Emma married Henry McNeil she insisted he construct both buildings away from the house so there would be no odor from the horses or cattle to permeate the manse when its windows were open. The old barn beside the house had been cleaned and was now used only for storage.

"Good morning, Millie," Maria said to the older woman as she drew near. "Where are you headed so early?"

"I need to milk the cow. Emma's taken off for town with Lang Redford, and Will Singer is repairing a leak in the inn's roof. And those two no accounts Lang hired can't be found anywhere. The poor old cow can't wait much longer." The little woman pushed some damp curls off her forehead, and Maria immediately regretted her earlier remark. Millie must have been up hours earlier, baking, cooking, cleaning and washing clothes for Emma. The woman was too polite to point out her error.

Abigail spoke, "Emma said there were old dresses in trunks in the attic we could look through to remake for ourselves."

"Use the back door and go up the kitchen steps to the attic," Millie instructed them. "It's faster. Look around. If you need help finding anything, I should be finished milking Blossom in a few minutes."

"When is Emma returning?" Maria asked.

Millie shrugged. "She said she was stopping at the General Store and going over to Sarah Watson's to try on some new hats. It will take most of the morning, I imagine, if I know Emma McNeil."

Millie started toward the barn, then stopped and turned back, glancing at Maria. "I heard what you did for River Roy's son, allowing him to go to school a couple days a week. It was right kind of you. His pa delivers wood to the manse for Emma, too. He told me you were riding one of Tye Ashmore's mounts."

Maria nodded. "Tye was very generous. It will take us a long while to get enough money to buy horses and tack."

Millie pursed her lips. "I'll talk to Lang Redford. Emma has two of your uncle's horses in the stables. He used to ride. I'm sure Lang would be happy to have you exercise them when you girls have free time. One's a big red gelding. The other, a docile white filly."

Maria gave her a wary look. "I don't know whether Aunt Emma would allow it."

Millie waved her free hand in the air, dismissively. "Emma has never had any love for riding. She used to despise your uncle when he went out and came back smelling like leather and the horse barn. Emma tolerates the carriage horses because she needs them to take her places." She drew in a breath and smiled, before turning back toward the barn. "What she doesn't know isn't going to hurt her."

****

As the girls climbed the hill and later the back stairs, Maria wondered why Millie Hanson continued to work for Emma. Millie was a spinster, having never been married. She remembered Uncle Henry would often mention her in his letters, telling them what a wonderful apple or blackberry pie the housekeeper had made. Was Henry a content man once he married Aunt Emma? Never once in his letters had he spoken of his personal happiness. He often wrote of other things instead. How the town and territory were growing. How statehood was just around the corner. How he was pleased the war was over. Or how the inn was doing and who had stopped by to stay for a night before traveling westward.

The attic was large, built of sturdy beams with two sloping and windowless walls, perpendicular to two end walls, each with a window. A planed, but unfinished floor held a motley assortment of junk and cast-off items. Trunks of all sorts lined the perimeter of the room in addition to old chairs with faded upholstery and broken legs. Old ledgers, vacant picture frames, and books were scattered among traveling cases, dress forms, hatboxes, and crates of old china and empty bottles.

Abigail went to a nearby trunk and lifted the dusty lid. "Oh, here are some everyday dresses." She knelt on the floor, her back to Maria, and started to root through the trunk and pull out garments. "And they look like they're cotton and hardly worn, perfect for us." She pulled out a yellow gingham dress and proceeded to inspect it for missing buttons and flaws.

Maria moved to a trunk at the far back of the room, tucked under the eaves to the right of the window. She opened it and peered inside. A folded Confederate uniform, along with what looked like a stack of letters and a saber, were inside, beside a pile of men's work clothes, shoes, and belts. Maria removed the top letter and was about to open it, when she heard footsteps on the attic stairs. Heart pounding, she quickly folded the letter, tucked it inside her pocket, then quietly closed the lid, moving across the room to another trunk and hurriedly opening it. It was full of blankets, quilts, and old sheets.

Millie appeared at the top of the steps. "Did you find what you girls are looking for?" She peered at Maria. "Most of the Emma's clothes are in the trunks up front here."

"I know, but I was wondering whether Aunt Emma could spare a few of these old blankets." Heart thudding, but relieved she was not caught snooping through the trunk under the eaves, Maria forced out a smile. "At school, once the cold sets in, these old blankets would be excellent to use for the bigger children who are in the back of my room away from the warmth of the stove. Actually, some of these could be given to some poor children who have little at home to keep them warm." She thought about Two Bears who had shivered in the cold rain and was just pleased to sit by the warm stove and sip some hot tea.

Millie pursed her thin lips. "I'm sure Emma wouldn't want them to be given to the poor. She believes it would only make them more dependent and helpless. She and your uncle always disagreed about money and people in need. But I say, take them. Emma doesn't even know these cast-offs are up here. The colors are faded or not quite right…or the threads are worn too thin to suit Emma's rich tastes. You'll have to remove them before she returns." She looked at them with a fearful gaze.

Maria nodded, both in appreciation and understanding.

"What about the dresses?" Abigail asked, her hands on her hips.

"We'll have to come back for the dresses," Maria said with a sigh. "We can't carry both."

"But we came for dresses, not old blankets."

"Abby, don't be difficult. The children need to be warm." Maria felt the letter in her pocket, and her only thought was to get out of the manse as quickly as possible. Her sister could be so trying at times.

"Here's an idea." Millie came to her aid with a wane smile. "I'll have Will Singer or Big Jake put a trunk of old blankets in the barn, and Will can take it to you when Emma returns. He has to take the buggy to the carriage house. I don't know what that woman was thinking when she convinced Henry to construct those buildings way down there. During the winter, the men must return the horses, sled, or buggy to the barns below and trudge back up through the snow to finish their chores at the house." She shook her head. "She's even having Lang Redford enlarge the root cellar in the basement. Heaven only knows why. We don't need to put up more vegetables for the winter with so few mouths to feed."

Under Millie's watchful eyes, Maria and Abigail quickly selected a few dresses from among the many in the trunks, thanked the housekeeper, and started back down to their cottage. On the way, Maria told Abigail about her meeting with Two Bears at the school. She was afraid the signals she had planned to leave for Two Bears could be ruined if Abigail unknowingly brought the bucket and dipper into the house. In turn, Abigail related to her what Brett had told her about the mine and ownership by their father. Both easily agreed it was best to keep all shared information a secret.

Back at the cottage, Maria grabbed the dresses from Abigail's hands, pulled her into the bedroom, tossed the dresses on the bed, and shut the door.

"What's wrong? Has the attic dust addled your brain?" Abigail's hands flew up into the air. "You've been acting strange and out of sorts since we left the manse."

Maria pulled the letter from her apron pocket. "The trunk in the back of the attic has Confederate clothes in it, along with a saber, other men's clothes and shoes, and a pile of letters. I took the top one from the packet," she whispered.

"You stole Aunt Emma's letters?"

"Letter. Not letters."

"Oh, Maria, how could you?"

"Think about it, Abby. Uncle Henry was killed with a Confederate button clutched in his hand."

Abigail's eyes grew huge and round. "Did you check the uniform? Was a button missing?"

"I didn't have time. Millie Hanson showed up before I had a chance."

Maria unfolded the letter. Heads bent together, the two women read the letter in unison:

My Dearest Emma,

How often I think of you and the few short days we spent together. How often I think of your exquisite face, charming wit, and exceptional Southern hospitality. You can't begin to understand how much I hold you in deepest esteem for sheltering me during those days when I was enroute to rejoin the Confederate ranks in Georgia.

Should you ever come east, you are most welcome in my home in Augusta.

Your humble servant and ardent admirer,

Capt. Charles Everhart

Maria looked at Abigail. "Aunt Emma had a romantic tryst with a Confederate soldier?"

"She harbored a Confederate soldier, you mean. Maybe even one who returned and killed Uncle Henry."

"Now, Abby. Let's not jump to any conclusions

until we find a way to get back to the attic and check out the uniform. And then we don't know if the uniform belongs to Charles Everhart. Let's not talk to anyone about this until we are certain we have some sound evidence."

Later, at bedtime, both girls were silent as they prepared for bed and a million thoughts swirled in their heads. So many, neither of them had a good night's rest.

****

Sunday was a rare autumn day, cool and crisp, when Maria walked to the schoolhouse after church, taking with her some books she had promised to lend to her older students. Along the path, late-blooming blue asters, goldenrod, and Queen Anne's lace nodded their heads while sumac stood boldly ablaze in red along the cemetery. Usually, she enjoyed the walk, but more recently, she had the odd sensation she was being followed. Behind her, she heard a twig snap and she stopped, feeling the fine hairs at the back of her neck rise. She turned, searching the shadows and woods behind her while the feeling persisted. When she saw nothing, she heaved a soft sigh and berated herself for being so silly and fickle. Of course the woods were filled with wildlife—birds, squirrels, and small animals—scurrying about, minding their own business, putting in their stock of food for winter.

Farther on, she stopped, placed her books on a nearby rock, and picked some chicory, Queen Anne's lace, goldenrod, and other blooms into a colorful bouquet before she sought out her uncle's grave at the back of the cemetery. She was surprised again when she approached the site to find someone had again placed a fresh bouquet of daisies, tied with a simple white ribbon. She stared at it for a few minutes, puzzled, and reminded herself to ask Abigail whether she had stopped by.

With quick steps, Maria proceeded to the schoolhouse, glad to know she could unload her burdensome bag of books and also pleased the older students were now taking a more active interest in reading. When she opened the door, she was not prepared for what greeted her on the slate board. In large white letters, someone had written: *Go home. You are not wanted here.*

Maria stared at the warning, her heart thudding. A niggling voice whispered in her ear: *Was this the malicious act of one of her students?* Or had someone, an adult perhaps, left her a poignant warning? Suddenly, she grew angry, and her fists clenched as tightly as her jaw. She would not be threatened in her own classroom. Promising herself she would get to the bottom of it, she went to the board, took an eraser from her desk, and wiped the slate clean. She had learned early in her teaching career student pranks were common, and someone in the class would eventually squeal on the offending rascal. She had only to remain silent and vigilant.

Later, returning from the schoolhouse, Maria found Abigail waiting for her on the front porch. Her arms were crossed at her chest and a scowl marred her usually animated face. She tapped the toe of her foot in irritation. "You ordered chickens?"

With a look of confusion, Maria peered up at her from the bottom step. "Chickens? What chickens?" She followed her sister through the house and out the back door where a wooden crate sat on the stoop and held a black rooster and four chickens—one red, one speckled white and black, and two of them pure white. "You didn't buy these?"

Abigail shook her head. "I thought you did."

Bewildered, Maria stared at the crate as the rooster crowed what seemed a colorful expletive, unhappy with his confinement. The only persons she had told about her desire to have fresh eggs were Abigail, Tye, and Two Bears.

"Well, these pretty ladies can't stay in a cage if we want eggs," Abby finally said. Together they lugged the crate to the chicken coop at the side of the shed and opened the door. "We'll have to get some feed. If they roost and lay as I think they will, we should have over a dozen eggs a week. And any eggs we don't need, I can buy from you for the inn."

"But we don't know where these came from. They could be stolen or delivered to us by mistake," Maria said.

"Oh, for Pete's sake," Abigail chided her. "Let's not look a gift horse in the mouth!"

Or a rancher or an Indian, Maria thought to herself.

Chapter Fifteen

The morning sun sent slanted rays into the window of the schoolhouse and warmed the room along with the stove Maria had earlier fired when she arrived. Thanks to Lenny Sanderson and his father, a huge pile of wood was stacked along the side of the schoolhouse and a wooden crate of kindling beside the stove.

The young boy, an eager learner, had appeared like clockwork every Tuesday and Thursday, never missing a day, always arriving early. Head bent, biting his lower lip, he was now concentrating on the arithmetic problems she had assigned him. He was a remarkably fast learner, too, able to keep up with many of the older students who attended every day. Often when he finished his work before his classmates, he quietly pulled out the sketchbook she had given him and proceeded to draw what she considered the most amazing pictures of animals and landscapes. The child was gifted. There was no doubt.

She was also pleased that he had made friends with Joseph Sarowski's quiet, polite grandson, Isaac, who was about his age. Both boys were good for each other, both of them being rather shy. She noticed he was still arriving each morning without a coat, and she reminded herself to ask Tye whether he or his brothers had any cast-off clothing. It would be a difficult chore to convince Lenny to take a coat, but she would try.

As Maria walked between the desks, checking the progress of every student, she thought about the first lesson she would have later in the afternoon with Two Bears. Why had she even agreed to help him? She remembered the look of shock on Abigail's face when she told her Two Bears had visited the school.

"You had *tea* with an *Indian* in the schoolhouse?" Abby had asked with dismay. "Did you serve him crumpets, too?"

"No," she told her sister. "Just a plain biscuit. It was all I had, but I put honey in the tea."

"Oh, what a cheery thought!" Abigail had lifted her mouth in a wry smile. "Well, it makes me feel so much better knowing your Irish manners aren't amiss even though your brain is taking a rest. Mother and Father are probably rolling over in their graves, and if Aunt Emma should find out about your antics, she'll have apoplexy."

Smiling at the memory, Maria looked out the schoolhouse window at the landscape where far beyond, mountains rose up with their ragged but colorful blue peaks lined with the green of lodgepole pine and aspen, their leaves turning yellow. How drastically her life had changed in just a short time.

She was now in a strange place, teaching a roomful of new children, and living in a small but cozy four-room cottage, surrounded by ranchers, egg-laying feathered friends, and an Indian who wanted to learn to read and write.

Her thoughts wandered to Tye Ashmore. He was a quiet, often withdrawn man with an unusual sense of humor, but not always a burning need for unnecessary conversation. Yet when they were together, time seemed to revolve in beautiful harmony, and the minutes flew by. Maria still had not discovered who her benefactor for the chickens was, though she doubted that it was Tye. A methodical man in all his daily chores and undertakings, he was not the type to drop off a gift and leave without saying a word. He had promised to take her to an early dinner tomorrow, and she had eagerly agreed, although she had no idea where he had planned for them to dine. That was one detail she had forgotten to ask him about.

She thought about the blackboard and the message she had erased on Sunday afternoon. None of the children had acted sheepish or guilty. All had greeted her warmly and looked her straight in the eye, impatient to begin a new week. A wave of apprehension swept over her. What if it wasn't a childish prank? She quickly brushed the thought aside. This was her classroom. She was the teacher of this schoolhouse. She was now part of the town and its people, and no one was going to scare her away.

****

Tye Ashmore loved working outside, especially on those rare autumn days when the days were hot and the nights were cool, and fresh cool breezes made the air smell radiantly crisp and clean. Overhead, a flock of geese honked, and he stopped from his task of breaking a bronc in the corral to watch them wing their way southward.

He was just about to mount the contrary critter again when Marcus rode up, kicking up a cloud of dust as he approached. He slipped off his horse, tying the mare to the top rail. "You just got your bum leg back in shape, and you're breaking broncs again?" Marcus rested his forearms on the rail. "Do you ever learn from your mistakes, or are you doomed to repeat them, little brother?"

Tye walked over to the fence, beating the dust from his hat on the side of his thigh. He ducked between the rails to stand beside him. "He who kills time buries opportunities, Marcus. I had some free time to kill."

"If not yourself." Marcus laughed, turned, and untied a bag from his saddle. "Corn muffins from Anna. I've been peddling them all over town and to every family member."

"You rode all the way out here to give me muffins?"

Marcus shook his head and pulled a piece of paper from his shirt pocket. "That wire you sent to Marshall Luke Ashmore came back with some answers. I picked it up at the telegraph office." He leaned against the fence and promptly withdrew a muffin and started eating it.

"I thought you said those muffins were for me!" Tye grabbed the bag and reached for the paper, but Marcus held the telegraph out of his reach.

"It seems," Marcus said and swallowed the food in his mouth, "that Emma's friend, companion, and carriage driver, Mr. Lang Redford, is a handyman, stable master…and gunslinger as well. And I bet you don't know where he came from?"

"What is this, Marcus? A guessing game? Give me the damn wire."

Marcus chuckled. "Georgia. And guess which side of the War he fought for?"

Resigned to his brother's antics, Tye took a muffin from the bag and bit into it. "The South, of course, which means he should have worn, at some point, a Southern uniform. That doesn't mean a thing, Marcus. Many men out here fought for both sides. Cullen Wade came from Georgia and was enlisted by General Lee to doctor for the South, against his wishes to leave and resettle here in Golden. Remember, Brett Trumble was found on the wrong side wearing Confederate gray."

"Has Brett been able to gather enough information to clear his name?" Marcus asked.

"He's still working on it."

Marcus nodded. "I still think it would be wise for us to keep a close watch on this Lang Redford. A gunslinger turned carriage driver and lady's escort puzzles me. Another thing, I learned was that Emma McNeil's first husband was a miller."

"I knew that," Tye said. "Folks said he drowned before their first anniversary in his own millpond. Accidents happen, Marcus, even to good swimmers. Look at me, I injured myself falling off a horse, and I've been riding since I could walk."

"And you're lucky you didn't land on your head." Marcus withdrew a cigar. "Don't you think it's strange a miller couldn't swim well enough to save himself? I don't know, Tydall. It sounds fishy." He chuckled and withdrew a match and struck it against the sole of his boot. "Do you know why it's so easy to weigh fish?"

Tye shook his head. "I have no idea, Marcus, and don't light that foul-smelling cigar!"

"Because they have their own scales." He laughed at his own joke. "Get it?"

Tye sucked in a long breath of air. Why, oh why, did Ma and Pa give him a brother who thought he was Mark Twain? His brother's humor was a penance they all had to endure. He watched his brother light the cigar despite his warning. "I thought you gave up smoking those smelly Havanas."

"Anna gave them up for me. She hates the smell. Take pity on your poor brother, will you? She won't let me smoke in the house and chases me out behind the barn." Marcus took a puff and blew out a series of smoke rings as his gaze circled the ranch yard and fell upon the barn. He stared at the front corner curiously. "You're going to need help with the foundation. Corner's sagging again."

"Yes, when you and Flint have a free afternoon I could use some help. Each time the rains come, they wash it out just a tad more."

Marcus nodded and laughed. "And I know who doesn't want to crawl under it and see what needs repaired." It was an ongoing family joke about Tye's distaste of small, dark places. "By the way, Betsy had me drop off a bag of chicken feed for Maria. Guess you finally got around to getting her those chickens she's been hankering for. Really romantic, Tydall."

Baffled, Tye squinted at Marcus. "I didn't get Maria any chickens."

"Oh-ooo, blast it all! Sorry, little brother. My mistake." Marcus's face turned a vivid shade of red, and he looked like he wanted to jump out of his skin and onto his horse as quickly as possible. Cigar clamped between his teeth, he moved to his mount, untied the reins from the top rail, and quickly changed the subject. "Anna's making a roast and all the fixings for dinner tomorrow evening if you're needin' a good meal under your belt."

Tye clapped his brother on the shoulder, attempting

to ease his brother's embarrassment and his own. "Tell Anna, thanks, but I have other plans." He paused and looked at the sky, then leveled his eyes at his brother. "How did you and Flint know you wanted to share the rest of your lives with Anna and Julia?"

A low rumble erupted from Marcus large chest. "Well, to be honest, Anna and I knew right off from the start. There was an immediate attraction to each other. But Flint had to jump through a few hoops to convince Julia she was in love with him. Is Maria giving you some grief? Didn't she like the shawl?"

"Trying to catch Maria is like grabbing a fistful of air," Tye said sourly. "She says she was hired to teach, and she's afraid a relationship might get her fired. She's so damn independent! I don't reckon gifts are the answer."

"Oh, swell." Marcus sighed. "Why is it all the women we get tangled up with have that peculiar trait? Maybe there's something wrong with us?" He chuckled. "I'll tell you what I told Flint once, give her a little room. Everything is new to her and her sister. Maybe she's just afraid of any type of commitment. Help her to fall in love with the town and the land so she's comfortable falling in love with you."

"That's what old Theo Sarowski said. Right now, Marcus, she has me so confused, my brain feels like scrambled eggs."

"Humph, that's a sure sign you're in love." He slapped his brother playfully on the shoulder. "Try not to scare her with your shenanigans, brother, and try to stay out of trouble."

"I try, but it seems to always follow me."

Offering Tye a hopeless shake of his head, Marcus

mounted and headed toward a small a lane leading to his ranch just over the rise. Tye watched him until he vanished from sight, leaving a trail of dust from the path and a cloud of smoke from this cigar. The idea of someone giving Maria some chickens gnawed at his thoughts as he returned to his chores and sent a wave of jealousy spiraling through him.

****

As soon as she arrived home from school, Maria gathered up a blanket, McGuffey's Pictorial Primer, some pencils and paper, and two corn muffins Marcus had dropped off with the chicken feed. She headed out the back door and around to the backside of the shed where Two Bears was already waiting. He had taken a bath, and his long, jet black hair gleamed in the sunlight and was pulled back and tied with a white strip of cloth at the nape of his neck. He wore buckskin trousers with high soft leather moccasins like Tye often wore. A rifle, a ring flask, and a tattered blanket lay beneath a nearby blackberry bush. He stood as soon as she approached.

Maria smiled. "I see you are an eager student, Two Bears."

The Indian returned her smile with a toothless grin. "I see you also watch the sun and know the days grow short, Ma-ree-a."

Maria handed him all the things in her arms and took the blanket, spreading it on the rock before she sat and motioned for him to do the same. "Tell me, Two Bears, did you leave chickens at my back door?"

His dark penetrating eyes were sharp and assessing. He searched her face and said quietly, "I did not steal them, white teee-cher, if that is what you are thinking."

"I didn't say you did," she rejoined and returned his stare. "Where *did* you get them?"

"It was eee-easy. I took a wild horse to a farmer beside the ranch of Old Mrs. Sarowski, the mother of Joseph. Mrs. Sarowski is...what do you say, growing loco?"

"Getting senile," Maria corrected him.

"Yes. Seeeeenile," he said the word slowly and nodded. "I helped her to get home when she picked berries this summer and was lost. But she is *not* seeenile. She is smart. She can speak *pole fish* and *rushing*. She just gets turned around when she is in the woods and doesn't watch the sun. She would not make a good tracker."

"Probably not. And yes, I believe she can speak *Polish* and *Russian*," Maria said the words slowly to him.

He nodded. "Yes, this is so. Did you know she can play one of those things you squeeze and music comes out?" He held his hands out and opened and closed them palms touching.

"Yes, an accordion. Let's get back to the chickens," Maria urged.

"Oh, yes. I traded horse for a pig and young calf. Old Mrs. Sarowski needed the calf. One of her cows is old like she is. I took calf to her. Jul-ee-a Gast Ashmore needed a pig. I took pig to her. Mrs. Sarowski wanted pottery. Jul-ee-a gave Mrs. Sarowski pottery, and Old Mrs. Sarowski gave her chickens. Julia gave me chickens for the pig."

Maria stared at him thunderstruck. She rubbed her forehead and felt a dull headache coming on. "You started with a horse, got a pig and calf, had Julia trade pottery for the chickens, then she traded the chickens back to you as payment for the pig?"

Two Bears nodded and smiled. "Yes, that is so. See? That is how Two Bears got the chickens." He thumped his chest. "Eeea-sy. You like?"

Maria raised an eyebrow and shook her head disbelievingly. "Yes, I like the chickens. Thank you, Two Bears." She handed him the muffins wrapped in a cloth napkin. He quickly withdrew one and sniffed it.

"These are for me?"

She nodded. "Corn muffins."

"You baked these?"

She shook her head. "Anna Ashmore did. And we need to begin so we don't lose light. How did you do with the letters I gave you at the school house?" She listened and was pleasantly surprised at how easily and fluently he repeated them.

He handed her the practice paper, and she wrote the final thirteen letters, instructing him on the sounds of each. Finally, she gave him McGuffey's Pictorial Primer and showed him how the pictures would help him to recognize words.

"I think that's enough for today," she said an hour and a half later and rose.

He also stood, his expression serious. "Are you still Tye Ashmore's squaw?"

"Squaw?"

"Woman. Are you his woman?"

"Yes, we are seeing each other." She groaned, thinking how she sounded like a piece of property to be bought, sold, or traded.

"That is too bad," Two Bears lamented. "All the Ashmore men get beautiful women. Your hair is like the color of mink. Dark and soft." He reached out and touched her hair that fell over her shoulder, then gently placed his hand on her forearm. "Listen to me," he said solemnly. "That man who runs the stables at the end of your path, do you know him well?"

"Lang Redford?" she asked. "Tall and thin? Yes, I know him."

Two Bears nodded and withdrew his hand. He sliced the air with the edge of his palm. "He is not a good man, Ma-ree-a. Be careful! He carries a gun inside his coat you cannot see. I have watched him from a distance. I do not like him. He has bad people who work for him."

"Thank you, Two Bears. I'll be sure my doors are locked and that I'm not alone with him."

"He also had a knife in his boot."

"As do half the men in this town, Two Bears. Tye Ashmore, too. I see you are not wearing one in yours."

"I did not want to scare white teacher." He looked at his pile of belongings, and Maria knew he had stashed his knife underneath the blanket. "You need to learn to shoot, Ma-ree-a."

Maria shook her head vehemently. "Oh, no. Tye Ashmore tried to teach me. I don't like guns."

The Utes's face was serious. His voice was firm. "Betsy Ashmore taught Jul-ee-a. She can teach you. Ask her. You must do it soon."

She smiled. "I'll think about it. Now go! I have dinner to prepare before my sister gets home from the inn."

"I will watch for the bucket and dipper." Two Bears turned and in one fluid motion slipped away into the forest.

Chapter Sixteen

With only a cape thrown around her shoulders, Abigail hurried up the path leading to the Mule Shed in the early morning fog. Earlier, Amos and Charlie Haney had sent a young girl who worked in the kitchen to fetch her, saying they needed to speak with her immediately. She wondered what the problem might be. Charlie was a valued and loyal bartender whose experience she had come to trust in all matters concerning the bar and clientele. And Amos was more than a dedicated friend; he was family as far as Abby was concerned.

She slipped into her office from the outside door, then into the hall, and onward into the back of the barroom. This time of the day was eerily quiet, except for the faint tinkling of glass. Only one guest was eating an early breakfast in the dining room. Charlie was behind the bar, drying and polishing glassware, and Amos was taking inventory of the liquor and wine. Both Amos and Charlie looked up when she entered. Worry marred their faces.

"Please bring us a pot of coffee and some cream and sugar," she instructed one of the girls from the kitchen staff and motioned for the men to come sit at a table near the doorway where she could see into the dining room, hall, and kitchen, and where they wouldn't be disturbed or overheard. They ambled over and pulled out chairs, their faces glum. A serving girl returned quickly with a tray bearing coffee and cups.

Amos excused the girl and poured them each a cup of coffee. "Tell me, Miss Abby, have you been taking money from the safe to pay for odd purchases, perhaps to supply missing stock for the kitchen?"

When she shook her head, Charlie spoke, "Then I believe we have a thief, Miss Abby. Someone has been skimming money from the safe either early in the morning or very late at night when the bar is closed and no one is around."

"Has anyone touched the cash boxes?" Both the dining and the barroom staff had separate cash boxes to collect customers' money. At the end of the day, it was collected, counted, and locked away in the safe. It had been Abigail's idea to keep the money separate for convenience and accounting purposes.

Amos shook his head. "Not that I can tell. All we know for sure is when we open the safe to replenish money for the bar and dining room for the start of the day, there's money missing."

"How much?"

Charlie Haney sat up straighter, leaned across the table, and spoke in a low voice. "At first, I thought it was my mistake and I was miscounting, so I had Amos double check the totals the past few weeks before I locked up. Some days, it's none. Some days, it's ten dollars or less. Other days, it's more."

"Who besides Amos, you, and me know the combination to the safe?" She stirred some cream into her coffee.

Both men shrugged this time. "Possibly your aunt Emma. But anyone might have seen us open it, and if they had a good eye, might have been able to figure out the combination," Amos admitted. "Luckily, at the moment, whoever is doing it thinks we haven't noticed. What I fear is he'll get greedy and clean us out after a good night."

Abigail took a sip of coffee, then leaned back and sighed. "Well, we can't let it happen. From now on, each of you divides the money. Drop one of the cash boxes at the cottage and lock the other in my office in my desk drawer. This person may have keys to the rooms as well."

"Then we can never find out who's responsible for such a low down dirty trick," Amos pointed out. "And the culprit will know we're on to him."

"You're right," Abigail agreed. "Leave a few handfuls of bills inside the safe so it will look as if we're using it. Let's keep watching to see if it continues." She smiled and patted Charlie on his hand. "Don't worry, Charlie, I trust you. Just go about business as usual."

****

Despite the fact that Tye was supposed to come calling for her in less than a half hour, Maria sat on the edge of her bed amid a tangle of clothing. She had tried on every dress twice she and Abigail owned, and nothing seemed right for a first dinner together. She didn't even know where they were dining which made the decision more frustrating.

Abigail found her minutes later, clad only in her camisole and petticoat, wringing her hands and glum-faced. A hairbrush lay on the floor, along with an abandoned assortment of hairpins and ribbons.

"Whatever is the matter with you? You've never

been fickle before." Hands on her hips, Abigail looked at the destruction Maria had done to her bedroom. "This room looks like it fell into the path of a strong northern gale."

"I can't decide what to wear if I don't know where we're going," she said with obvious distress in her voice. "Oh, Abigail, and I've never been in love before. I want to look perfect."

Abigail picked up the hairbrush. "You always look perfect. I have it from a reliable source you'll be dining at Tye's ranch house."

"How can you be sure?"

Abigail smiled. "Oh, Maria, I have my sources. Brett is incapable of keeping a secret where Tye is concerned. Put on the pretty green gingham dress you remade from Emma's and take my white shawl. But hurry, he'll be here shortly." She bent and collected the ribbons and handed them to her. "And leave your hair down and tied back, for heaven's sake. You don't need to look like an old maid with a lumpy bun planted on your head like a head of wilted cabbage."

At the door, Abigail stopped and turned back toward her sister. "Maria, by chance do you know of anyone who might know the combination to the safe in the barroom besides Amos, Charlie, and me?"

Maria shook her head. Her hand stopped in midair from trying to untangle her hair. "Did you ask Aunt Emma?"

"She's the next person I intend to talk to."

"I'd love to hear that conversation." Maria rolled her eyes toward the ceiling. "Oh, Abby, I hear a buggy. Quick, go stall Tye while I get ready!"

Minutes later, Tye Ashmore arrived with a chestnut

horse pulling a covered, one-seat black buggy. It rattled into the yard sending two of the hens squawking and scurrying to get out of his way. Abigail hurried out to meet him. He had discarded his usual buckskin clothing and was wearing a white shirt under a brown leather vest and dark brown trousers to match his hand-tooled boots. Abigail noticed his gun was still strapped to his hip and a buckskin jacket was thrown on the seat of the buggy. "Maria needs a few more minutes," she said. "She is usually very punctual, but she had trouble deciding what to wear. She didn't have a clue as to where she'd be dining."

He nodded, saying nothing, leaning against the buggy.

Exasperated, Abigail continued, "You know, you two could spend a little more time conversing about details." When she got a nod and silent gaze again, she waved both hands in the air. "Oh, for goodness sake, Tye Ashmore, if you had told her where you were going, it would have made her selection of dresses a little easier, and you wouldn't be standing here staring at me like a big lout. You've sent her into a dither, and trust me, Maria doesn't do dither very well."

This time he smiled. "Yes, ma'am."

"Oh, what the devil am I thinking? You *both* are hopeless!" She flounced back into the house.

"Thanks for helping," he called out after her. She turned, and he motioned to the back of the buggy where two picnic baskets were perched behind the seat. "Your kitchen staff at the Mule Shed have outdone themselves."

"My pleasure, I hope you enjoy it," she replied and disappeared into the house.

****

The late autumn afternoon was bright and clear when Maria climbed into the buggy with its plush upholstered red leather seats. Fluffy white clouds hung in the sky, and the air was unusually warm and balmy for autumn as they passed through town on their way to the Ashmore ranch. Tye was unusually pensive, lost in his own thoughts. They continued onward along a small country road lined with a canopy of brush and trees blocking out the sun and allowing only filtered light to penetrate. Around them, everything fell silent, except the gentle clip clop of the horse's hooves on the hard-packed ground.

Finally he spoke, "I see you now have chickens."

"Yes, and eggs and custard." Maria nodded and bit back a threatening smile. Should she tell him about Two Bears? She quickly brushed the thought aside. It was best if her teaching endeavors with an Indian were kept a secret. The last thing she wanted was for the townsfolk to get wind of it. She could put her teaching position in jeopardy.

Face impassive, he drawled, "Should I be worried?"

"Because I now have eggs?" Maria enjoyed his discomfort.

"I think you know what I mean."

"Ahhh…that I have a secret admirer?" She regarded him with an amused look. "Actually, they were given to me by a friend who owed me a favor." She watched the relieved look on his face and was glad he did not question her further. Settling back against the plush seat, she relaxed, enjoying the play of shadows through the trees cutting the road in half and the flame yellow of golden rod along the roadway forecasting the autumn season. "This buggy makes for a pleasant ride."

"Yes, it's well-sprung and easy to handle. We bought it for Betsy when she started working at the General Store. We didn't want her handling a wagon and team of horses to deliver smaller goods around town. Now it sits idle at the ranch since Betsy owns the store and others deliver for her."

"You and Betsy are very close, aren't you?"

"You could say that." His face took on a playful, radiant look. "Betsy was adopted by my parents as an infant. Mother had just delivered me, the last of four boys, so you can imagine her joy at finding a baby girl abandoned in our stables. Betsy and I grew up together and played together—almost like twins, and we conspired to aggravate the lives of our older brothers. We now make it a point to keep up the habit."

Farther up the road, Tye slowed the team as they approached a spot in the road where a fallen tree limb blocked the buggy from passing. Stopping the horse, he tied the reins to the brake. "Stay seated." He jumped down to drag the offending branch from the road.

"No. Let me help." Maria hiked up her skirt and climbed down, following him.

"Maria, stand back." He picked up the thick end and began to drag it across to the side. The words had barely left his mouth when two rattlesnakes slithered out from a gunnysack held shut by the weight of the leafy bough. One curled up in warning in the middle of the road, buzzing loudly. The other glided away from them and up the road toward the grassy edge. In a flash, Tye dropped the branch, wrapped an arm around Maria's waist, and slammed her hard against his solid chest. At the same time, he drew his gun and fired twice, sending the head of each snake flying up onto the dusty road. Startled by the shots, the horse bolted, the motion of the buggy dislodging the loosely tied reins on the brake. With the whites of its eyes bulging, the horse went flying past them with the buggy bumping along behind.

"Nooo-ooo!" Maria screamed and tried to break loose to run after them, but Tye's arm held her fast, her back plastered against him.

"Wait!" Gun still drawn, he swore softly under his breath near her ear. "Stop fighting me! We don't know how many snakes were in the sack. There could be more."

"I can't breathe," she choked out.

He released his grip, and she slipped down onto her knees in the middle of the road near his boots, heedless of any dirt soiling her dress. She sucked in a lungful of air. Cold fingers of fear pressed along her spine. She dropped her head into her hands as misery reared its ugly head. Again, they were without a horse and miles from the ranch. "How many enemies do you have, Tye?"

He stared down at her, his eyes dark and expressionless before he moved away to check both sides of the weedy road. "I'm serious, Tydall! How many?" She watched him gather a stick, pick up the limp bodies of the snakes, and toss them onto the gunnysack at the edge of the road.

"I don't know, maybe it's the same person." He walked to her and held out his hand to help her up.

She slapped it away. "Get away from me! I hate this God-forsaken land!" Tears welled in her eyes and spilled down her cheeks. "I told Abigail this would never work." She swiped at her face with the back of her hands. "We should have never come here. I could have put in a request for a teaching position back in Albany where there are civilized people who respect each other. I could tell in Uncle Henry's letter that Aunt Emma had no love for his relatives. Why, oh why, did I listen to Abby? Now here we are stuck in the middle of a snake infested land with all types of vicious creatures like lynx and people without scruples!"

Patiently, without speaking, Tye stood above her and listened to her rant. Minutes seemed to pass like hours until he squatted in front of her and handed her his handkerchief. "At least life here is never dull, Maria," he said in a soft voice.

She wiped her eyes and face, and let out a nervous laugh, trying to compose herself. "No, at least life *with you* is never dull."

He stood and offered his hand again, and she let him pull her to her feet. "Let's walk, Maria. The horse will either stop farther up the road or end up in the ranch yard. And let's hope the baskets of food weren't thrown out in the ruckus."

"With our luck?" She begrudgingly set out, walking beside him.

They had barely covered a few yards when they heard a rider approaching from behind. Gun drawn, Tye pushed her off to the side of the road and behind him. Moments later, around a bend, Marcus came thundering up, and Tye stepped out to halt him. "You are sight for sorry eyes, Marcus."

Marcus drew up his mount and looked at Tye with wrinkled brows, then back down the road where he had pitched the two headless snakes and the gunnysack. "From the look on your face, your afternoon is on a downhill slide, Tydall—to hell. Please, don't tell me you lost the horse *and* the buggy?"

"Long story. And jokes would not be well received at the moment." Tye threw a cautious sideways gaze at Maria a few feet away. She was shaking dust from her dress. Her hair had come undone and framed her face in a wild, disheveled array.

"Holy Mother in heaven, she looks like she could scare bats out of a cave!"

"Marcus!"

"All right, stay calm," Marcus said in a low voice. "Tell me what in blue blazes happened."

Tye squinted up at him. "Someone hoped we'd tangle with a few rattlers. What are you doing out this way?"

"The kitchen staff forgot to pack the dessert for your dinner tonight. I was leaving the barroom and heading home, so I said I'd make the delivery." Marcus's saddle creaked as he dismounted and untied a basket from behind it. He handed it to Tye. "I'll take a ride up the road and see if I can recover your horse and rig."

"Be careful, Marcus, someone planted that gunnysack."

Marcus snorted, thumbed back his hat, and studied the shadowed forest around them. He heaved a weary sigh. "You know, Tydall, life with you has never been dull."

"Someone already told me that," Tye replied sourly.

"Where's your dog?"

"I left him with Betsy. I was tired of vying with him for Maria's affection."

"You sure have your share of problems, brother." Marcus shook his head and mounted.

"Just find our rig, Marcus, before I shoot you, too."

****

Later, at the ranch house with the horse and buggy secure and the excitement of the earlier dilemma waning, Maria left Tye outside to send Marcus home and went inside to try to put herself in order. Knowing she must look frightful, she took a seat by the kitchen table and combed her hair with her fingers, trying to dislodge the tangles and gather it into a bunch at the back of her neck.

"Here, here. There's a better way." Tye quietly strode inside and stood over her. He motioned for her to follow him into a bedroom and pointed to a bench with a pink satin cushion sitting before a lady's dressing table with an attached mirror. Undoubtedly, it was Betsy's bedroom when she stayed at the ranch.

"Sit," he ordered and when she reached for a brush, he pulled it gently from her hands. "Just relax, I know how to do this." His callused hands gently turned her head toward the vanity mirror, and with her back to him, he brushed the snarls from her hair with long efficient strokes. The calm motion felt soothing after her teary cry, lulling her into serenity.

His low voice and warm breath near her ear startled her back to reality. "What is your wish, princess? One braid? Two braids? Or a chignon?"

"Are you serious?" Her cinnamon eyes found his dark ones in the mirror.

He smiled and continued to work each lock, taking

care to stop every time he hit a snarl and gently untangle it. "I assure you, my dear, Maria, I am the best. When Betsy and I were growing up, I had to wait for my mother to do my sister's hair before we were allowed to go out to play. At about the age of eight or so, I realized if I could comb and braid the mane on my horse, I could fix Betsy's hair, and we would get outside a whole lot faster."

He looked at her in the mirror with a steady penetrating gaze.

"So how did you learn the chignon?" she asked. "It's certainly not something most men would know."

He continued to comb her hair. "When my mother died, Betsy and I were fourteen and had just come out west. One day, my father found her crying for hours in the bedroom…from grief or from loneliness…or maybe from both. But the whole crying spell began when she couldn't properly put her hair up to go to town. She wanted to look older as if she were the woman of the house. Which, in truth, she was."

"So what happened?"

Tye took a comb from the vanity, parted Maria's hair in three sections, and began to loosely braid it. "Pa offered any one of us a gold eagle and a new rifle if we could get her to come around. I went into the bedroom, found out the problem, and dared her that together, we could make this so-called chignon if she helped and told me what to do. She had a picture of it from an *Arthur's Home Magazine.* I also offered her the gold eagle to quit crying."

"You *bribed* your grieving sister?"

"I had to." He grinned a lopsided devilish grin at her in the mirror. "I wanted a new rifle. I was tired of hand-me-down shirts, boots, and weapons from my three older brothers. Anyhow, fifteen minutes later, Betsy was smiling, and we were on our way to town to buy supplies—and a new rifle." He laughed. "It didn't take much thought afterwards to use my sister and her weakness against my older brothers. Every time I had a chore I didn't like, I told them they could help her do her hair, and someone always stepped forward to do the task for me. Little did they know she had mastered the chignon herself after a few tries."

"Now I see why you and Brett are friends." She watched while he reached for a ribbon from the vanity and tied the end of the braid. "You are both laid-back and self-assured. You don't place much faith in the theory there are jobs meant only for men or for women?"

"Not much, I reckon—not after growing up with Betsy who had to learn everything we did. She can rope, ride, and shoot as good as my brothers. And once she started working at the General Store when she was sixteen, each of us had to take turns cooking for the family." He smiled. "Now if you go around town telling everyone I fix women's hair, I will be forced to deny it and tell everyone you're having strange visions brought on by the exceptionally warm weather." He winked and pulled the braid. "Come, I want to show you the ranch."

Together they walked outside, and she could see he was proud of the well-maintained sprawling ranch house and its three barns for horses and domestic animals, carriages, and storage. The air smelled of hay, dust, moist earth, and cattle as they walked to the corral. The horses trotted over to the rail begging for some affection or a treat. Tye was silent as he stood beside her and watched her rub the forehead of his favorite mare. Maria suspected the earlier antics of the day had taken its toll on both their energies. She, too, was weary and had to stifle a yawn.

With daylight fading, they walked to the ranch house. Tye started a small fire in the fireplace while she lit candles and lanterns and unpacked the picnic baskets. Over a dinner of roast beef, mashed potatoes, and the inn's best dessert of apple crisp with whipped cream, they tried to put the earlier incident of the day behind them. Later, after they finished storing the remains of the food, Maria went to the fireplace in the living area and stood staring at the dancing flames of yellow, orange, and red.

Moments later, Tye approached her from behind, and spoke in a low voice, "It's much too lovely an evening to occupy ourselves with thoughts of what happened earlier today." He pushed aside her braid and kissed her tenderly on the nape of her neck.

"Tye." She turned to look at him. "This is the second time someone has tried to frighten us. If they had wanted to kill us, don't you think they could have?"

"Do we have to talk about this now?"

"Yes." She was not going to be distracted.

"What are you getting at?"

She pulled away and stepped back, staring at him. "The only time you've been shot at is when you're with me. Maybe it's me someone is trying to scare."

"Why on earth would someone want to frighten you?"

She shrugged, and he stepped closer again. She wondered whether she should tell him about the warning on her blackboard but decided against it. She was certain it had to be the prank of a student. "Maybe someone is disgruntled with Abby running the inn, and if I decide to go back to Utah or head east, they know she'll leave, too. Maybe it's somehow connected with the death of my uncle."

"Like I said, it's much too complicated to sort out now." He drew in a breath and let out a long sigh. "If it's worth anything, Frank Norwell had the sheriff checking out a former hired hand of Lang Redford's who was using a wallet like your uncle owned. He goes by the name of Jebb Masters."

"What did he find out?"

"Masters said he bought it from a peddler who came through town a few weeks ago."

"So the sheriff really hasn't found anything new surrounding my uncle's death?"

"No, and it's much too beautiful an evening to speculate about death, Maria."

She frowned and nodded. "You're right."

Gently, his hand cupped her chin and tipped her head back. He looked into her eyes. "The night is beautiful, but nothing is as beautiful as you are," he whispered as his lips found hers.

When the kiss ended, she pulled away and leaned her forehead on his chest. "Were you ever homesick when your father first brought you here?"

"Are you?" he whispered in her hair.

"A little," she said, her voice muffled by his shirt. "I worry I won't be a good enough teacher. I worry the inn won't be successful. I worry I won't be able to adjust to this harsher kind of living. I really worry I might find this was one big mistake Abby and I made."

"Ah, Maria, it's no mistake." He pushed her gently

away, his hands on her shoulders. "Let me show you the most spectacular spot on this earth, and you decide whether there's anything to match the Colorado Territory." He went to the bedroom and returned with a quilt over his arm, then led her out to the stable where he tossed only a saddle blanket over his horse, and pulled her up behind him to ride bareback.

They took a path beside the house leading to Cherry Creek. The evening was filled with the night sounds of insects and somewhere far off, the hoot of an owl and the cry of a coyote. Minutes later, they arrived at a huge willow beside the gurgling creek and he slid off, helping her down. He tied the horse farther up the bank, parted some low-hanging abundant branches, and laid a quilt on the soft grass, then tugged her down beside him, leaning his back against the massive tree trunk and pulling her back against him. Between the leafy undergrowth, they could see the sky above with it mass of twinkling stars starting to appear in the night sky and out in front of them, fireflies emerged to dance and dart through the ferns and reeds along the riverbank.

"When I first moved here, after my mother died just months before back east, I found this spot. It was the perfect place to sneak away, to think, to mourn, to be homesick, to forget my worries, or just to be by myself, away from the noise and hectic life of a ranch. This is where I fell in love with the Colorado Territory. Have you ever seen such a spectacular light display put on by God and nature?"

"No," she whispered and watched in awe as the night grew inky black and the world lit up before her eyes. Millions and millions of more stars sparkled overhead and hundreds more fireflies frolicked around them. "It's magnificent. Simply stunning."

"No, you're stunning." He turned her and tilted her face up to touch his lips gently on hers. The kiss became more insistent, and Maria found herself pulling him closer as fiery sensations flooded her body. Just before she felt as if there was no more air in her lungs, he pulled away and pressed fevered kisses over her face and forehead. "Maria," he whispered, "let me make love to you under the stars. Stay with me tonight."

"I can't stay, Tye. You know why."

"Please let me make love to you and hold you all through the night." His voice was tender, but insistent. His eyes never leaving her face, he reached around and untied the ribbon from her braid and worked his fingers through her hair letting it spill onto her shoulders and back. "I promise to make this night special, more special than all those stars in the sky."

She shook her head. "I'll make love with you, but you must promise you'll take me home. I don't *want* to leave you, but I can't stay. I can't risk ruining my reputation." Her hands traveled to his chest. She could feel the heat of his body. He smelled of sweet dried hay, sunshine, and a hint of bay rum.

"Are you sure?" His gaze searched her face. He covered her hands with his.

She looked into his eyes, dark and earnest and remarkably serene. She pulled away, reached up and tunneled her fingers through his hair and kissed him, then dropped her hands to start unbuttoning his shirt. She realized she loved him with a passion that frightened her with its intensity.

"Am I sure I love you? Or sure I want to make love

with you? Yes, to both." She smiled.

He kissed her long and deep and hard, and when it ended, he quickly removed his clothes, then slowly disrobed her, his dark eyes full of burning passion and tenderness. He started with her face and slid his hands gently down her cheeks, the sides of her neck, then down her shoulders to her ribcage, caressing her. His hands explored the plane of her back, her small waist, and her narrow hips. His mouth dipped to close over her breast. As his tongue explored each one, he moved his hand to gently stroke her inner thighs and find her most erotic spot, his fingers exploring and tormenting her until she was soft and damp.

Maria gasped in sweet agony and felt an unfulfilled yearning spiral down to the core of her body as his hands and mouth worked magic on her body. A feeling began to overwhelm her, a feeling so intense she could hardly stand it. It was the age-old desire of woman needing man and man needing woman. She grabbed him by the sides of his face and pulled him to her, kissing him and clawing at his back, needing him to come to closer and satisfy her hunger.

He broke away and looked down on her with a knowing smile. When, at last, he stretched above her and buried himself deep inside, he waited for her to become comfortable with the fullness. He kissed her gently on her the side of her throat and whispered, "I love you."

The moment of pain lasted only a few seconds before the unfulfilled longing consumed her again. Slowly they moved in perfect rhythm together, each trying to reach that unknown pinnacle. When she felt waves of euphoria wash over her and fling her up and up and up into a blinding brightness, she was certain a million more stars exploded around her as she felt herself falling over the cliff of contentment and sublime relief, carrying Tye along. He spilled his seed within her, calling out her name as his hard body went slack and satisfied against her.

He rolled off her, gathered her close to him, and positioned her head on his shoulder. Gently, he kissed the top of her brow as he flipped part of the quilt to cover her body from the night air. "You have me bewitched, Maria," he whispered in her ear.

"And you have taught me how perfect love can be," she said.

Content to be together—if even for a few hours, they lay together in a warm embrace watching the heavens above and nature below put on a show that could only be meant for lovers.

Chapter Seventeen

The morning was a breezy one, perfect for hanging wash on the line. Abigail took another pillowcase from the laundry basket and snapped it viciously to dislodge the wrinkles before attaching it to the clothesline with equal vengeance. With two clothes pegs clamped between her lips, she hurried down between the filled lines with a dishtowel about to receive more of her anger.

From atop his horse at the side of the yard, Brett watched with curious concern. She wore a simple blue cotton dress, and her hair, a mass of luscious thick curls, were tied upon the top of her head with a simple piece of white rag. He dismounted, and carefully removed the basket behind his saddle, and set it near an alder tree where he tied his horse. He walked between two long rows of sheets coming to stand a few feet from where she was stabbing pegs onto a bed sheet. He picked up the basket of wet laundry lying near his feet.

"You trying to kill that sheet?"

She jumped at his voice, eyes wide. "The last thing I need is your humor, Captain Trumble. You scared me."

"Brett. Remember? My name's Brett. And dang, my timing must be off because you seem to be in a less than joyful mood every time I show up." He held the laundry basket while she took out what looked like a curtain and proceeded to hang it beside the pillowcase.

"You can talk about it," he urged. "It sometimes helps to blow off some steam, darlin'."

"Darlin'? Don't call me your darling! You want to talk about it?" she mumbled with a peg in her mouth. When she realized she was talking garble, she removed it. "You want to talk about it? The girl who was supposed to do the laundry for the inn's bedrooms didn't show. Aunt Emma has run up an enormous bill at the General Store on doodads, baubles, and useless nonsense. Maria and Tye were threatened with a gunnysack full of snakes last night on the way to the Ashmore ranch. Someone is stealing money from me. I paid off the loan at the bank only to find out Emma believes she's entitled to even more of the Mule Shed's proceeds." She wagged a finger at him. "Less than joyful, I should think!"

"Whoa, looks like you're riding a runaway bronc here. Let's finish killing these last two pillowcases and take a break." He watched her grab four clothespins, jam two between her lips, throw one pillowcase over her shoulder, and expertly hang one and then the other.

When she was finished, she glared at him.

"Come, let's sit on the back stoop in the sunshine and get a glass of water," he suggested and removed his hat.

While she fetched the water, he retrieved the basket from beside his mount and set it beside the first step. Abigail returned within minutes with a tray filled with two glasses and two sugar cookies on a plate.

"This is all the food I have at the moment to offer." She slumped down beside him with the tray between them. "Unless you have something wonderful hidden under the lid of your basket."

"Actually, I have a gift for you and Maria from Tye. He planned to deliver this to Maria tonight, but was called out by the army to interpret for a group of Indians passing through south of here, and didn't know how long he'd be gone." Brett opened the basket's lid and took out a squirming little puppy with a black and white brindled body and with ears, eyes, and upper face so coal black he looked like he was wearing a mask. "This little boy is one of Swamp's. Seems Swamp was kicking up his heels and doing a little more than just herding for Tydall. He made friends with Frank Norwell's kelpie who had five of these lively little creatures three months ago."

"Made friends or mated?"

Brett shrugged. "Oh, a little of both, I guess. I should add the kelpie was a purebred and Swamp is…well, let's just say we're using some creative guesswork with Swamp's bloodlines."

"Why, he's adorable!" Abby set the tray aside and took the squirming puppy he handed her and laid him in her lap. "What's his name?"

Brett shrugged and scratched his head. "Whatever Maria and you decide to name him."

"Is he old enough to be weaned?'

Brett nodded. "Over twelve weeks or more." He could see Abby had already begun the bonding process. The pup snuggled belly up in her lap, and she was alternately petting him behind his ears and rubbing his stomach while he gazed up at her with his big contented brown eyes. Oh, how Brett wished he were that puppy! He and Tye had spoken about getting the women a watchdog. Both of them were not pleased the sisters were living in a cottage at the edge of the forest where there might be more than simple wildlife underfoot. Neither were they happy with Lang Redford and his shoddy hired men.

"We'll need things to make this little one a bed." She laughed joyfully, still playing with the puppy.

Brett rose and reset his hat on his head. "Well, I'd better get back to the lumber yard. Betsy is sending over a wooden crate, some table scraps, milk, and water dishes. All you'll need is an old quilt to throw into the crate for a bed." He looked at her with concern. He hated to bring up her earlier worries especially since she was now in a joyful mood. "Is there anything I can do to help you with all your other problems?"

She shook her head and sighed. "Wait!" she said as he started to walk away. "Just wait here a moment." She handed him the pup, hurried into the house, and returned with the letter Maria stole. "I implore you to not divulge the information in this letter, but I'd like your opinion. It's a letter Maria found in a trunk under the eaves in Aunt Emma's attic. Along with a packet of letters, it was packed on top of a Confederate uniform with more clothes beneath. You know it was believed Uncle Henry died by the hands of a rogue Confederate sympathizer?"

He placed the puppy on the ground near his feet, opened the letter, read it, then folded it, and handed it back. "The War's over Maria. A lot of people on both sides detested it and weren't fussy about helping a wounded soldier when ended up in enemy-held territory. They cared little about whether he fought for the North or South."

"Yes, but Uncle Henry was killed with a

Confederate button left beside him. All I want to know is whether the uniform in the trunk has all its buttons."

He raised an eyebrow while he weighed her comment. "Well," he finally said, "let's find out. Let's pay a visit to your dear aunt Emma."

"And tell her we want to see the uniform?"

"No, let's use the ruse of showing her your new pup."

"My good man have you been drinking?"

Brett snickered. "Who knows? Maybe even old hard-nosed Emma will melt under this little one's charm, and he'd be enough diversion so one of us can look in the trunk." He winked.

Abby grinned, then grew serious. "I'll say we're there to ask Millie to give Maria and me some additional milk each day, or maybe borrow an old useless quilt for the dog's bed."

"Sounds desperate, maybe a little too deceptive, but we can play it out and make up the rest as we go along." He glanced down, too late to stop the pup who had relieved himself over the toe of his boot. "Good grief! These boots are almost brand new." His face crumpled in disgust over the ripple of laughter from Abigail. He swiped his boot on the grass. "You're going to have to teach this little mongrel some manners."

Together they walked up the hill, past the stables, to the old manse with the puppy riding safely in the basket. Millie met them at the door.

"Is Aunt Emma here?" Abigail asked.

"Yes," Millie nodded, then whispered, "but she's on a rant about the seamstress. It seems the dress she had ordered is too tight. She can't get it buttoned. This may not be a good time."

From behind Millie, Brett and Abigail heard, "Who is it, Mildred? Some pitiful soul wanting another hand-out? Bid him farewell and shut the door on the sniveling creature."

"No, it's Abigail," Abby called over Millie's shoulder. She bit her lip and grimaced at the housekeeper.

Emma replied, "Might as well be a waif! Well, show her in, Mildred. Don't stand there like a dolt with the door open."

In the foyer, Emma stood like a proud statue, her back to them. Her blonde hair shot with gray was done up in a mass of curls on her top head and spiraled down the back of her head. She wore a sapphire blue silk dress. "I was just about to go to town to return a dress the seamstress incorrectly altered for me. Altered miserably with little skill, I might add." She turned, looked up, saw Brett, and brightened. "Oh, and what do I owe the pleasure of your company, Captain Trumble?"

"I'm just accompanying Abigail. It's a pleasure to see you again, Mrs. McNeil."

Inside the basket, the puppy whined, and Emma's gaze locked onto it.

"Oh, Aunt Emma, Maria and I have a new puppy. We wanted you to see it." Abigail lifted the lid and took out the squirming puppy and held it in her arms.

"A dog?" Emma snapped and backed away. "You wanted me to see a *dog*?"

"Yes," Abby forged on, turning to Millie. "I was wondering if we could have a little extra milk each day?"

"For the dog?" Emma frowned. "My dear, I'm not about to start feeding all the stray animals wandering around your doorstep."

"Mrs. McNeil," Millie said, "the old jersey cow gives us close to seven gallons a day. Even when we send milk to the inn, we still have too much. We can only make so much butter, whipped cream, and cheese."

"I'll remind you, Mildred, you are hired and paid to do as I instruct you to do."

Millie Hanson lowered her head and nodded.

Irritated by her aunt's haughtiness, Abigail interrupted, "I know Millie is always busy, often milking the cow twice a day when the men aren't available. What if Maria or I agree to milk Blossom in the evening in return for an extra quart of milk? It would give Millie more time here at the manse?" She watched her aunt consider her offer.

"I already give milk away to you and for the inn's meals, and I imagine the staff there drinks it as well," Emma said.

Abigail fought the urge to explain to her that half the Mule Shed Inn's profits were going to her without *any* of her help. And what type of person would ever deny the hired help or a stranger a glass of cold milk, especially when there was too much?

Brett spoke, his voice smooth like velvet. "Now, Mrs. McNeil, there must be some sort of solution. What if Maria and Abigail could send up a few fresh eggs a few times a week?"

Emma looked at Abigail in surprise. "You have chickens? Nobody told me you had chickens."

Abby nodded. "Oh, yes. Or rather, Maria does."

Outside they heard a buggy pull up in front of the house. "Well, I suppose it would work. Thank you, Captain Trumble, for your brilliant suggestion."

"My pleasure, Mrs. McNeil. Please call me Brett."

Emma smiled radiantly, then motioned to Millie to get her cape from the peg beside the door. "As you can see I must be on my way to that wretched, wretched seamstress. Why don't you work out the details with Mildred?" With that, Emma O'Neil dashed out the door.

At the sound of the front door slamming, the puppy in Abby's arms whined. "I think he's hungry," Abigail said to Millie. "I have no idea how long it's been since he was taken from his mother. I also came to see if we could get another old quilt from the attic so I can make him a bed."

"Come into the kitchen," Millie said. "Let's get him a saucer of milk immediately."

"If you don't mind, I can send Brett up into the attic to get the quilt while we take care of the pup." Abigail trailed behind Millie. She turned and raised her eyebrows at Brett.

"Of course, what a good idea," Millie called over her shoulder scurrying down the hallway. "You can use the back stairs in the kitchen, Captain Trumble, while I make some tea and warm the coffee. It's so nice to have company. Come, come sit. I have custard pie, too, if you'd like. The little one is hungry. What have you named him?"

"I'm waiting for Maria to name him." Abigail followed Millie to the kitchen. As she passed the parlor, she looked at the sheet-draped furniture, eerie-looking in the fading light. She took a seat by the table. "The

War is over. Isn't it time for Emma to take those hideous sheets off the furniture in the parlor and stop worrying about the wear?"

Millie put a kettle on the back of the stove. "Oh, she only covered the furniture right after Henry's death, not before the War started. I was down in Colorado Springs for my sister's funeral when Henry was killed. She draped the entire room herself—like she was in mourning and was paying tribute to his memory. She hung that enormous picture of Henry above the fireplace, and only left the spinet and loveseat uncovered. She still refuses to even let me go in there to clean. It's some sort of personal shrine of hers."

"Shrine?"

"Yes." Millie shook her head disapprovingly. "And poor Henry's marriage to her was little more than a long series of rants and spats. It near drove us all crazy."

"What did they fight about?" Abigail set the puppy next to the saucer of milk Millie placed near her feet and watched him shove his little nose into the milk and begin to lap it up.

"It was always money." Millie sighed. "My, oh my, Emma knows how to shop. Pity the seamstress today. The dress she's returning was ordered six months ago, when Emma was ten pounds lighter."

Later, as Brett and Abigail walked back to the cottage, Brett told her he found all the buttons still attached to the Confederate uniform.

She shook her head sadly, holding an old quilt to her chest as he carried the basket with the puppy. "I thought maybe we had a clue to help us discover who killed my uncle." There was disappointment in her voice. "All that sneaking around for nothing."

Brett reached out and encircled her shoulders with his free arm. "We're not giving up yet, Abby. Do you want to hear the good news?"

"What?" she asked.

"I stole the rest of the letters in the trunk."

Chapter Eighteen

It was always an exciting day, a day of celebration, whenever it was the birthday of one of the student's in Maria's class. It was especially so, when Maria discovered Lenny Sanderson's birthday was coming up, and he would be attending school that day.

Earlier in the week, she had arranged with the cook at the inn to bake a cake and have it delivered to the schoolhouse. She had helped Millie, an expert knitter, to select yarn to make a hat and scarf for the boy. They had finally settled on black for the hat, but more colorful yarns for the scarf. It was a task Millie had been unselfishly doing for the last three years for all the schoolchildren when their birthdays arrived.

Maria also knew Lenny Sanderson needed something warmer to wear than the few flannel shirts he wore each day, and when she mentioned her concern to Betsy, a hefty package was delivered along with the cake.

For the last two weeks, with autumn sending its chilly fingers over the countryside and leaving the morning frosty and cold, Maria had arrived at the school house only to discover the stove was lit and warming the classroom. Although she had never enlisted the help of anyone, she knew it was Lenny Sanderson and the blacksmith's grandson, Isaac, who were sharing the task. She suspected Tye gave them a few coins each week for their work.

Careful not to embarrass the boy, Maria waited until the party was over and the last of the children were leaving when she presented Lenny with the gifts. His father was planning to deliver another load of wood after school, and Maria knew he was also taking the boy home with him afterwards.

"I don't know how to thank you." Lenny looked in awe at the store-bought woolen coat and the hat and scarf. "I don't know whether my pa will let me keep these."

"He won't." River Roy stopped inside the doorway, removed his scruffy lumberman's cap, and stomped his feet to get them warm.

Maria rose from her seat behind her desk and smiled. "Ah, Mr. Sanderson, welcome to my classroom. And thank you for the wood." She waved him inside. Despite the man's gruff appearance, Maria suspected deep down inside there was a man of character. "Come, sit by the warmth of the stove, and let me get you a piece of Lenny's birthday cake and show you some of his schoolwork."

Warily, River Roy proceeded to one of three chairs Maria had placed beside the stove and accepted the plate and fork she handed him.

Maria took a stack of papers from the top of her desk and took a seat beside him.

"I do thank you, Miss O'Donnell, for telling me about the inn needing wood delivered this winter. Words out, and Lenny and me now have regular customers in town. Even your aunt has requested a few more loads. I can barely keep up, and the money is sure a help."

"You're most welcome." Maria smiled at him. Unaware of whether Sanderson was capable of reading, Maria showed him his son's homework in arithmetic, history, spelling and grammar, all marked with an "A" on top right corner. "Lenny is one of the brightest students in my class, and he only attends two days a week. These are the best grades possible."

"He still can't take no gifts." A shadow of annoyance crossed his whiskered face.

"Mr. Sanderson, I beg you, do not disappoint me or others with your stubbornness. Millie Hanson knits every child a hat and scarf for his birthday, even those children with spring birthdays will get something to wear later in the year. I am not about to tell her she can't do this, do you understand?" Maria looked at him and set her chin in a stubborn line. "The coat is a present from Betsy Ashmore who said if you don't let Lenny accept it, and I quote, 'tell the cantankerous coot I'm going to knock him alongside his head with a broom the next time he comes in to the store for supplies.'" Maria watched a faint smile kick the side of River Roy's mouth to wrinkle his whiskered face before he broke into a deep rumble of laughter.

She removed a package from her desk and handed it to Lenny. "And my birthday present is a new sketch pad and pencils which I absolutely *forbid* you to deny him." She gave him the most stern teacher's look she could muster. From the bottom of the stack, she withdrew a sketch she had framed. It was the one Lenny had drawn the first day of school when he arrived and had been instructed to draw a picture of what made his father happy. River Roy and his son, fishing poles over their shoulders, walking down a narrow path through the woods toward a pool in a rain-swollen creek. Exquisitely drawn, it was shaded, and detailed, so real a person could step off the page and into the woods.

"My son did this?" Sanderson asked in a bewildered voice.

"Yes, your son is talented way beyond his age." She rose. "I'm going to take time to try to teach him how to use pen and ink. Your son has an exceptional mind and memory for recreating detail. And for a child so young. The picture is yours as a gift. It would surely look nice on the wall of your cabin." When he opened his mouth to argue, she wagged a finger. "No, no, no, Mr. Sanderson. Don't be stubborn!"

He smiled and stood. "I guess you ladies have pretty much made up your minds, and there will be no room for me to disagree. I want to thank you for all you've done, Miss O'Donnell."

"I have done nothing, Mr. Sanderson. I just take a child's talents and work with what he has. Your son has been blessed with many talents. As for the gifts, you must realize we've all fallen under his charming spell." She grinned, then paused a moment, thinking. "Oh, I almost forgot. Abigail needs wood at the inn. She said they have more overnight guests than she originally planned and will be burning wood in the fireplaces. She wanted to be certain there's enough for the kitchen and barroom stoves since she's expecting additonal guests to arrive later this week. She's taken a fancy to the sweet smell of the dried apple you delivered a few weeks ago."

River Roy grunted. "It's good to see the Mule Shed Inn busy again. I saw Emma coming out of the backdoor the other morning when I delivered some kindling for the kitchen stoves and was stacking it nearby. It wasn't even daylight yet. She was headed home, lantern in hand. She said she was checking on the linens and guests."

Maria shrugged as a niggling thought surfaced in her head. Last weekend the Mule Shed Inn didn't have any guests. Last weekend she had helped Abigail clean rooms and organize the wine cellar. Check on the laundry? Abigail was doing the laundry today.

Later, after River Roy and Lenny had left, Maria tidied up her desk and set out for the cottage, meeting Tye on the path heading her way. He removed his hat and wound his hands around her waist lifting her off her feet as he soundly kissed her. When he came up for air, Maria laughed. "Put me down before someone sees us."

"I don't care if the whole world sees I'm in love with you." He kissed her again but set her on her feet. "I just helped with the most spectacular birth in an Apache camp near here, and I'm hankering for a slew of kids."

"Don't you want to work for the army?" she asked. "You could probably help a lot of people. Brett said you're very talented with languages."

He shook his head. "Nah, once you've lived on the land and understand its moods, its sounds and smells, its seasons, it gets in your blood. I can never leave ranching."

Together, they continued to the cottage and found Abigail and Brett sitting at the table reading a stack of old letters. They looked exactly like the ones she'd seen in the trunk in her aunt's attic.

"How did you get those?" Maria asked.

223

"Shhh…" Abigail pointed to the crate beside the cook stove where the puppy slept.

"A puppy," Maria whispered in awe and knelt by the crate. "Is it ours?"

"Yes. Shhhh!" she whispered. "We let him have the run of the kitchen, and the poor little thing was so confused he kept crashing and smashing into everything. I think he wore himself out."

"He's a gift to you and Abigail from Tye," Brett explained as his gaze moved to Tye. "How'd it go with the Apaches?"

Tye smiled and gave an evasive shrug. "Just a small band left behind from a bigger one moving south who needed some help with a mother having trouble delivering twin boys. Ironically, Cullen Wade moved in to town a couple of weeks ago and was agreeable to take a ride with me to see if he could help with the delivery. Both mother and squalling sons are going to be fine. The band is allowing them a day's rest and then is moving onward tomorrow morning. The tribe sees the twins as a good omen. I only wish the mother could get more rest." He shook his head.

Maria stood, grinning from ear to ear, and wrapped her arm around his waist. "The puppy's beautiful, Tydall. Thank you." She stood on tiptoes and kissed his cheek.

He nodded, and the slightest smile formed on his lips. "He may be a handful. Swamp wasn't easy the first year. He was a bundle of motion and nerves." He looked curiously at the letters on the table.

"Brett stole them from the trunk in Aunt Emma's attic," Abigail explained.

"What do you mean by *I* stole them?" He looked

up with narrowed eyes. "You were running the diversion in the kitchen, keeping Millie busy."

Abigail related the conversation and their antics at the manse. "And there were no Confederate buttons missing from the uniform either."

"Nor is there any useful information in these letters that could help us discover who killed Henry McNeil." Brett frowned.

Tye's gaze circled the group. "You two hooligans stole them for nothing? I'd love to hear your plan for getting them back in Emma's attic."

"It gets better." Abby turned to Maria. "We have to milk Aunt Emma's cow every evening in order to get an extra quart of milk for the puppy, and we have to give her a few of our eggs."

Maria slumped down in a chair by the table and held her head in her hands. She couldn't believe what she had just heard. Before her Abigail and Brett grinned at each other like bumbling simpletons, each looking like the proverbial cat swallowing the canary.

"And these two run businesses?" She looked at Tye with a bewildered frown.

"Yep, unfortunately."

"They connive. They steal," she said in an exhausted voice, "and the results of their shenanigans mean more work for *me*?"

"Yep, it does appear that's their plan."

"I beg you, Tydall, do not leave them alone ever again. Do you hear me?"

****

It was dark when Maria and Abigail headed to Aunt Emma's stable with a lantern and pail to milk the cow. They took the old worn path winding through the backyard and lined with dense growth to the barn where the earth smelled of damp earth and sharp pine. Earlier, Maria had given Two Bears another lesson behind the shed. An avid, quick learner, he was getting very proficient in recognizing word combinations and figuring out sounds without much help. When the lesson had ended, Maria had confided in Two Bears about the warning she'd received on the chalkboard. He wouldn't betray her trust, and she desperately needed someone else's thoughts and advice. The recent happenings made her feel as if she swallowed an ornery cat, and it was clawing its way upward.

"Two Bears," she had said, "my father always told me to make friends before you need them."

"He was a wise man." Two Bears nodded and put his book aside. "What is bothering you, teea-cher?"

"I've received a threatening note on the chalkboard in the school house telling me to leave Golden and go home. I think the first time Tye Ashmore and I were shot at on the mountain and later the bag of snakes along the road—"

"—were meant for you?" His sharp, dark eyes looked at her intently, wordlessly. His face was sober like granite and revealed nothing of what he was thinking. Finally he spoke, "You may well have an enemy."

Maria nodded and felt a wave of apprehension sweep over her. "I believe I do, unless it's a student playing tricks on me."

"Even one enemy can be harmful."

"Yes, and to make things worse, I don't have any idea who the enemy might be, Two Bears."

"Abigail? Has she received threats?"

226

Maria shook her head. A cold knot formed in the pit of her stomach, and she fought to keep her trembling hands steady as she clasped them around the edge of the book in her lap. "I have to learn to shoot," she admitted. Tears welled up in her eyes.

Two Bears laid a hand on her trembling ones to still her. "Listen closely. You must tell Tye Ashmore and those you trust. You must always carry a weapon. Do not take chances. Do not be foolish. Foolish men are the first to die. Take a different path to the school each morning. We need to find your enemy."

"I don't know how." Maria gave a choked, desperate laugh. She watched Two Bears stare with a hawklike gaze at the forest leading toward the stables of the manse, then let his eyes encircle the entire wooded area at the edge of the yard.

Finally he spoke in a calm steady voice, "Enemies are not always wise enemies. They get careless. Then we will find him…or he will reveal himself."

Now, as she and Abigail walked down to the barn, she relayed all the information she had told Two Bears. "Let's discuss it some more when we're back at the cottage," she warned as soon as they arrived at the barn. She didn't want anyone to eavesdrop. Swinging open the solid double doors, she folded both back against the building, propping them open with rocks. Then she remembered Two Bears warning about not taking chances. She bent, lit her lantern, then proceeded inside where she lit three more lanterns hanging on hooks beside the stalls. Yellow light spilled down the rows of stalls on each side of the barn. She picked up the three-legged stool along the way, went to the cow, settled herself, and began milking. The steady swish and ping of the milk hitting the pail filled the barn with a calming, repetitious noise. Farther down the middle walkway, she heard Abigail say, "Brett thinks he might be able to get us a nice carriage and horse at a good price. A family is headed to California in the next few weeks, and Joe Sarowski is selling it for them. He's going to see him tomorrow."

Abigail strolled to the end of the barn and started back, looking into the vacant stalls on the opposite side. "Will Singer is sure we can use one of these stalls if we clean it out. I'll check to see if I can find one without a lot of junk piled in it. We can take a weekend morning to work. I can't believe this is in such a disastrous state. Lang Redford has two men to help him."

"I can't imagine Aunt Emma allowing anyone to keep anything at the house or in the barn next to it," Maria replied and stood, talking over the back of the cow. "All the junk was probably brought down here or stored in the attic."

"Yes, and a lot of this gear and belongings are from the men who work for Emma or the Mule Shed. We try to keep the inn's stables as clear as possible for guests' mounts or carriage horses."

Maria set the pail aside, smoothed down her skirt, and grabbed a pitchfork. She took a forkful of hay from a nearby pile and tossed it in the cow's manger. "There you go, Blossom," she said soothingly. She patted the cow on the neck. "Have a good night, you ol' gentle girl."

"Over here," she heard Abigail call to her. "Bring the lantern, will you?"

Pitch fork still in hand, Maria went to the open stall where Abigail had disappeared.

"Look!" Abigail explained. "A trunk!"

"And not ours." Maria shook her head, leaning against the pitchfork, its tines dug into the barn floor. "Haven't you learned your lesson from the escapade with the letters in Aunt Emma's attic?"

"Oh, horsefeathers, Maria." A grin spread over Abigail's animated features. "Aren't you curious?"

"The trunk has a lock on it," Maria warned again.

"But this is all abandoned rubbish—dry-rotted, rusted, and without any sensible order."

"Still, the trunk doesn't belong to us." Maria watched in dismay as Abigail removed a hairpin from her hair and bent over the rusty lock. In a matter of seconds, she had sprung the lock and removed it from the hasp.

"I mean it, *Abigail*..." She blew out a disgruntled breath. "Oh, please don't ever tell anyone you pick locks."

Abigail waved her hand to silence her. "Hush. You know how to do it, too, only you're always so afraid of getting caught!"

"Thus, a good reason *not* to do it," Maria countered.

"But this is worthless junk." Abigail threw open the trunk's lid. Inside piles of men's shoes, belts and clothing were packed away with wool blankets, old tin plates, and a battered hat. From the corner of the trunk, Abigail pulled out a Confederate coat and held it up to the lantern's yellow light. She stared at it a moment, her face bleaching white. "Oh, my. Oh, dear," she said in a low breath. "It's missing a button."

The whinny of a horse approaching from outside the barn sent them scrambling to refold the coat and jam it back into the trunk, snapping the lock into place. With only minute to spare, they hurried outside the stall and shut the door.

Leading his horse, Lang Redford came sauntering into the barn. He stopped short when he encountered both women. His dense, little ratlike eyes looked suspiciously at them. He spit some chew onto the barn floor. "I wondered why all the lanterns were lit."

"We came down to milk the cow," Maria stammered.

"The cow is over there." Redford jerked a thumb over his shoulder and down the aisle toward the front of the barn where Blossom had already lain down for the night.

"We've already milked her," Maria said.

"Then what were you still doing here?"

Abigail came to her rescue. "Brett Trumble is hoping to get us a carriage and horse for a good price. We thought we could stable it in one of the empty stalls once we clear it out. There's no room at the Mule Shed, and we only have a lean-to at the cottage."

"And where would you two ladies get enough money to buy a horse and carriage?" Redford scoffed. "I hear, the Mule Shed is barely making ends meet, and you, schoolmarm, are lucky you make enough to put a sack of potatoes on the table."

"Where did you hear such nonsense?" Abigail stepped forward brazenly. "We are doing just fine at the inn. Every day we get more people for dinner and more people stopping for the night to rent a room." She looked at Maria. Her face was clouded with an uneasy, unsettling expression.

"Let's go, Abby." Maria pulled her sister by the

arm. "I doubt Mr. Redford wants us to bore him with the operations of the inn. We've milk to put away in the spring house, and we have to feed the pup."

"Now you don't have to hurry off, little ladies, on my account." Lang Redford stepped forward and blocked their escape.

Maria could smell the whiskey on his breath. She wished she had a gun in her apron. Tye and Two Bears were right; she needed to be armed. She tipped the pitchfork upside down, tines pointing upward, handle on the barn floor. "You need to bed down your horse, Mr. Redford. Looks like he's had a long ride."

When Redford made no motion to let them pass, she warned in a confident voice she hardly felt. "I have school work to do." She gestured for Abigail to leave and started to brush past him, following her, when his hand shot out to stop her. It was at that very moment a large yellow tabby cat came sailing through the air into the barn as if it had wings. The old she cat let out a long, low screeching sound, tumbled under the horse, before righting herself and scrambling out between the its front legs. Startled, the horse reared back, almost tearing the reins from Lang Redford's hand. In the ensuing commotion, Maria managed to grab the milk pail, set the pitchfork aside, and slip out the door with her sister, leaving Redford struggling to calm the agitated horse.

Chapter Nineteen

Maria hurried along the path toward town as the rising sun crept down the hills and stretched itself in a sleepy yawn, chasing away the morning mist. She hoped to speak with Betsy whom she surmised would be already awake and getting ready to open the General Store. The other day when she had arrived at the schoolhouse before Lenny or Isaac, she found a note, folded in half, lying on her desk. When she opened it, only one sentence scrawled in bold, black letters glared back at her: *Go home, teacher, if you know what is good for you!* Hands shaking, she had tucked the note into her pocket and busied herself arranging papers and starting a small fire in the stove with kindling. She now considered the note a cause for alarm. After two threatening incidents and two warnings, it was clear someone wanted to scare her away instead of Tye Ashmore as earlier thought.

The town was empty when Maria approached the boardwalk, still shrouded in a foggy morning gloom. Shopkeepers had not yet come out to sweep their walks or turn their signs from closed to open for business. Far up the street, she heard a wagon plodding toward the center of town, its iron-banded wheels crunching on small rocks. From somewhere behind her, a skinny brown dog raced past, skimming the side of her skirt. She skidded sideways in surprise, shivers running up her arms. She clasped her hands to her chest beating like a war drum.

"Looks like someone's a mite jumpy this morning," a scratchy voice said.

Lang Redford stepped out from the mining office with Jebb Masters and Pat Wenson. "Well, lookie here, gentlemen, if it isn't our new schoolmarm. And what could you be doing in town so early in the morning?"

"I have business to attend to with Betsy Ashmore." Maria looked warily around, but there was not a soul in sight.

"The sassy hell-cat with the broom who runs the General Store? And what might you be wanting to buy? Some baubles and ribbons, per chance?" Lang Redford took a step forward and raised a hand to touch her face.

"Don't touch me!" Maria shied backward and heard the other men chuckle.

"My, you're not really very hospitable to those who work for your dear auntie."

"Maybe Miss O'Donnell is just not in a hospitable mood this morning, boys," a deep voice said. Maria turned to see Frank Norwell step up on the walk and tip his hat. His old weathered face was framed in snow white hair. His hand rested on his gun strapped to his waist. "I would suggest you all move along...and have a good day."

"We don't want no trouble." Jebb Masters rubbed his jaw.

"If you do what I say," Norwell said, "there won't be any trouble, I assure you."

Jebb jerked a thumb over his shoulder. "Come, Lang, let's get out of here. Wherever Norwell shows up, his men are always close by. Right, Pat?"

Maria watched the trio turn and stalk up the walk.

Norwell turned to Maria and squinted down at her. "Isn't it a little early for you to be out and about?"

She nodded. "I was hoping to talk to Betsy Ashmore before school. Those men caught me by surprise, Mr. Norwell, and I thank you for coming to my rescue."

He nodded. "Yes, sometimes surprises are welcome. Sometimes they are not, Miss O'Donnell."

"Please call me Maria."

He looked down at the boardwalk for a moment, then looked up and smiled. "Did a young man come by asking you to help him learn to read?"

"Yes, and we made arrangements for Eli to stop twice a week at the end of the school day for an hour's lesson. His sister, Margaret, is one of my older students. It works out well. He has an excuse to come by, then take her home after his lesson. He appears to be a very bright lad."

"That he is."

Maria pursed her lips. "Tell me, how long have you lived here, Mr. Norwell?"

"A long, long time." He chuckled. "Anyway, at my age, it seems like a long time, my dear. Is something troubling you?"

"And you knew from the start you wanted to live here?"

He took her gently by the arm and steered her to a nearby bench. "You're having doubts?" A puzzled expression appeared on his old weathered face.

"Maybe," she agreed, sitting down. She watched him take a seat beside her and remove his hat, hanging it on his knee. "Even if I'm sure I want to stay, I'm not sure others in this town believe my sister and I should."

"Is someone trying to scare you away?"

She withdrew the note from her pocket that she had received yesterday and watched as he read it.

"This is rubbish, sheer rubbish, my dear." He looked at her with a disgusted expression, refolded the note, and handed it back to her. "This is the work of some spineless coward. There's something you should know, Maria. The people who choose to stay aren't afraid to take a few chances now and then. The losers sit around and wait for the odds to improve. When it doesn't happen, the losers leave. Winners expect to win in advance and believe life is a self-fulfilling prophecy. They are brave, they are fearless, but they are wily and smart." He smiled at her and rose. "I hear you are an exceptional teacher, and I think you're a wily and smart young lady, for what it's worth." He patted her shoulder in a fatherly fashion.

She blushed and looked down at her hands. "Thank you for the advice."

"However, my dear, I would take any personal threat very seriously."

She nodded, then stood. "I will. Oh, and I want to thank you for the puppy, we are still trying to find an appropriate name for him. He's a bit rambunctious."

Norwell scowled. "Well, let's hope he lives up to your expectations."

"Tye said he'd help train him."

"If he's as good as the mongrel Ashmore owns, you'll have an excellent watch dog. Every man in town wishes his dog was as devoted as Swamp is to Tydall."

Maria smiled. "I guess I'm not supposed to know, but I did find out you were responsible for my beautiful dress. I felt like the belle of the ball at the opening of the Mule Shed."

He stared at her a moment with a thoughtful, kind gaze. "Always my pleasure, Maria. Always my pleasure." He took her gently by the arm. "Come, let me walk you to your destination before you get yourself into more trouble."

Minutes later, when Maria knocked on the back door to Betsy Ashmore's living quarters, she heard quick steps hurrying to open the door. Betsy greeted her with her warm signature smile. She was a petite, energetic woman whose mouth and eyes laughed together and often. She was dressed in a crisp brown cotton dress beneath a many-pocketed, clean canvas shop apron.

"Come in to the kitchen. I just put on a pot of coffee and took bread from the oven." She led her through the parlor, her long golden braid swinging in rhythm to her walk as she passed through an archway into the kitchen. Farther beyond, a door led into the store. "I'm expecting my brothers to show up later this morning, since I haven't seen them in a few days. Here, sit." She motioned to the huge kitchen table surrounded by eight chairs positioned next to a large, black cast iron stove with six burners, a warming oven, and a tank for keeping water warm.

"I don't mean to bother you," Maria said, "but I wanted to thank you for providing the birthday gift for Lenny Sanderson. The child was thrilled. He never celebrated a birthday before, at least not with cake and presents."

"No bother." Betsy opened the door to the firebox on the stove and threw a few pieces of wood on the hot coals. "I'm always happy to help all our students when given the opportunity. Don't hesitate to ask me. Education is going to be important to Golden, especially with statehood around the corner." She retrieved two cups from a cupboard nearby and set them on the table. "I'm glad Lenny liked the coat. Old man Sanderson is a hard worker, even with his ornery disposition. It's sad with his wife's death, he can't seem to pick up the pieces and properly father his own son. Both are in need of a break in life."

"Yes, they are." Maria watched Betsy pour two cups of coffee and set sugar and cream on the table before taking a seat. "I need another favor. This time it's for me." She blushed and felt the red heat creep up her neck.

"Then spill the beans." Betsy spoke in her no nonsense voice she had perfected over the years after living with four brothers underfoot.

"I need to learn how to shoot a gun."

"I thought Tye was going to teach you?"

"He tried," Maria admitted, feeling the heat of her blush deepen. But how to tell her his nearness only seemed to make her more nervous? "But I had just arrived in Golden and everything was so new and overwhelming." *And now I need to learn to protect myself from someone who wants me to leave the Territory or maybe wants me dead.*

"Ah, men!" Betsy said with a laugh. "They always go to extremes with instructions and details whenever it's something to do with mechanical parts, especially weapons. Sure, I can teach you, and I have a double shot derringer in the store perfect for you to carry undetected. It's small and has beautiful ivory handles. I carry mine in my garter."

"While you're minding the store?"

Betsy nodded and rose. "And I have a revolver behind the counter, too." She went into the parlor and came back with a small, double-barreled derringer. The ivory scrimshaw handles on the gun were etched with delicate roses, and the gun's frame and barrel were engraved with intricate scrollwork. "This is mine. My brothers had it specially designed in France." She set the gun on the table. "You never know when you may need to defend yourself. When do you want to learn?"

"Soon."

"Is there any special reason why you need to learn *soon*?" Betsy scrutinized her more closely as if she could read her mind.

Maria shook her head. "Whenever you have a free moment." She didn't want to alarm Betsy with the notion she thought someone was following her. In fact, she couldn't be sure it wasn't her imagination running away with itself. And she didn't think she should say anything about the warning on the chalkboard and the note until she had time to talk to Tye. She decided upon another approach. "Well, Two Bears, actually suggested it."

"Two Bears?" Betsy's face registered surprise. "Land sakes, how'd you meet that rascal?"

How do I explain to someone why I'm teaching an Indian to read and write? Maria smiled. "I met Two Bears when Tye and I were shot at the first time we were on the mountain visiting the Sanderson homestead. We had a small conversation about petroleum jelly which he initially tried to convince me was bear grease."

"Oh heavens, that sounds like crazy Two Bears." A flash of humor crossed Betsy's face. "I remember giving him some when he had some scrapes on his arms and stopped by to see Julia one day at the Gast ranch. It came into the store as a sample. It's a derivative of oil and is now becoming very popular for cuts and burns."

Maria checked her watch pinned to her dress and stood. "Oh, golly. I have to get to my classroom. The children will be arriving soon. Thank you for the coffee and your help." She turned to leave, then turned back. "I would appreciate it, Betsy, if we kept our conversation strictly between ourselves."

Betsy nodded. "I'll send one of my delivery boys to tell you when and where we can meet."

****

Minutes later, true to their word, Betsy's rowdy brothers arrived for a free breakfast. She was always delighted to have them come visit, and even more joyful to see them leave—especially when they arrived with Swamp, Brett, and Doc Wade in tow. Now she had five mouths and a dog to feed instead of the usual three. Swamp quickly took his place in the corner of the room near the stove where Betsy had placed a blanket for his many trips to see her. She handed Marcus a crock of butter, a knife, and two loaves of bread to slice while she finished a pan of bacon and started on a dozen eggs. There were times when she was more than glad she owned a store. Feeding a bunch of scalawags like the noisy ones before her was no small task.

"Do we get to tell you how we want our eggs?" Flint slouched down, reaching out and yanking the back of her braid, as he winked at her.

Resisting the urge to throw the fry pan at his head,

239

she shook her spatula instead. "No! Everyone gets fried eggs this morning, both sides flipped, and you all better hope I don't break any yolks. Then you'll get half scrambled, and no, you don't get to decide who gets that sorry mess. You want a special order?" She gestured to the door. "Go over to the Mule Shed and pay to eat in the dining room."

The kitchen filled with laughter. Dr. Wade and Brett grinned and Marcus raised his hands in mock defeat.

Tye spoke, "See what we have to put up with? And does anyone wonder why my sister is not married? Who'd marry someone with a temper hot enough to tan a hide while it's still on the horse?"

Betsy's gaze circled the table—from Cullen to Brett to Tye. "I don't see great throngs of womenfolk hankering to hitch up with the lot of you three." From the corner, Swamp gave a small whine and looked up at all of them. "See, even the dog agrees with me."

"Careful, Tye," Brett warned. "You're going to get the broken eggs." He smiled solicitously. "You wound me, Miss Ashmore, with your harsh comment."

"I'll wound you with that knife once Marcus is finished." She pointed at him with her free hand. "Please refill everyone's cup with coffee. The more hands, the lighter the work. And toss that poor dog a slice of bacon for his wisdom."

But it was Cullen Wade who pushed back his chair and reached for the coffeepot. "Allow me, Betsy, since I'm honored to be able to just sit here and enjoy a good meal, the company of a fine lady, and the ribald humor of your misfit brothers." When everyone groaned, he added, "And of course, let's not forget that Brett is all decked out in new duds this morning with the sole intent of convincing the town council to purchase his lumber for the new jail. He shouldn't be handling anything he can spill on himself before he spins his spectacular spiel."

"Oh, heaven forbid, Captain Trumble gets himself dirty." Tye didn't try to disguise his sarcasm.

Dressed in a new sack coat, striped trousers, and a brocade vest, Brett looked at Tye with a sour face. He pointed at Tye's buckskins. "At least my clothes can be washed without me in them."

Tye snorted. "At least some of us really *work*. Now Doc, here, was up most of the night delivering a baby for Joseph Sarowski's eldest daughter, Eleanor. A big, healthy boy."

"And her second son," Betsy added, smiling. "Joe will be pleased as punch since all the other daughters have given him eight granddaughters. He longs for grandsons to teach them the trade. Until last night, Isaac—who hangs around with Lenny Sanderson—was his only grandson."

Dr. Wade laughed. "Joe was so excited he reverted to speaking Russian, and the only thing I understood was the glass of vodka he pushed into my hand while he mumbled some heavenly incantation his son-in-law later translated as 'God bless you, Doctor.' Then shortly thereafter, someone came running and said Lang Redford needed his arm sewn up, so I had to leave the festivities." He laughed. "Good thing, too. I could have been sporting a terrific hangover."

"Lang Redford was knifed?" Betsy asked. "By whom?"

"A misunderstanding in a card game, according to

him." Cullen set the coffeepot back on the stove and sat back down. "When he's not gambling at the saloon, he's at a back table in the barroom playing with some old cronies who hang out there. I don't know how he fits his work in between card games."

Betsy put the platter of bacon on the table and took everyone's plates one at a time as they handed them around the table to her. Leaving her two eggs in the pan, she filled each plate before she took a seat next to Cullen Wade who rose and politely poured her a cup of coffee before sitting again to resume eating.

"Tell me, Dr. Wade, what do you know about Emma McNeil?" She buttered a piece of bread. She suspected her brothers had already told him about Emma's unsettling exit when his name was mentioned at the opening of the Mule Shed Inn.

"It's Doc or Cullen," he said gently while smiling. "I've known these idiot brothers of yours for far too long for you to be formal." He took a sip of coffee. "I knew her cousin who served in the War as an assistant to our medical staff." He shrugged. "We once briefly discussed Emma's first husband's death. He said he was there when they found the body, pulling it from the millpond some three days later after he'd been missing. We discussed the outward appearance of a body having been in the water for a lengthy time—" He looked around the table and then focused his gaze back on Betsy. "Should we be discussing this at the breakfast table?"

"I assure you, Cullen, there is nothing these foolhardy brothers of mine haven't discussed at the table that would cause me any distress. You were saying…"

Cullen shrugged again. "It appears, from the information the cousin provided, Emma's husband was killed initially, then thrown into the millpond where he was submerged for a short time, rather than three days. However, the death was ruled as a drowning."

Marcus leaned back in his chair. "Tell us, Tye, have you had to duck any more bullets or dodge anything lately? Every time you take the little schoolmarm on an outing, you get into some sort of trouble."

"It's not amusing," Betsy admonished above the chuckles around the table.

"Pretty soon she's going to dump him for someone who's a tad bit safer," Marcus added.

"Stop it, right now." Betsy gave Marcus a warning look and was glad he relented. Despite the big man's physique and his jovial nature, his persistent humor could be wearisome at times.

"Maybe someone's trying to scare Tye away from Maria." Flint stared at the group with a concerned look.

"Or maybe, someone is trying to scare Maria away from Tye," Betsy muttered uneasily. She decided she'd have to tell Tye about Maria's recent visit to learn how to handle a firearm. But she would have to wait until she could get him alone.

Marcus looked at Betsy's plate which held only a slice of bread she had been nibbling on. "Aren't you going to eat those last two eggs in the pan?"

Betsy shook her head and rose, sliding an egg on Marcus's plate. "Anyone else?" When no one spoke, she dropped the last one on the big man's plate as well. "I have no idea where you stow all this food, Marcus. Your poor, poor wife."

"Luckily his wife is an excellent baker." Tye grinned.

They were interrupted by a sharp rapping on the parlor door. Tye, closest to the door, rose to answer it. He found a harried-looking Maria on the other side.

"What's wrong?" Eyebrows knitted, he reached out and pulled her inside.

"Both Lenny Sanderson and Joseph Sarowski's grandson, Isaac, didn't show up for school today," she said in a frightened voice. "They started the schoolhouse stove and then must have left."

"Boys skip school, Maria," Tye said in a reassuring tone.

Behind him, Flint, Brett, Marcus, and Cullen came through the archway and stopped.

"Not these two," Maria insisted. "They are my best and brightest students. They've never missed a day of school." She bit her lip and wrung her hands. "Isaac's father stopped by the school this morning. In all the excitement of the new baby, Isaac forgot to take his lunch pail. When he didn't find his son with me, he was most upset." She looked at Tye with pleading eyes. "We have to look for them. I have Abigail at the school house watching the rest of my students."

"Then we better find those boys quickly," Brett said in a droll voice, "to rescue the rest of the class from the hands of your sister. She would have more luck teaching a bear to drink whiskey than instructing those poor innocents."

Tye whistled for Swamp and laid a reassuring hand on Maria's arm. "Brett and I will meet you at the school house with horses. We'll try to track the boys from the schoolhouse onward. Marcus can go up the mountain and check on the Sanderson homestead to see if Lenny returned there. Flint can round up a couple of men and search the town and surrounding area, then fan out to the woods to the north. Doc should stay in town in case we need him. Three rapid shots in the air means we found them."

"I'm going with you," Maria insisted. "I feel responsible."

"Get something from the classroom he's touched," Tye instructed her.

Later, as Tye and Brett drew up in front of the schoolhouse with Swamp trotting along beside them and an extra mount behind Tye, they found Maria waiting. She was dressed in a split riding skirt and held a ring flask, a lantern, a rope, and a sketchpad in her hands. "The boys tell me Isaac and Lenny often talked about the old mines and finding gold," she said. "I dismissed the class for the rest of the afternoon and sent Abigail to the inn to alert the men there to help Flint round up some search parties."

"Everyone dreams of finding gold," Brett said. "Every boy dreams of having adventures." He looked at the sketchbook with a puzzled gaze.

"This is all I have of Lenny's," she said with a shrug.

"Swamp doesn't need much to make a connection." Tye dismounted. Behind his saddle, he had tied on another lantern and a shovel. He took Maria's lantern and rope and fastened it to her horse, then took the offered sketchbook and called the dog, letting him sniff the paper. "We need to *find* him, boy." He patted the dog on his head. "*Find* him," he repeated and waited as the dog smelled the sketchbook yet again, then sniffed the ground around the doorstep of the school before barking and taking off toward a copse of aspen behind the school.

They mounted and followed until they came to a clearing slowly taken over by bright yellow plumes of goldenrod and blackberry bushes with a splattering of late berries wildlife had yet to find. Entering a small path lined with bull thistle and half-dried weeds, they climbed up and over a hillside toward higher ground, always vigilant of the route the dog was taking.

Suddenly Tye pulled up and the others stopped beside him, leather creaking. His frisky horse snorted and danced sideways, eager to proceed. He looked at Brett and Maria with a disturbing gaze and brought his mount under control. "If Swamp does have their scent like I reckon he does, then those boys are headed for the old caved in mine Lenny's dad owned. You know the one, Brett—where he buried his wife when the mine caved in?"

A rumble of thunder above their heads brought them all to attention. Clouds began to gather in the sky, turning black, looming dark and threatening. Around them the sunshine had disappeared along with the trill of songbirds. Nighthawks and swallows prowled the sky, wheeling and diving, catching insects gathering before the storm. Far off, they could hear the roll of thunder.

"You should go back, Maria." Tye checked the sky with a nervous gaze. "This is going to be a wet one. A dandy."

She shook her head and nudged her horse forward. "I'm not quitting until we find those boys. They were my responsibility." Together, they watched Swamp lope easily up an embankment and over a ridge.

"Yep, it's the old mine." Tye kicked his mount forward.

They reached the spot just as the first fat drops of water fell from the sky. Tye was the first to slip off his horse and approach the cave from the front. Swamp was running in circles and barking at the piles of slag and rubble barricading the entrance.

"Lenny! Isaac," he yelled above the rumble of thunder. He started up a small spoil pile footpath winding its way upward to the top of the mine with Swamp in front of him. "There's an air shaft up on top leading straight down into the mine if it hasn't caved in by now," he shouted to the others. He turned and motioned to Maria to take his horse and circle around from the other side where a better path led to the top of the mine. She and Brett reached it about the same time. Tye knelt before the opening and shouted down the long dark shaft lined with timber. "Lenny and Isaac, can you hear me?"

The faint sound of "help," like a distant echo, filtered up from the mine shaft between the rolls of thunder from above.

"One of us has to go down there," Tye said to Brett. They barely exchanged glances when Tye scrambled up and hurried to the horses. He removed a rope, a pair of leather gloves, and the two lanterns.

"Since I know your wish is to overcome your fear of caves and dark, small places, I think you should have the honors." Brett took a tin of matches from his coat and handed it to him. He grinned his cocky grin. When Tye shot him a sour expression, he plucked at his new sack coat. "What?" His hand flew up in the air. "You know I was planning to meet with the town council today at the lumber yard."

Tye shook his head and cursed softly. For a fleeting second, he thought about throwing him head first down the chute. Instead, he dropped to the ground, removed his hat, made a lasso in the rope, and pulled it over his head to settle at his waist. "Any idea how far down this shaft goes?" he asked no one in particular.

Maria was already lighting a lantern and tying it onto a rope she had taken from her saddle. "We'll lower this first lantern down to try to determine the depth," she said as a bolt of lightning flashed across the sky. "We may be able to get an idea of how sound the timbers are lining the chute." Her hair had come undone and whipped about her head and shoulders, blowing strands into her eyes as the wind began to pick up in strength with the incoming storm. She knelt in front of Tye, hands on her knees. "You need to signal us if you need help, if someone is injured. Pull once on the lantern rope. Leave it at the entrance to guide you back to the chute. I'll have it in my hands to feel the tug. One of us can come down. Pull twice on the other rope when you need us to pull someone up."

He reached out and carefully pushed a tendril of hair out of her eyes and tucked it behind her ear. They stared at each other without speaking. Finally he said, "I don't want you down there under any circumstances, do you hear me, Maria? Send down fancy pants over there in the new duds. I don't give a damn about his going-to-the-meeting clothes. Use my horse to pull us up. Dreamkeeper's a good cow pony, and he knows what he's doing even in the worst situations. That's why I brought him. He's steady, and he won't shy from a rope."

"Please be careful, Tye," she said, her voice cracking. "Remember, yank twice on the rope when you need us to pull someone up."

He took off his hat and handed it to her, then raised a hand and cupped the side of her face. He could see her spirits sagging. "Hey, don't worry. How hard can this be? No one will be shooting at us, and I can guarantee there are no snakes in that blasted cold mine down there." He touched his lips to hers and kissed her quickly.

She pulled away and sighed. "Don't joke."

Chapter Twenty

Tye slipped down the hole into the inky blackness, pleased to find Maria's lantern sitting at the bottom, casting a dim light to illuminate the floor of the mine. As soon as he hit bottom, he tied his rope to a nearby piece of rotted timber and lit the second lantern he had secured at his waist. Above him, he heard Brett fire three rapid rounds from his gun to signal their whereabouts and to alert other search parties they had found the boys. Beside him, he heard the steady drip, drip, drip of water coming from a crack in the rock ceiling and hitting the mine floor. He surveyed the gloomy walls around him and yelled the boys names again, waiting patiently for a response.

From somewhere down a long low tunnel to his right, a voice called out, "Here! We're over here."

"Can you see the light?" Tye shouted. He held the lantern higher.

"Yes!" Lenny replied from the depths of a long tunnel in front of him. "Isaac's foot is caught under a fallen rock."

Tye closed his eyes and sighed. He thought about the barn at the ranch and the dark crawl space under its foundation where he had sent Flint instead of himself to check the foundation. Now, even the barn space looked better than the narrow, black, gaping mouth ahead of him ready to swallow him up. He stepped over a puddle of water and stooped to peer into the tunnel. The ceiling was low, and its walls were slimy and black. A drip of water fell on the back of his neck and slipped under his shirt. He cursed, took a deep breath, and ducked down, moving into the tunnel's entrance. Inching forward into the blackness, he felt the rock ceiling graze the top of his head. Another drip fell down onto the back of his shirt as he crept along, taking care not to stumble or dislodge any debris from the sides.

Slowly, carefully, and minutes later, he found the boys in a small clearing in the mine high enough to allow a man to stand upright. It was heaped with rock, shale, and ore rubble. Black-faced, filthy, and wet, Lenny sat on a flat rock, and beside him, Isaac lay on the ground, his foot wedged under a large bolder that had slipped from the heap surrounding him. With the help of a fallen timber, Tye pried the rock upward enough to allow Lenny to pull Isaac's foot from beneath it.

"Can you walk?" Tye heaved the boy up by his armpits.

"I think so," Isaac said, wincing and shivering. "It's my ankle, but I don't think it's broken."

"Then let's hobble out of here," he said. *Before this whole damn tunnel falls down around our heads.* "Here, lean on me. Lenny, take the lantern, hold it high, and lead the way."

With the help of Brett and Maria, both boys were lifted up the shaft to safety followed by Tye. Maria helped him loosen the rope from around his waist as he tumbled onto his knees, then onto his back in the wet grass. Never had he enjoyed the sight of open air, despite the rumble of thunder and light rain beginning

251

to fall. He gazed up at the stormy, gray sky. Nearby, he heard the snicker of a horse coming around the mine from the trail below. Beside him Swamp whined and complained about getting wet, but loyally hunched down beside his master.

"Are you all right?" Maria asked with a worried frown. "You're going to get soaked lying on the wet grass."

He laughed cheerfully. "Maria, my dear sweet Maria, just to lie here and breathe in the clean air and be surrounded by miles…and miles…of space…is a blessing." After a minute, he rolled to his feet, patted Swamp on the head, and surveyed the two boys huddled nearby.

"That's Pa coming, and I'm going to get a licking for sure." Lenny shivered and hung his scruffy head.

"Why did you two go in there?" There was a stern timbre to Brett's voice. "Mines are a dangerous place to play, boy." Behind them, Roy Sanderson rode up, slid off his horse, and glared at the boys, also waiting for an answer.

"I wanted to see if I could talk to my ma." Lenny's face was sullen, and his eyes grew misty. He fought to control the tears and swiped at them with his sooty hands making muddy-looking puddles on his cheeks. "Pa never talks about her. I thought if her spirit was there, she'd talk to me. I hardly remember her." He looked at Tye. "It wasn't Isaac's fault. I begged him to come with me."

Roy Sanderson started forward. "I ought to—"

Tye waved him away. He knelt in front of Lenny. "I lost my mother when I was just a little older than you. I know the loss and pain, even though I have a few memories. But you have to remember your ma's spirit isn't just down there in the mine, her spirit is everywhere. Her spirit is with you when you wake up in the morning and when you lay your head on your pillow at night. She hasn't left you." He thumped his chest. "She's right here with you...in your heart...*always*."

He rose and looked Roy Sanderson square in the eye. He shook his head sadly. "Maybe, old man, you need to start talking more with your son, instead of *at* him. He's all you've got. He's searching for answers to questions about his mother, and he deserves to get them. A man can't rightly live a healthy life without having a few good memories to hold onto. The boy needs someone in his life he can turn to when things get tough. Wake up, man. He needs you."

Grimly, he took the hat Maria handed him, jammed it on his head, and walked away with Brett beside him and Swamp trotting behind them.

"Come," Maria said to Isaac, "let me help you." She put her arms around the boy's shoulders. "Hold on to me. You can ride behind me. Let's get you to your mother and father. They must be sick with worry."

Alone, Roy Sanderson stood on top of the mine, staring at his son as the sky opened up, pouring torrents of rain upon them as if it was crying its heart out.

****

Later that afternoon when the rains had stopped and skies had cleared, Brett was surprised to see Tye come thundering into the yard at the lumber mill. From his office window, he could see the man was not in the best of moods. He had changed his blackened, wet clothes and was wearing new buckskins and knee-high boots and what looked like a new tan hat. He dismounted and tied his horse at the rail and, ignoring everyone around him, stormed directly into Brett's office.

"It's not often I have the privilege or pleasure of your company on the south side of town." Brett watched Tye slump down in a chair across from him and cross a leg over the top of his knee. The ivory handle of a knife protruded from his boot. "By the way, that was a nice job out there in the mine this morning."

His face sullen, Tye removed his Stetson, tossed it crown side up on Brett's desk and grunted. His vexation was evident. "Is your fancy suit still spotless?"

"Still clean as a whistle." Brett brushed at the front of his vest like he was dislodging some specks of dirt. He felt a faint twinge of humor forming on his lips and forced himself not to chuckle. "See you have a new hat. About time. So what can I do for you? I'm going to guess you're not interested in discussing my clothes or buying lumber today."

"I need some help, and I don't want my brothers involved."

Brett heaved a sigh. There was never any beating around the bushes with Tye Ashmore. He looked at the gloomy man with a wary expression. "I smell trouble. Haven't you had enough excitement for today, Tydall?" He raised an eyebrow. "Does this *help* involve me getting wet, dirty, or hurt?"

Tye shook his head. "No, you just have to hold my hat."

"Hold your hat?"

"Well, it's a new hat, and I don't want to get it soiled on a filthy saloon floor. And it would help if you could train a gun on some of Lang Redford's friends if they make a misstep while I have a short discussion with him."

When Brett looked at him half in anticipation and half in dread, Tye continued, "It seems Redford's been pushing his weight around with the O'Donnell sisters, and I aim to have him stop. He and his men are over at the saloon, and I figure we should have a little talk with the galoot while it's fresh in our minds."

"We?" Brett's voice rose an octave.

"Take it easy, compadre. I have a plan."

"Oh, hellfire." Brett sighed. "I hope it's better than the one we had on the flatboat. And if I'm holding your hat, what the devil will you be doing?"

"Depends upon Redford. I'll try to be reasonable and diplomatic."

Brett snorted and rose from his desk. He couldn't help grinning. "Well, what are we waiting for?"

When the two men rode into town a quarter hour later, the day was drawing to a close. Soon darkness would fall, and the tinny sounds of the piano would echo from the saloon. But now, the air still hummed with the sounds of rattling harnesses, children's laughter, and adult voices. A few carriages and wagons still remained on the street, drawn up to the hitching posts and tied with a set of reins. Women with baskets hurried along the sidewalk, heading home to fix supper while children, fresh out of school, rolled hoops and skipped rope.

Brett and Tye dismounted and tied their horses to the rail outside the saloon.

"I really don't want to make this into a gun fight, unless necessary," Tye warned.

"Unless necessary? What the devil? I thought you said you had a plan." Brett threw him a quick look of dismay.

"I do, but it has room for changing horses in the middle of the stream, so to speak."

Brett grunted. "Just give me a signal if you're going to jump on my proverbial horse so I'll know ahead of time if I have to swim." They grinned at each other remembering the mailbag and the flatboat.

Together they walked through the batwing doors, taking time to let their eyes adjust to the smoky, dim interior. Only a few people were at the bar. Across the room, Lang Redford was playing poker with Jebb Masters, Pat Wenson, and an unshaven man who appeared to be a drifter.

"Redford, we need to have a little talk." Tye removed his hat and handed it to Brett.

He walked toward the table and stopped a few feet away.

"Sorry, Ashmore, but I have a card game to finish here. And it looks like I'm ahead."

"No, it looks like your luck's run out." Tye crossed the distance and grabbed him by the front of his shirt and yanked him upward as if he was tossing a sack of feed. The other men at the table scrambled up, reaching for their guns.

Brett stepped forward, his gun already drawn. "Easy, easy, gentlemen." He trained his revolver at them. "This is a friendly discussion between Tye and Redford."

"Get your hands off me, Ashmore!" Lang Redford spit out. He pushed himself away, straightening his suit coat. "Such uncivilized behavior! Is this about the little schoolmarm you've been keeping company with?"

"Stay away from Maria *and* Abigail," Tye ordered. A muscle flicked angrily on his jaw.

"Is this a warning, Ashmore? Or a threat?"

"Call it what you want, but stay away from the women if you know what's good for you."

"What? You keeping both of them for yourself?" Redford grinned. "Isn't that a bit greedy? Maybe some of us would like a little whirl with them. They sure are lookers, and I aim to have a look under their skirts myself."

Before Brett could even utter the words, "Your goose is cooked." Tye stepped closer, and his right fist came flying up, hitting Redford's left check with a solid, bone-jarring crack. He followed it with a quick left hook that caught Redford on the right side of the face, below his eye, and sent him tumbling backward and onto the floor with a heavy thump. The man lay unconscious in a heap at his feet.

Tye's icy gaze circled the wide-eyed men at the table. "You tell Redford, if he comes close to either of those women again, the next time I see him, he'll have a choice of knives or guns—and I'll make sure he won't be able to open his eyes to look at anything except Lucifer. And the warning goes for all of you." Tye stalked to Brett who was backing slowly out the door with his gun still drawn. He snatched his hat, jamming it on his head.

"Well, I wouldn't certainly call that your best diplomatic moment, Tydall," Brett muttered under his breath and followed him toward the hitching rail and their mounts.

Chapter Twenty-One

It was Friday, but there was no school. Maria arose and began to tidy up the cottage and kitchen while an applesauce cake finished in the oven and a pan of cornbread cooled on the counter. The whole town was in a state of constant motion, and excitement was high as they prepared for their annual harvest celebration to be held on Saturday. Farmers from around the area would be bringing in livestock and fall vegetables to sell, and the women of Golden were making baked goods to sell and cakes to auction off to the highest bidders. A variety of music would be presented under the trees near the blacksmith shop, and a barn dance was planned for later in the evening. During the week, Maria had helped the children organize a small parade through the town at noon complete with wagons, homemade flags, and songs.

Late last night, Abigail had left for the Mule Shed, a bundle of quilts under her arms, determined to find whoever was stealing from the safe. She intended to sleep on the floor of the barroom after it closed for the evening. Normally, Maria would have been worried, but when Brett heard about her antic, he insisted upon accompanying her. Maria hoped Abigail furnished him with some good whiskey while they sat on the hard wooden floor waiting for a thief who might never arrive.

The wuffle of a horse outside the door brought the puppy to attention, and he started yapping at the door, tail wagging.

"Shhh." Maria tried to hush the dog dancing excitedly around her feet.

She opened the door to find Swamp and Tye standing on the porch.

"You should at least ask who's there before you open your door," he scolded, a frown on his face.

"Emerson knew it was someone friendly," she shot back with an indignant look.

"Emerson?" He removed his hat and a flash of confusion crossed his face.

"The pup."

"You named the dog Emerson?"

Maria smiled. "Yes, after—"

"After Ralph Waldo Emerson, I presume. The poet and writer. Good thing you didn't force the poor little guy to respond to Waldo."

"I knew you'd get it!" She grinned. "Come, come in. Bring Swamp. I've fresh coffee on the back of the stove and a pan of cornbread cooling. Abigail spent the night at the barroom trying to chase down the safe thief, and she's not back yet. I have some blackberry cobbler left from last night, too."

He stepped inside, put his hat on the peg beside the door, and motioned to Swamp who sat quietly at his side even with the puppy tumbling around their feet. "It's ok, boy. You can tangle with the little scamp." He pointed to the pup, and Swamp went over to it, nudging it as it rolled over submissively onto its back, but then brazenly started to bat a paw at the older dog's muzzle.

Tye pulled out his chair, but before he sat down,

his arm snaked out and pulled Maria into his lap. "It's not often we have any private time to ourselves, Miss O'Donnell." He stole a quick kiss. It quickly grew into a more demanding one before she pushed at him.

Breathless, Maria struggled to her feet. She felt her face grow hot as she stepped away and poured him some coffee. "Cornbread or blackberry cobbler? Which do you prefer?"

"Which one is sweeter?"

"The cobbler."

"The cobbler then." He grinned. "If I can't have you."

"Tydall Ashmore, you have a sweet tooth." She spooned some cobbler on a plate, then cut some squares of cornbread, and put them on another one. He grabbed her around the waist again and pulled her back down. "The cobbler can wait. Time alone with you is so very, very scarce." He reached up and tucked the errant lock of hair that always fell into her eyes behind her ear. "When are you going to marry me?"

She kissed him and scrambled up, laughing. "You just sweet talk me, Tye, when you know the kitchen is full of good things to eat."

"And I'll sweet talk you some more since we have the entire cottage to ourselves, praise the Heavens above!" He looked over at the stove. "Is the applesauce cake yours or Abigail's?"

"Does it matter?"

"It does if I'm going to lay down money tomorrow at the auction to get it." He took a spoon and stirred some sugar into his coffee.

"It's mine. I seriously doubt Abigail even plans to bake today." She looked at the knuckles on his right hand. They were swollen and bruised. "What happened to your hand?"

"Nothing." He scowled. "It was a diplomatic moment needing a tad bit of persuasion."

"A *tad* bit?" Maria frowned.

A knock on the door made Tye groan as both their gazes flew to the front door. "Don't open it," he whispered. "Please, don't open it. This is the only time we've had to ourselves for days. They'll go away if we're quiet."

Laughing, Abigail moved to the door and behind her, she heard Tye heave a long disgruntled sigh. She was surprised to find River Roy Sanderson standing on the other side, hat in hand, and holding a small wooden box. His face was ruddy from the cold ride down the mountain. His clothes were washed, his hair neatly trimmed, and his face, clean shaven. Around his neck, he had a new russet scarf, and Maria recognized the yarn from the lot Millie kept on hand. They stared at each other for a moment before Sanderson broke the uncomfortable silence.

"I have to deliver a load of wood to Millie Hanson, and I saw Tye Ashmore's horse outside your cottage. I figured I needed to thank you and him for rescuing my son yesterday."

Maria stepped back. "Please come in where it's warm. I was just cutting some fresh cornbread and have coffee already made."

"I don't want to be no bother." He looked at the floor.

"I assure you, Mr. Sanderson, you are no bother. Now, come and sit. We are warming the outdoors standing here with the door ajar. Hang your hat and coat on the hook there." She motioned to the coat rack beside the door. "How's Lenny?"

Sanderson nodded. "Fine, just fine. A few scratches is all. He's running some errands around town for me." He walked to the table and pulled out a chair. "I'm beholden to you, Ashmore, for going down the mine to get those boys." From behind him, Emerson came bounding over, but Tye scooped him up, reached back, and dropped him in the crate beside the stove. He signaled to Swamp, lying beside the back door. The older dog moved next to the crate and lay down, head on his paws, guarding the rambunctious pup unsuccessfully trying to crawl out.

"It wasn't me alone," Tye admitted. "Brett and Maria helped. It was clever of Maria to decide we needed two lanterns. One to keep a glow at the entrance of the tunnel."

Maria handed Sanderson a cup of coffee and set a fork and a plate with a piece of cornbread in front of him.

Sanderson nodded his appreciation. He pulled the box he had balanced on his lap and handed it to her. "These are letters I received from the U.S. government after Walt died. I don't rightly know what they say, since I can't read. They've been lying in my cupboard for years now." He blushed a bright red and hung his head in shame. "But I'm guessing at least one of these has to do with Brett Trumble, since it has a government look to it. It would be a kindness to me if you would read them and tell me what they say." He hesitated. "When I lost Walt, I had no desire to find out what the U.S. government or anyone else had to tell me."

"I can understand your pain." Maria removed five

letters from the box, handed two to Tye and put two in front of her, and laid the last in the middle of the table. While Sanderson tackled his cornbread, she and Tye glanced over the papers.

She opened the first envelope and withdrew a letter, taking time to read it twice before she looked up, her eyes misty. "This is from the government telling you officially of your son's death," she said quietly and looked up into the man's sad eyes. She picked up the other letter, withdrew it from the envelope and quickly scanned it. "This one says your son, Walter, died a hero's death trying to save others and was awarded a medal for his bravery." She looked over at Tye.

He cleared his throat. "This one here explains that your son never collected his final wages, and there is money owed to you." Tye set the letter aside. "Maria, perhaps, can help you write a return letter. This other letter states the government had lost contact with Brett Trumble who enlisted with Walt. These are Trumble's orders from the Union Army and sent to your son's address to be forwarded to Brett." Tye let out a long breath of air and leaned back in his seat. "Brett has been looking all over the countryside for these orders to prove he was not a deserter from the Union Army when he went behind Confederate lines to spy for the North."

"Can you see that Trumble gets it?" Sanderson asked. "I'm sorry, but I don't think the man would enjoy seeing me."

They stared at each other for several moments. Tye waited for him to continue.

"It was too painful. Losing a wife and son." With callused fingers, Roy Sanderson toyed with the rim of the plate. "Lenny was only a little boy, and there I was without a wife to help raise him, without a grown son to help me make a decent living. I hated Trumble for coming home without Walt. When I got these letters, I just dropped them in this box and shoved them on a shelf." He picked up the last envelope and withdrew two sheets of paper and handed them to Tye. "I think these are important. Henry McNeil gave them to me a few months before his death and told me to keep them in case something happened to him."

Pensively, Tye shuffled through the sheets, glancing at them, then handing them to Maria. She scanned them and looked curiously at Tye. "This looks like the deed and information for the Irene M mine that Abigail and Brett have been searching for." She smiled at River Roy. "Did you know you had the deed to the mine Henry McNeil bought for his brother-in-law, himself, and Brett Trumble?"

"I knew it was a deed for the Irene M, sure," River Roy admitted. "Henry bought the mine years ago and set me up with mules and equipment to check it out and see if it was showing any color." He paused. "In return for my work, he said he'd give me a cut of the mine's worth, once it was decided when operations should begin. It was rumored they were planning two stage roads into the area, and the railroads were itching to get connected to Victor and Cripple Creek."

"He gave this deed to you?" Maria looked puzzled.

"Henry told me he didn't trust anyone with the deed. Said he didn't want to leave it in his office and would never leave it in his house." He paused. "Whenever he was talking about Emma, he acted nervous-like. You know, as if he didn't quite trust her. Around town, it was said she was spending every nickel he made. I don't think he wanted her to know about it. Then he added the second sheet to the deed. Even rode up the mountain to give it to me."

Maria nodded. "Yes, here it states Henry, Brett Trumble, and our father owned the majority shares, and you would have ten percent, but in the case of his death, his shares would be equally divided to you, Brett and my father, giving you 20 percent, and Brett and my father each a total of forty percent each."

Tye grinned. "If the mine pans out, Roy, you will be able to have a very comfortable life and will not need to work the woods or mines again."

A knock at the door interrupted them.

"You planning on having the entire town drop in today, Maria?" There was a mischievous glint in Tye's eyes when he glanced at her. He rose, went to the door, and opened it. "Well, well. If it isn't the little mischief-maker himself. Come on in, Lenny. Maria has fresh cornbread. You hungry?"

"I'm looking for my pa," he said, "but cornbread does sound mighty good."

"Well, you've come to the right place for both."

Chapter Twenty-Two

Brett and Maria sat on the floor of the barroom, hidden back in the far corner, both awake, but sleepy and disgruntled. They had spent the night on the hard, cold, wooden floor and shared a bottle of the best French wine and waited and waited and waited. Inside, it was still dark, but outside the night was beginning to fade from black to dark gray.

Earlier, when they arrived, they found Charlie Haney closing up the bar and restocking the wine and liquor beneath the bar. When questioned about the barn, the trunk, and other belongings in the stables, Charlie said the only people storing possessions there were Lang Redford, the stable master, or Big Jake, the bouncer. Will Singer, the old stable master and handyman, lived in a house outside town and stored his belongings there, he told her. Abigail surmised the trunk had to be Lang's. When asked about Big Jake, Charlie told her he always had his clothes specially made to fit his huge, robust frame, and Abigail immediately concluded the Confederate uniform was way too small for him. Charlie reluctantly left them then with a tray of food from the kitchen, wine glasses and wine—and a stern warning to not get shot.

"Well, it looks like no one is going to show." Brett yawned and stretched, raising his arms above his head.

"I was certain with everyone getting ready for

Saturday's big Harvest Festival someone would try to get money from the safe." Abigail frowned, removing the ribbon from her hair. She gathered the errant locks into a smooth bunch and retied them at the nape of her neck. She was just about to stand up, when the hinges on the door leading into the barroom from porch squealed. The door opened slowly and a burst of cool breeze followed the figure who slipped inside and headed behind the bar. Abigail heard the scratch of a match against a surface, smelled the phosphorous, and saw the glowing tip quickly disappear to be replaced by the low shine of a lantern sitting atop the bar.

From her seat on the floor, Abigail felt Brett's hand come around and cover her mouth just in time to prevent her from gasping at the sight of a woman. "Shhh," he whispered in her ear, "let her open the safe first and withdraw some money so there will be no doubt she's caught in the act."

Abigail nodded and Brett removed his hand.

Minutes later, when the bills were on the bar, Brett stood. "The last person I expected to find stealing from anyone would have been you, Millie Hanson." He strode toward her, his large frame casting eerie shadows on the wall.

Millie's face in the dim light faded to a ghostly white as she stared at him.

Abigail rose and followed Brett.

"I...I...I can explain," Millie replied. "She made me do it." Her gaze flitted fitfully from Abigail to Brett.

"Who made you do it?" Abigail's tone was quiet, but firm.

"Emma. She gave me the combination and told me if I wanted to keep my job, I would do as she requested.

She threatened to fire me if I didn't." Millie hung her head, and her hands came up to cover her face. She started to weep. "I had no choice. She said when I threatened to quit, she'd make sure no one in town would give me a job. I have no way to support myself. I have no husband. I have to do whatever she asks."

Abigail heaved a long sigh. "Why is Emma stealing the money, Millie? She could have asked me if she needed some. Heaven knows I already give her more profits from the inn than she's entitled to, and I've been stuck with some of her bills around town, just to save face."

"I...I don't know." Millie shook her head. "What are you going to do? Are you going to tell the sheriff?"

"She should," Brett snapped.

Abigail heard the seething anger in his voice and laid a restraining hand on his arm. Something about Emma McNeil didn't make sense. The woman was a puzzle. A nasty one, she reminded herself, but a puzzle nonetheless. "Tell me, Millie, did Emma ever come down here and take money from the safe herself?"

Millie nodded. "Yes, a few times, but then she decided to send me. She was afraid to get caught." Still visibly shaken, she said, "Please, please Miss Abby. Please don't get the sheriff. I'll lose my job. You don't know how mean Emma can get. Last time I displeased her and baked the wrong pie, she threw the pie at me and threatened me with a butcher's knife."

Abigail shook her head. "No, Millie. Take the bills, go back up to the manse, and give the money to Emma."

"You're going to let the old witch get away with this?" Brett's voice raised an octave.

"You…you won't tell anyone I'm a thief?" Millie asked.

"No, I won't. Just give me time to think this through." She ignored Brett's outburst. She watched as the woman shoved the money in the pocket of her apron and scurried to the door. Millie was just about to leave, when Abigail called to her. "Millie," she cautioned, "keep your eyes open and ears to the ground. We need to find out why Emma needs so much money."

Later, as she and Brett walked back to the cottage, he asked, "Do you have any idea what's going on here? What don't I understand about all this, Abby? Is there something amiss at the manse?"

Abigail shook her head. "I don't. It looks like we have another mystery to solve."

"It's not like we don't have enough already." He snorted. "We still don't know how Henry died. We don't know who shot at Maria and Tye and put snakes in the road. And we don't know why Emma is stealing money."

"Nor do we know whose Confederate uniform is lying in the trunk in the barn."

"Uniform?"

"Yes, a Confederate uniform with a button missing. Maria and I think it's Red Langford's, but we can't be sure."

"What were you two doing pawing through Langford's belongings?"

"Milking the cow." When Brett looked skeptical, she added, "We poked around the stalls in Emma's barn when we finished the task. We were looking for a stall to clean out so when we finally had a horse and buggy, we'd have a place to shelter them. Unfortunately,

Langford showed up, and we couldn't explore further."

"Explore further? What the devil are you thinking?" Brett blew out a breath of air. "Stay away from Redford, will you? There's nothing good about him, and he seems to be in cahoots with your crazy aunt and those two unsavory characters he hired to lollygag with him."

"Brett, it's been over two months, and we still are no closer to finding my uncle's murderer. The sheriff has come up with nothing." *And we don't know who's threatening Maria and writing warnings on the school's chalkboard.* She wished she hadn't promised to keep the warnings a secret, but she had sworn to Maria she wouldn't divulge a word to anyone.

"Tree by tree and board by board, a house is built."

"I know, and a handful of patience is better than a sack of brains," Abigail muttered. "But if you're thinking I have any patience, I can assure you mine has just about run out. I want answers, and they're buried in this town somewhere!"

Brett shifted the quilts he was carrying in his other arm and pulled her close. "Take heart, darlin', we have the ideal time to find some answers tomorrow when the Harvest Festival gets under way."

They reached the end of the path and entered the kitchen to find River Roy, Tye, and Maria seated at the table. On the floor, Lenny played with the pup while Swamp, head on his paws, watched cautiously from a distance. River Roy stumbled up as soon as he saw Brett come through the door. His chair toppled to the floor. Brett stopped abruptly. The two men stared at each other with guarded, wary expressions.

"Sit down, sit down, both of you," Tye admonished

them with a wave of his hand. He reached down and righted the chair. "No sense in everyone getting all fired up."

When River Roy looked at Brett holding the pile of quilts, Abigail spoke up quickly. "We were just getting some old quilts out of the inn to replace them with others." The last thing she wanted was for the whole town to know she spent the night alone with Brett on the floor of a barroom. She looked from Tye to Maria, but neither of them gave away their night's escapade.

"Good news, Brett." Tye again motioned for him to take a seat. "Thanks to River Roy, we finally have your Union orders and your name can be cleared. And you and Maria and Abby have the deed to the mine as well." He handed him the envelope. Brett looked at him curiously and sat down.

Maria stepped forward and poured Brett a cup of coffee and placed a plate with a large square of cornbread on it before him. He nodded his thanks as he scanned the papers.

Roy Sanderson cleared his throat. "I owe you an apology, Trumble." He rose again, his chair scraping on the floor as he pushed it back. He nervously glanced at Tye. "You can explain the rest to him, Ashmore. I gotta go."

"No, might be best if you did."

"You know I can't read." River Roy stared at the floor, and his face colored a deep red. "When the letters came in I just thought they'd be about Walt, not you, Trumble." He looked up at everyone.

Maria said softly, "You know, I can teach you to read, Mr. Sanderson, if you'd ever like to learn."

"It's not a bad idea," Brett agreed, his forehead

wrinkled, his eyes still scanning the papers. "If you're going to be part owner of the Irene M, you'll need to know how to read to help run the business. You're lucky. You have a very talented son who can help you learn when Maria is not available."

"Yes sireeee," Tye drawled with distinct mockery. "You've got the perfect opportunity and an excellent teacher. I'll bet Maria could teach an Indian to read if she set her mind to it." He looked at Maria with a stony expression. Her face grew scarlet. She bit her lip, but said nothing.

"I'll think on it." River Roy motioned to his son. "Come, Lenny, there's a wagonload of wood that needs delivered."

"You don't need to rush off," Abby said.

"Sun's almost up," he replied. "I thank you for the cornbread and coffee."

While he and Lenny shrugged on their coats, Maria spoke. "Don't forget the Harvest Festival tomorrow, Mr. Sanderson. And Lenny, I'm counting on you to read the passages we practiced. Loud and clear for everyone to hear, you hear me?"

"Yes, ma'am." Lenny nodded and silently followed his father out into the chilly morning.

****

Later in the afternoon, Maria collected her school supplies and shawl to take out back with her. Once her lesson with Two Bears was finished, she was headed back to the schoolhouse to check her materials for the children's program the next day at Harvest Festival. She had promised Two Bears she could only meet him for a half hour and was not surprised to find him there early, seated on the rock behind the shed. Over the past

272

weeks, they had made tremendous progress, flying through the materials Maria had available for teaching. Two Bears, it seemed, was as good a student as he was a warrior. He soaked up the lessons like a water-starved man in the burning sun.

"You are early, Two Bears." She sat, putting her book bag beside her. In his hands, he held an Oliver Optic book she had lent him.

"Was it too difficult?" Maria asked.

Two Bears shook his head. "I stopped at old Theo Sarowski's house this week when her calf got away, and I spotted it in the forest nearby. She helped me with many of the words which I put here." He tapped his head.

"Memorized." Maria nodded. "You already understand how the letters are strung together. You can pronounce most words almost perfectly now. You just need to understand the meaning of them. Very good, Two Bears!" Beside her, the tabby cat from the barn came slinking around the corner, leaped onto the back stoop of the cottage, and surveyed the area around her like a queen on her throne. Abigail had been leaving a pan of milk at the cottage and feeding the cat at the inn to coax it into staying and catching mice. Suddenly without warning, the tabby sniffed the air, cocked its head, and spotted Two Bears. Hissing, she arched her tawny back and backed up a few paces, then vaulted from the stoop onto the path leading up to the Mule Shed. Two Bears and Maria watched her golden tail disappear.

Maria looked warily at Two Bears who was scratching his head. A faint smile played across his face. "For some reason, the cat doesn't like you, Two

Bears."

"I do not harm animals. White men say a cat has nine lives, is it so?"

Maria shrugged and continued to gaze at him as a thought flitted through her mind. She touched his forearm and noticed a faint latticework of scratches, then eyed his other arm and saw the same pattern. "Poor Priscella almost lost one of those lives the other night under the hooves of Red Langford's horse, didn't she?"

"If you say so," Two Bears replied solemnly. "Prissss-ella? You call that she cat Priscella? Claw Face might be better name."

"You might want to put some bear grease on those scratches on your arms." She smirked.

He stared at her, only his dark eyes showing any trace of humor. "Do you know bees and dogs can smell fear? Cats not so much."

"But it does appear cats have a memory." She tapped her head.

"Can I keep the book for a few days? Theo Sarowski is willing to help me read it. She said it is good practice to speak the words out loud."

Maria nodded. "Yes, keep the book. And thank you, for the other night." She rose. "Come, walk with me to the school house, Two Bears. I can teach you rhyming words and their meaning while we walk. We'll use the back way through the woods. You're only going to follow me anyway."

Two Bears grunted. "That is so."

Chapter Twenty-Three

The town's Harvest Festival was a time of gaiety, motion, and commotion as townspeople and farmers in the area came together to celebrate a good year and a bountiful harvest. The Sarowski barn, next to his blacksmith shop, served not only as the town meeting house and polling place during the year, but also as the dance hall for the festivities each October. Folks from all around gathered a few days before to help sweep out the barn, set up chairs and tables, and ready the area for the festive weekend event. While the women saw to the food, the men kept watch on the drinks, assuring everyone the beer and whiskey would never be scarce.

The opening activities started with the children marching down Main Street at noon, carrying flags and banners, and singing the songs they had learned in school. The march culminated in the center of the street where a makeshift dais was constructed, its lower perimeter covered with blankets and where the children kept their props when they recited poetry, performed small skits, or read from their favorite books.

The O'Donnell sisters along with Betsy Ashmore now stood on the sidewalk in front of the General Store, directly across from the dais, ready to help the smaller children needing assistance or help finding their parents once their part in the performance was finished. Brett and Tye crossed the street and sauntered up behind them, tipping their hats to the town folk as they approached. A guitar was slung around Brett's shoulder.

"Ladies." Brett touched two fingers to his hat brim, propped a foot up on the boardwalk, and turned to Maria. He surveyed the huge crowd surrounding the dais where a pretty blonde girl was reciting a poem by Robert Browning. "Looks like you've outdone yourself, Maria. The children are having a great time, and from the radiant look on the faces of the parents, they are, too. Are you prepared for the finale?"

Maria winced. She didn't know whether she was going to dread the ending or enjoy it. Lenny, Isaac, and her older students had begged her to let them arrange a surprise presentation for the finale. Reluctantly she had agreed, knowing when children often take on creative responsibility it teaches them a lesson far greater than a lesson in a book. "It looks like you might be part of it?" she asked skeptically.

"Well, they needed a few musicians, so I volunteered." He shrugged and followed it with a sheepish smile. "I can't say no to a young'un. And Tye would have my hide if I said no."

While Lenny finished his final recitation of the day, all the children scrambled away from where they stood with their parents and disappeared beneath the dais. Like a conductor of a major play, he stepped forward, cleared his throat, and addressed the crowd. "These last two presentations are a surprise for our new teacher, Miss O'Donnell, whom all of us admire for her humor, her artistic talents, and her caring nature." He cleared his throat again, nervously, "And I should add for trusting us to perform in acceptable fashion even though she has no idea what we've planned." Over the chuckles of the crowd, he signaled to Betsy who turned and waved to a group inside the General Store. A group of musicians exited and gathered on the wooden sidewalk, waiting for the proper signal.

Maria was surprised to see children had enlisted adult musicians from the townsfolk. There were two fiddlers, and from inside the store, a piano player. Maria also noticed River Roy Sanderson holding a banjo.

As the group struck up a the lively tune of the "Yellow Rose of Golden," to the tune of the "Yellow Rose of Texas," all the children marched out from under the dais, circling it, singing, and holding yellow flowers. When the song ended with the words, "But the yellow rose of Golden is the only one for me," each child presented a flower to their parents or family members. Then quickly, like a flock of sheep, they clambered back underneath the dais and disappeared for the last song, "Buffalo Gals." Minutes later, after the musicians played the first line of the song, Maria found herself grinning from ear to ear. The male students, wearing cowboy shirts, vests, and hats and holding yellow cut-outs of the moon paraded out first, followed by the females—from the tiniest first graders to the oldest eighth graders—dressed in old worn dresses and wearing holes in their stockings. Together, they danced by the light of the moon. At the end of the song, Isaac presented Maria with a large bouquet of fall flowers, and Lenny gave her a basket of apples as the parents and crowd roared in approval.

"Well, that's going to be a tough presentation to beat next year." Tye smiled and looked at Maria whose eyes were misty. "Oh, no," he lamented, "please don't tell me you're going to cry."

"I'm so proud of them," she said, sniffing. "I'm so happy."

"You cry when you're happy *and* sad?"

She nodded and gave a resigned shrug.

"Well, I, for one, am going to have to get used to that side of you. But for tonight, I plan for us to dance by light of the moon." Tye steered her toward the sidewalk where the crowd was dispersing. "You have no idea how many people Isaac and Lenny roped into helping with the performance. Betsy bought all the boys a shirt. I canvassed the barroom and town saloon and offered everyone with the correct head size to match one of the boys, a free drink if he'd lend the kid his hat. Millie helped all the girls round up dresses and stockings and helped them with their hair. Oh, and she made all the matching cloth vests. Brett pulled together the music, and Abby fed all the kids after school on the days they held a practice in the dining room at the Mule Shed."

"Feeding them was fun," Abby said, eavesdropping as she followed behind with Brett. "I also had the agonizing pleasure of listening to Brett practice the "Yellow Rose of Texas" and "Buffalo Gals" over and over and *over* again last night before darkness fell, and we camped in peaceful silence inside the barroom."

"I didn't know Lenny's dad could play a banjo," Maria said.

"Neither did I," Brett said. "It seems it's one more enigma about River Roy. I understand he quit when his wife died, but it looks like your little lecture, Tydall, pushed the poor man into realizing he was neglecting his son."

"Did you know he's sparking Millie Hanson?" Abigail's gentle laugh rippled through the air.

Tye raised an eyebrow and looked at the group. "Millie Hanson and River Roy?"

"Behave." Maria nudged him with her arm and smiled. "Everyone is entitled to their own happiness."

They had stopped at the corner to watch a wagonload of beets, potatoes, and fall vegetables pass by. The horses pulling the wagon were a perfect matched set of bay-colored Belgian draft horses at least sixteen hands high. The chains on the traces jingled as they pranced in synchronized step.

"And speaking of joyful people, here comes Emma McNeil." Brett frowned and looked up the walk. "Come, everyone, I think we should head over to the bakery and check out what Anna Ashmore has baked special for the Harvest Festival." He turned and tried to pull Abigail away from the group.

"Wait!" Maria was growing weary of her aunt as much as Abigail. Abby had been paying her bills around town, but even she was occasionally stopped and asked to remind Emma about her overdue accounts. Last week it was for something she bought at the millinier's.

Emma approached in a light gray dress with a matching parasol and surveyed the group with a reproachful gaze. "Well, well, was everyone at that silly little play those children were putting on up the street?"

Beside her, Maria felt Tye tense, his face unreadable.

"It was well done," Maria said. "I'm sorry you missed it."

Emma huffed. "I saw part of it, my dear, but I needed to see about a new hat."

"Yes, we need to talk about new hats among other things," Abby spoke up. "I'll meet you at the manse sometime soon, sometime this week."

Lips thinned in anger, Emma stared at her. "You'll not be telling me, Missy, what I can or cannot buy." She turned on Maria and scowled. "And it might be best if both of you keep your nose out of my business and out of my barn. If you want to stable a riding horse or harness horse and buggy, it will not be on my land or in the inn's stables either. Yes, we are going to have to talk. It's about high time you both start paying me rent for the cottage."

Tye's nostrils flared with anger. "You forget, Mrs. McNeil, that the school board paid for all the materials and made all the renovations on the cottage with the assumption the town's school teacher would have a place to stay. You agreed to it."

"Well, how unfortunate for them." Emma sneered. "It's time the school teacher paid for the roof over her own head. Abigail could easily live in a room at the inn, and I could rent my cottage out for a monthly charge."

"You'd better speak with the school board," Tye suggested.

Emma let out a shrill demented-sounding peal of laughter. "What? I don't have to answer to any school board and especially to any Ashmore." Rudely, she pushed past them, her skirt swirling in anger around her ankles as she proceeded down the street.

****

The Sarowski barn was filled with noise, laughter, music, and gaiety when Maria and Tye arrived later in the evening only a few minutes before Abby and Brett. Outside the air was still warm, but growing cool and damp with the scent of fall. Their group had dispersed later in the afternoon, the women returning home to get ready for the big evening ahead. And it appeared the entire town had come to the outing.

Maria looked across the crowd and picked out her Aunt Emma with Lang Redford, Patrick March, Frank Norwell, Will Singer, and Charlie Haney. Even Big Jake was whirling some little gal effortlessly around the dance floor. Now, standing beside Tye who was leaning against the doorframe of the barn, Maria tapped her foot in time with the music.

"You seem more cheerful than I would've expected." Tye tipped his hat back to peer down at her face.

"You mean for someone who might not have a place to live?" She smiled and lifted a shoulder in a half shrug.

Abigail and she had discussed their dilemma only hours ago. Brett had told them he was working to get the Irene M opened up to mine come spring. The two stage roads and a rail line were almost completed into Cripple Creek and Victor. There was no reason why they couldn't make a new life in Golden, the sisters decided. They were young, strong, and capable, and if Aunt Emma decided to sell the Mule Shed Inn, Abby would find other employment. They would not starve, and they would not bend to the silly will of their obtuse, unkind aunt or anyone who threatened them and wanted them to leave.

"We've decided to look for a larger house with some land near town where I can raise chickens and have an apple orchard," Maria said. "Our father had one when we lived in the East, and it was filled with McIntoshes, Winesaps and Northern Spies. Abby is itching to have a real barn to house some horses and a buggy. We might have to wait a year or more, but we plan to save our money. If Aunt Emma throws us out of the cottage, we'll manage with a room at the inn."

Tye smiled down at her and pulled her close, her back to his chest. He kissed the side of her forehead. "I love you, Maria," he whispered in her ear. "You know, it's time for me to settle down. You don't have to live in a room at the inn or a house with your sister. My ranch house is too large for one man. Let's get married. We could raise some cattle for me and some chickens for you. And a passel of kids for both of us."

"And I'd lose my job. You know the school board is opposed to having a married woman for a teacher." She twisted her head up to look at him.

"Forget the dang school board—"

"Tye—" Maria glanced at the dance floor and spotted Millie moving toward the door on the other side of the barn. She wiggled free from his embrace, turned toward him, and pulled his face down to meet hers, her lips touching his. She kissed him soundly, brazenly. "Hold that thought, Rancher Ashmore. We need to discuss this, but there's something I have to do right now. Right this minute."

"What? Hell's fire! Where are you going?"

To catch a murderer. Maria smiled. "I need to talk to Millie Hanson. It's really important."

"For the love of Pete! Why now?" he asked in disbelief. "Maria, I'm trying to propos—"

"Please, Tydall. Not now. I've waited all evening

to corral Millie and talk to her alone, away from the clutches of Aunt Emma." Before he could utter another word, she slipped away and disappeared across the barn floor, threading her way among the dancers.

"Millie," she called out.

Millie whirled and moved to the edge of the far doorway and waited. Maria saw a flicker of apprehension course through her. Earlier, Abigail had told her about Millie's trip to the barroom's safe.

"You did a wonderful job with the children's final musical presentations," Maria said sailing up. "I don't know how I can thank you enough."

Millie smiled. "It was a pleasure. Children are so easy to work with. So full of laughter. So full of excitement."

"Yes, they are." Maria took Mille by her forearm and pulled her outside, around the corner of the barn, out of earshot of others. "Millie, I need a favor. A huge favor."

The woman looked at her warily.

"Do you have any idea what happened to the button found alongside Uncle Henry when he was killed?"

Millie nodded. "It's still sitting on the top of the spinet."

Maria heaved a sigh and pushed away wisps of hair falling in her eyes. "I need you to go get it and meet me at the stables."

A look of tired sadness washed over Millie's face. "You'll only stir up trouble, Maria, if Emma finds out. It's not good to be on the wrong side of that woman."

"I don't intend for her to find out. This is the ideal time while she's at the festival." She paused. "Look,

Millie, I know you loved Uncle Henry. I suspect it has been you who has been regularly putting flowers on his grave, hasn't it?"

Millie's voice broke miserably. "She never loved him. Never! All she did was harp at him and demand more money, more jewelry, and fine clothes. He was a good man, Maria. He didn't deserve to have a shrew for a wife." She hung her head. Her eyes filled with tears and splashed down her cheeks.

"All the more reason to find the answers we need about Uncle Henry's death." Maria gripped her arm firmly and pushed her toward the manse. "Hurry, let's get this over with," she urged. "Meet me at the stables while there's still some daylight."

Minutes later, when Millie returned to the stables, Maria had already picked the lock to Lang Redford's trunk and removed the Confederate coat. She took it to a window and looked closely at it in the fading light. The thread holding the lost button to the material had been severed clean with a knife or scissors. Maria took the button Millie handed her and compared it to the others on the coat. A soft gasp escaped from her throat. "It's a match," she said. Their eyes met and widened in surprise and fright.

"I never trusted that man," Millie admitted and shook her head.

Behind them, the door opened and they both jumped. Abigail slipped silently inside. "What are you doing?"

"Goodness gracious, Abby, you scared us," Maria said. She showed her the coat and unattached button.

"You mean Lang Redford killed Uncle Henry?" she asked, her expression grim. "Now what do we do?"

Millie looked at Abby with frightened eyes. "This time maybe we'd better get the sheriff."

"No, I suggest we all take a little walk up to the manse," a voice said from behind them. They all whirled and watched Lang Redford stalk out from behind a stall, gun drawn and pointed at them. He had obviously been drinking. His face was scarlet, and he squinted at them through a swollen, black right eye. "My, my it's going to take some thinking to decide how to get rid of this many people at one time."

"You'll never get away with it, Lang," Abigail said. "Too many people know we've left the festival. They'll come looking for us."

His face went from pink to beet red. "You daft women! You both never give up! You just keep turning over rocks, again and again and again, until you stumble on hidden secrets that don't concern you. You're as dumb as tree stumps." He turned to Maria and persisted, "Wasn't a bullet near your head and a bag of snakes enough warning to leave things alone and hightail it out of here?" He waved the barrel of his gun toward the back of the barn. "Now we're all going to go up to the manse through the back door so as not to arouse anyone's suspicions. Lucky for me I came to check on the horses after I dropped your aunt off."

Minutes later, he marched them into the parlor where Emma was seated at the spinet. "My, my," she cackled. "What have we here?"

"Three women who know where the button came from." He kept his gun trained on them.

Emma picked up the crystal dish and a look of rage passed over her face when she realized it was empty. "Where *is* the button? Who has the button?"

All three women stood mute staring at her.

She rose from the spinet and stormed toward them. This time her voice rose in hysterical anger. "I asked for the button!"

"Button, button, who has the button?" Abigail said in a sing-song voice. "You remember that old childhood game, don't you, Maria?"

"You little smart-mouthed harlot! You'll get what you deserve." She looked at Lang Redford with eyes like a rabid dog. Spittle flew from her mouth as she ordered, "Give me the gun and go to the kitchen and get me a knife. One of these women is going to talk, I assure you. I want that button!"

"Now, now, Emma," he said. "Who cares which one of them has an old button?"

She shouted at him, her eyes wide and crazed. "I said get me a knife!" She ripped the gun from his hand and pointed it at the women, then took a step toward Maria. "You, stupid, stupid school teacher. Can't you read?" She laughed shrilly. "You couldn't heed the warnings to get out of town? I couldn't have made them any clearer."

"Oh, she did," Abby replied. Her voice was calm and steady. "We had a few laughs over them. The whizzing bullets and message on her slate board were a real treat. The snakes? Well, we're both not fond of snakes."

Instantly, Maria knew Abigail was trying to goad their aunt, trying to get her to step closer. It worked. Emma strode forward and pointed the gun at Abby's nose. "I should shoot you this very instant, you little trollop! I told Henry I never wanted his nieces here when he was alive, and I certainly never wanted you here now that he's dead. You girls are a noose around my neck!"

With a desire for vengeance she never knew she had, Maria sent her foot flying, soundly kicking Emma in her knee. As she stumbled forward to try to catch herself, Maria lunged and ripped the gun from her hand. Emma tumbled to the floor and landed in a heap, her legs tangled in her petticoats and dress.

"Owwwwh!" Emma righted herself screaming, "Lang! Lang, get in here. Help me! Now."

Maria stepped back and trained the gun on her. "Get up and move back, Aunt Emma, before I use this. I have no desire to hurt you, but it means nothing to me if I do." For once, Maria decided, she was tired of being afraid. She would no longer be scared of this demented, sharp-tongued woman. She would no longer be afraid of using a firearm. And she would no longer worry about making a home in the Territory. She and Abigail were not going back to Utah, and no one was going to force them to leave.

Emma scrambled up and backed away. Her nostrils flared with fury. "You sniveling little strumpet. Why, you don't even know how to use a gun." She laughed. "I heard about your silly little performance at the picnic when you arrived in Golden."

"Maria, give me the gun," Abigail said. Her voice was low and insistent. She held out her hand.

Maria smiled and shook her head. She couldn't believe how calm she felt. She waved the barrel at the picture of Emma on the wall. "I never understood why Uncle Henry liked such a lurid, horrendous portrait of you. Did any of you ever wonder about it, too?"

"Give me the gun, Maria," Abby pleaded. "Please.

Before one of us gets hurt."

"Oh, none of us will get hurt, I assure you." Maria's eyes never faltered as she looked at her aunt and spoke through gritted teeth. "You know, Emma, the portrait doesn't do you justice. I've always hated it. The dress is offensively hideous, and you have enough powder on your face to dust three babies' bottoms!" She pointed the gun at the portrait, took aim with both hands, and squeezed the trigger. Amid the sound of the blast, the bullet severed the thin cord on the portrait. It came crashing to the floor, pieces of glass splattering against the wall. Maria saw Emma flinch and then heard her gasp. Her eyes grew big and round as she gawked at the hole in the wall and her ruined picture on the floor.

From under her breath, Millie whispered. "Maybe we ought to let your sister keep the gun, Abigail. She's doing a right fine job at the moment."

Maria turned to the housekeeper. "Millie, please go over and take all the covers off the chairs and settee."

"No-oooooo," Emma screamed and clutched the sides of her head, tearing at her hair. "Leave the room alone!"

Maria kept her gun trained on her. "Calm down. Don't make me shoot you, Emma."

Hands shaking, Millie hurriedly circled the room dragging the sheets from the chairs and dropping them on the floor. When she got to the wingback chair in front of the fireplace, she pulled the sheet to reveal upholstery splattered with large blood stains, now dried and brown colored. Her face reacted in utter surprise. "Is this where Henry was *killed*?"

In the kitchen, they heard a scuffle and the voice of

Tye telling Lang Redford to join the party in the parlor. When they entered, Maria spoke. "Looks like the game is over, Lang; it's your button, your uniform, and all the evidence for the murder of my uncle leads back to you."

"Don't be ridiculous," he said and followed it with a hiss. "I ain't taking the fall for something I never done. I never killed Henry McNeil. It was Emma. She drugged his drink, then stabbed him with a knife."

Emma waved her hands. "Shut up, Lang! Just shut up!"

"No, I never thought you did it," Maria admitted. "Aunt Emma knifed Uncle Henry, but then she needed help to put the body in the cemetery. You realized you'd have to keep quiet about the button and murder, and it would be the perfect opportunity to blackmail her and squeeze every penny you could from her. After all, it's no secret you like to gamble. So she paid to keep you quiet and from going to the authorities. And that's why she kept pilfering money from the inn's safe."

"How'd you figure it out?" he asked.

Maria glanced at Abigail. "We figured it was Aunt Emma who wielded the knife and gave you those stitches on your arm, but we didn't make a connection until Millie told Abigail that Emma had once threatened her with a knife. When Dr. Wade sewed your arm, Abby and I searched out all your cronies who play cards with you, and we couldn't find one who had witnessed a knife fight. We couldn't find a single soul. Now wasn't that odd?"

Tye nudged Lang in the back with the barrel of his gun. "You must have really riled the old gal for her to take off on you."

Maria took a deep breath. She stared at her uncle's portrait. Now all she needed to know was why Emma killed their uncle. Abby beat her to the question.

"Why?" Abigail asked. "Why Uncle Henry? What did Uncle Henry ever do to you?"

"He was weak," Emma said scornfully. "He was cheap. He'd give to others before he'd let me buy something new." She poked at her chest with a finger and spoke with bitterness. "It was me who was supposed to have everything." She waved her hands in the air. "He knew I hated Golden. He knew I wanted to go home to Georgia where the people were cultured and refined and where people cared about wealth and status. I begged him to take me back east."

Tye let out a long audible sigh. He spoke to all, but only gazed at Maria. "We need to fetch the sheriff. I have the feeling this is going to be a long night."

"I'll go," Millie Hanson said quietly.

Chapter Twenty-Four

"How did you know to come to the manse?" Maria looked at Tye who was seated at the Mule Shed Inn's kitchen table, along with Abigail, Brett, Marcus, and Betsy.

It was late that night, and they had just finished with the sheriff. No one felt in the mood to return to the festival, so they had gathered at the inn for coffee. Anna had sent over a huge plate of pastries. The kitchen glowed with the light of three lanterns strategically hung on the wall to shine on the table. The woodstove fire drove the chill from the air and made the kitchen feel cozy and warm.

"Betsy saw you leave the barn dance with Millie, and once I realized Abigail had also disappeared, it wasn't difficult to conclude you both were up to no good," Tye said. His words were calm, but the look he and Maria exchanged indicated he was barely concealing his anger. "I sent Brett to the inn to look for you and Marcus to the cottage. I headed over to the manse. I hope you realize you all could have been killed."

"What will happen to Aunt Emma?" Abby's attempt to deliberately change the subject did not go undetected. Tye and Brett sat at the table and glared at them, frowning.

Marcus rubbed his jaw. "She'll go to trial for the

murder of her husband and probably for the murder of her first husband as well. Then she's headed to a life-long stay at an asylum. Imagine the person who has the job of trying to untangle her mind." Marcus shook his head. "He'll soon discover Emma plays with a set of dice without all the dots."

"What will happen to the manse and the Mule Shed Inn?" Maria asked.

"The will the sheriff requested from your uncle's lawyer tonight indicated all his holdings and belongings were to go to your father upon his death," Brett said. "Therefore, Attorney Wright is confident Abigail and you will own all of it. Luckily, since Emma was intent on covering up Henry's death and trying to chase you back to Utah, it never crossed her mind to look for Henry's will, and she undoubtedly, and erroneously, assumed everything was hers. Had she discovered its contents, you both may have ended up like poor Henry."

"It looks like you will not have to worry about a place to stay." Marcus's gaze came to rest on the two sisters.

Maria shuddered. She thought about the dreary house, the bloodstained chair, the sad songs from the spinet, and the ugly portrait of Emma. "I will not ramble around in that cold, pitiful place."

"Nor I," Abigail agreed.

"Sell it, or have Millie Hanson turn it into a boarding house," Brett suggested. "Amos and Roy Sanderson can help her get it started. Why, the other day, Amos told me he was getting bored. The Mule Shed was running too efficiently."

Marcus pursed his lips and nodded. "It's a good

sound idea. The town can always use more places for people to stay when they come into the area." He rose from the table. "It's time for me to fetch Anna and get back to the ranch."

Betsy rose with him. "I'll go with you. Tomorrow might be another long day when the sheriff starts sorting things out. I'd hate to be in Lang Redford's boots."

"Yeah, there's another one who's about as sharp as a marble." Marcus chuckled.

Brett rubbed his hand over his face. "Come, Abigail. I'll walk you to the cottage. *We need to talk.*"

Abigail grimaced. "I'm hearing the same worn out lyrics from the same old song, Captain Trumble. But I'm betting we don't talk."

"You're right, darlin'. You're about to listen to a real lively solo from me." Brett's sarcasm was not lost on the group. "Now wish your dear sister good luck, 'cause you're both going to need it. Tydall has the God awful look like he could strip bark from a pine tree with his teeth."

When everyone left, Maria shifted nervously in her seat, uncomfortable under Tye's direct scalding gaze. "You're angry."

Both eyebrows shot up, and his nostrils flared with fury. "Oh, please, Maria. Angry doesn't begin to describe what I feel."

"I'm sorry."

"For what?" This time his expression was one of pained tolerance. "For ignoring me? For ignoring a man who was trying to propose? For leaving the festival? For not telling me where you were going? For going off unarmed to face a killer with a gun. Or a killer with a knife? For not telling me someone was threatening you, not once—but twice? Which one, Maria? Just which one are you sorry about?"

"All of them?" She hung her head. A sensation of desolation swept over her. "I couldn't let the murderer of my uncle get away with it. I just couldn't, Tye. I couldn't tell you about the message on the slate board because at first I thought it was a student. It wasn't until I got the second note, I became truly frightened. Can't you see? I wanted to try to handle it myself."

He sat there for a moment, then heaved a sigh, stood, and went to the lanterns, extinguishing them one by one. He walked to the door in the dim light of the moon shining through the kitchen window. "It's a full moon. Grab your shawl and come take a ride with me. I want to show you something."

Without speaking, he led her to a buggy tied out back and helped her in. The full moon overhead lit up the night and the roadway as they proceeded through a curtain of pine and aspen. The trees seemed magical, whispering to one another as the night breeze ruffled their leaves.

Before he reached the ranch, Tye turned the horse along a narrow path leading to a grassy rise looking down over a rolling field. The moon's golden rays made the field glow like amber. He stopped the buggy.

"What do you see, Maria?"

"A field. A beautiful field in the moonlight?"

"Yeah, under a glorious Colorado moon. Amazing, isn't it?" He tied off the reins and leaned back against the seat. Maria could see the sharp outline of his face. They sat in silence for several moments. Finally he spoke, "I see an orchard with rows and rows of apple trees. Johnathans and Macintoshes. Cortlands from New York. It's time for me to plant some roots, Why not some apple trees? What do you think?"

"Oh, Tye." There was hesitancy and resignation in her voice. "If I marry you, I can't be certain the school board would approve of a married woman teaching their youth. And I haven't proven myself yet to warrant the board considering such a bold idea. I'd probably lose my position."

"Depends upon the vote of the board. Times are changing, Maria. Betsy owns a store. Julia has her pottery business. Anna runs her bakery. You saw how excited the kids were today to please you. Do you think the parents of those children would let you leave without a fight?" He paused. "You could always start your own school and tutor adults who want to learn to read and write. There's a lot of people pouring into the Territory—lots of people who would be eager to learn how to write only their names on a legal document. I figure if you can teach an Indian, you can teach just about anybody."

"How did you find out?" She was glad it was dark, and he couldn't see her blush.

"Old Theo Sarowski mentioned to Julia she was helping Two Bears to read aloud from his McGuffey reader. Now, I ask you, how would Two Bears get his hands on a McGuffey reader? I had a deal with that fool Indian to make sure you got safely to school each morning, but I never dreamed he'd sweet talk you into teaching him to read and write."

Maria smiled. "If the school board will permit me to teach as a married woman, would you allow me?"

"Allow you?" He looked at her in disbelief. "The

Judy Ann Davis

way you handled that gun today, I don't think I'd stop you from doing anything you wanted to do. You're going to be a hero in school on Monday. No child will get out of line once he hears how you shot Emma McNeil's picture off the wall by its cord."

"Betsy deserves the credit. She's a patient teacher and skilled in weaponry." She felt a warm glow flow through her. She put her hand on his forearm. "Oh, Tye, I don't want to fight." Her gaze locked with his, and her mind reeled with a multitude of thoughts. This was the man she loved. Why couldn't she have everything she wanted? She could chart her own path. She could make choices. She didn't have to give up her love of teaching, nor her love for Tye Ashmore. She didn't need to be afraid anymore. "I love you," she said in a whisper and felt him gather her up in his arms and pull her to him.

"I love you, too, schoolmarm." He met her gaze and smiled into her eyes, a tender smile that wrapped around her heart. He caressed her back and kissed her gently. "Just say you'll marry me, we'll work everything out. I promise."

"I'll marry you, and we *will* work everything out," she said, feeling relieved and blissfully happy.

"Please say you'll stay with me tonight."

"Tye Ashmore, I'll stay with you forever."

He kissed her long and deep before he gathered the reins to the horse and sent them on their way…along the moonlit road lined with autumn flowers where only the sound of the buggy wheels crunching on the rocks broke the evening silence. And where an empty ranch house under a starry sky was waiting to be filled with love and laughter and a family.

A word about the author...

Judy Ann Davis began her career in writing as a copy and continuity writer for radio and television in Scranton, PA. Throughout her career, she has written for both industry and education.

Many of her short stories have appeared in various literary and small magazines, and anthologies, and have received numerous awards. Nineteen of them are now collected in *Up on the Roof & Other Stories*.

Under Starry Skies features the Ashmore family and many of the same characters in *Red Fox Woman*, her first novel, which was a finalist in the International Book Awards and USA Book News Best Book Awards.

Key to Love, her second novel published by The Wild Rose Press, is a contemporary romantic suspense.

When Judy Ann isn't behind a computer, you can find her looking for anything humorous to make her laugh or swinging a golf club, where the chuckles are few. She is a member of Pennwriters, Inc. and of Romance Writers of America and lives with her husband in Clearfield, PA.

Visit her at:

www.judyanndavis.com

and

www.judyanndavis.blogspot.com

You can find her on Facebook:

Judy Ann Davis

and on Twitter:

@judyanndavis4

Thank you for purchasing
this publication of The Wild Rose Press, Inc.
For other wonderful stories of romance,
please visit our on-line bookstore at
www.thewildrosepress.com.

For questions or more information
contact us at
info@thewildrosepress.com.

The Wild Rose Press, Inc.
www.thewildrosepress.com

To visit with authors of
The Wild Rose Press, Inc.
join our yahoo loop at
http://groups.yahoo.com/group/thewildrosepress/